Veins of Darkness

ELIZABETH DRYSDALE

*For Danny,
who made many deals to save me*

One

DEATH'S long shadow hovered over me long before today. Yet the chill spreading over my skin tonight whispers how it would have saved me from this fate, if only I had given it another chance.

My little black dog, Willa, rides in the carriage with me, but even she can't stop the dark thoughts involuntarily storming my head. She rests her small chin against my leg, but I barely feel it through the heavy layers of purple skirts I donned before leaving home. These ostentatious clothes were meant to create a favorable impression, which now seems so very trivial in the face of impending darkness. If the Lord had really cared that much about what I looked like, he would have waited until I was an adult woman before making the deal with my father.

The thought of it alone makes my fingers clench tighter around the ball of paper in my fist. My father's letter. His words continue to pierce through my mind despite the speed with which I rejected them. Even from the distance created by this carriage, he still threatens to find a way to make me care for him as the words drift through my mind.

. . .

Cora,

Your absence will be felt in our home, and I hope you know this. As your father, it has been my duty to express the complexity of the emotions that swirl within me as I reflect upon the decisions which have led to our current circumstances. Life often propels us down unexpected paths, and the choices we make, well-intentioned or otherwise, inevitably shape our destinies.

In light of recent events, I find it necessary to extend my heartfelt acknowledgment of the challenges this arrangement has presented. The intricacies of our relationships have brought about circumstances that, while not immediately anticipated, are unavoidable consequences of the history we share.

It is my sincere hope that you, my beloved daughter, possess the resilience and adaptability to navigate the intricacies of this new chapter in your life. The past, with its decisions and agreements, cannot be undone, but I trust that you will forge ahead with the strength and grace that are inherent to your character.

May the challenges you encounter serve as stepping stones toward your growth. My thoughts are with you, and I know, with time, we will be reunited.

Your Father

I thrust the ball of paper onto the floor of the carriage and grind it under my heel. His words are the same as always, long rambling sentiments with nothing in them. No final preparations for me, not even an apology for putting me in this situation.

The gravel's rhythmic crunching under the wheels grinds to a halt, and my heart beats harder against my restrictive bodice. Clutching Willa's collar, I tighten my grip. If the door swings open, she could take off and I'll never see her again. In this unfamiliar and foreboding place, her fear has no boundaries.

"Don't worry," I whisper to Willa even as my hands clutch her tighter. "We'll be out soon."

Time stretches agonizingly but the door still doesn't open.

My hands sweat and I rub them against the velvet seats. The Lord's carriage, devoid of windows, leaves us utterly shrouded in uncertainty. *Have we arrived? Or is something blocking the path and we simply can't move?* I tap my foot against the floor to relieve some of the tension from my chest.

If we *have* arrived, opening the door myself would hardly be considered a refined introduction. The teachings from *The Lady's Book of Manners* I've had drilled into my head a million times feel like a mockery of my current situation. Not that it matters. I don't know why we've played this charade for even a second, let alone the years we've done it. It's preposterous, considering I've never had a choice in this situation at all.

But even more ridiculous is sitting in this carriage for a second longer. Infinite patience, an excellent virtue extolled by Nanny Irma, has never been one of *my* virtues.

The cold touch of the metal handle penetrates my white kid gloves. It was still late fall at home, but the Lord's dwelling lies much farther north— an enigma among the few details I know about him. Father only decided knowing his location and sending me here on my seventeenth birthday was the only thing that could save him from complete ruin.

How fortuitous for me. Trapped in the impending shadows of a destiny I never chose.

The desperation has only grown over the years as I've waited for my fate, driving me to court danger for eight long years. The limited time I've had before being sent here has spurred me to come up with increasingly creative escape plans. Being more obvious might have been quicker and could have brought me closer to my goal, but it also would have led to capture or exposure

In my relentless pursuit of freedom, I've left behind a tapestry of scars as proof of my purpose. Each mark on my arms and legs standing as a testament to my struggle. Father would be horrified if he knew. Nanny Irma was adept at shielding him from any unpleasant truths about me, including the time I got tangled in ropes and was left hanging from the tree outside my bedroom for six hours.

With reckless resolve, I wrench the carriage door open, my grip on Willa unyielding. The cold bites at my skin, instantly clouding my vision with each exhale. As the frosty air settles, the world reveals itself in shades of white— a snow-crusted courtyard sprawling before me. A black stone castle looms, its windows and doors devoid of life.

Stepping onto the icy ground, my boot slips to the side, my grip on the handle the only thing preventing me from hitting the ground. *Well, at least I'm not stuck on the side of the road.* Yet the question lingers, will this desolate black expanse be my new home? This place devoid of even the man who orchestrated my forced arrival? *What is the point of any of this?*

Willa tugs at my hand, urging me forward. I release her collar and take her by the leash. No welcoming party will be waiting for me here. They have to know I'm here. After all, the Lord sent for me in the first place. But no one has come out of the castle. Why would he force me here only to forsake me to this desolate expanse of rock and snow? The void of time stretches before me, tightening its grip on my already shrunken heart.

A yearning to retreat claws at my mind, urging me back to the sanctuary of the carriage, with its deceptive warmth and the simple illusion of safety. But I can't stay concealed within its dark walls forever. Someone *has* to know I'm here. The carriage didn't just arrive at my house under its own free will. *Did it?*

The horrifying thought digs deeper: *what if it did?* What if it was given its magic to bring me here long ago and then something terrible happened and now no one lives here? Perhaps a plague swept through the Lord's estate, leaving behind a realm of frozen corpses.

My heart races and my throat feels tight. My hand trembles as I force myself to use the knocker once more. If silence greets me, I may finally get my death wish after all.

The door opens on silent hinges, revealing a yawning darkness within.

"H-hello?"

My voice falters as my throat grows even tighter. "Is anyone there?"

Willa tugs on the leash, trying to get inside the castle. I hesitate. It wouldn't be good manners. I know this. But it's not good manners to ignore your guest, either. And I'm definitely not willing to freeze to death for the sake of a favorable first impression. I take a tentative step into the unknown, my shoes clicking against the polished black tiles while Willa pads around, nails clacking against floor.

"Hello?" I repeat, the darkness slowly yielding to my adjusting eyes.

A grand staircase adorned in dark wood stretches up to unreachable heights, dominating the foyer. Archways to unknown rooms line the walls on either side of the foyer, draped in black curtains. The stillness is palpable, as if humanity itself has never dared to disturb this desolate abode.

I can't get my heart to calm down, it pounds relentlessly against my chest, desperate to scale my throat and make an escape. Willa slinks back towards me, a low growl reverberating through the air as she seeks refuge within the folds of my skirts.

"What did you find?" I ask, keeping my voice quiet in the nothingness.

Willa isn't usually one to growl or make a scene without reason. Something is here with us, even if I can't see it. My legs grow weak, and I crouch down beside her, holding her in my shaking arms.

"If someone is here, this is… this is extremely rude."

Calling them out seems the only way I can find my voice. The oppressive atmosphere demands a response. "Is this how you treat your invited guests? You should… you should be *ashamed*."

"Invited is a stretch," retorts a rich, male voice, sending shivers down my spine.

I recoil, falling to the floor. The voice emanated from the direction of the stairs. The cadence of my heartbeat intensifies, reaching a crescendo of panic. Willa's growls transform into plaintive whimpers as a shadowed figure, clad in all black, descends the staircase. It is a physical embodiment of the feeling in this forsaken place.

"Di-did you… were you not expecting me?" I swallow the lump in my throat to get my words out.

"Oh no," he says, shaking his head wistfully. He stretches out a pale hand to the banister as he reaches the bottom step. His silver hair mirrors the ice's crystalline sheen outside and his clothing has a fashionable cut, despite its ability to meld seamlessly with the shadows. Struggling to discern his face, an unsettling intuition whispers that there may be no face lurking there to reveal. I'm in a castle of ghosts. "I knew you were coming," he continues. "However, your presence here was never something I *asked* for."

I pull myself to my feet, refusing to be a weak puddle on the floor any longer. Hope flutters within me; perhaps my dreams of escaping this place could come true after all. "Then where is the Lord who signed the contract that brought me here? Surely *he* wished me here, and if not, I am more than glad to return to my home and rid you of the unpleasantness my presence has created."

He chuckles, the sound low in his throat as it pulls at me in a way that raises the hair on the back of my neck. "Oh no, neither you nor I will get out of this so easily."

"So, *you* are the Lord?" Disbelief taints my voice. The air hangs heavy with the unspoken, leaving me to wonder why he, if he truly is the Lord, would choose to personally address my unwelcome arrival. *Why didn't he send his butler or another member of staff to greet me?*

He shrugs, an unnatural motion for his stiff frame. "The contract was made and must be honored." He steps closer, his face still veiled in shadow. "You belong here now."

The slamming door behind me echoes the closing of the door on my former life as the stark reality settles like a lead weight in my chest—*I'm truly trapped here.* The prospect of never returning home looms like shadow over my thoughts. Perhaps the Lord only agreed to my father's deal *because* he had no servants here? Maybe all those lessons Nanny gave me will go to waste as I learn instead how to cook and clean and care for this recluse of a man.

I can't stop the burning of tears in my eyes, and more than anything I want to run away, find an escape, maybe even—

"I hope you don't find it *too* distasteful," he says, as though he can sense the emotions building within me. "After all, it could be worse."

His words send steel through my spine.

"And how exactly could it be *worse*?"

He cocks his head to the side. "This is something your father should have explained to you."

"And if he didn't?" It takes every ounce of my training to keep myself from grinding my teeth.

"Then the time for such education is long past."

The Lord descends the steps, his lips twitching in a half-smile while I stand before him in the semi-darkness. I clench my fists in my skirt as he stares. Willa whimpers and shifts behind me. *The coward.*

"I hope you find your time here adequate." He gives me a nod and disappears through the curtains shrouding a room on my right.

I remain in the foyer, uncertain of my next move. *Do I follow him? Do I go upstairs and hope for a clear sign to decipher where my room is?* Maybe I'm expected to just stand here until I turn to dust.

The thought causes my jaw to clench together. *What kind of Lord doesn't have servants on hand to take care of his guests?* The absence of servants must be recent, or else he would have had to learn how to care for guests himself— a skill set he obviously hasn't acquired.

Willa moves to sit beside me, pink tongue hanging out of her mouth.

"Nice to see you again, traitor."

I bend over and give her head a pat all the same. If running and hiding had been an option for me, I might have been equally tempted to follow her lead.

The Lord has defied any of my possible expectations. In my dreams, he was an old cantankerous figure akin to my father. Nightmares painted him as a sinister suitor, seeking to claim me as his bride. This new reality — a man much younger than my father but just as disinterested in me — brings me no comfort, regardless of my heartbeat returning to its normal rhythm.

The wait in the foyer echoes the futility of all the past moments I've spent waiting— in the carriage, on the front step, in the tree at home. Each instance seems to mock my powerlessness. Yet I can't just stand here forever. My back aches and my body cries for rest after the long journey. Surely the Lord must be aware of *that*.

If he chooses to disregard propriety, then I shall abandon the shackles of manners as well.

Taking a deep breath, I suppress the urge to bite my lip as I advance toward the curtained doorway the Lord disappeared through. My footsteps echo in the silence, disrupting the stagnant air. It's probably just a men's parlor he's gone into, a forbidden realm similar to the one in my father's home, reserved for his solitary escapes. If my father were here, he would insist this was what the Lord desired and I should oblige. But my father isn't here. And I'll most likely never see him again.

I wait for the familiar pressure in my chest, the weight of obligation and expectation, but instead, an unexpected lightness settles upon me. I refuse to worry about what he thinks any longer. I've fulfilled the contract he created, and it has torn me from him physically and torn my loyalty as well. My father's influence can no longer dictate my decisions. His opinion no longer has any bearing on me.

Still, my hands betray a subtle tremor as they forcefully draw back the curtains, revealing a room as dark as the foyer, as though the Lord forgot he had any windows at all. A pervasive blackness hangs in the air, akin to the heavy breath of death. But my initial thought of what the room would be is correct. A symphony of chairs sit facing each other, smothered in their darkly upholstered fabrics, with a solitary desk in the corner and a heavy rug swallowing the floor. It mutes my footsteps as I enter. The aroma of dead fires and old cologne linger in the air, as if a party had taken place just the night before. Something about the Lord tells me that isn't true. Everything in this castle is just a shadow of living, a weak exhale of what life should be. *Will I also turn into a shadow the longer I stay here?*

That, more than anything, makes a desire to flee claw at my insides.

But I can't leave, not when I haven't gotten any answers. My gaze sweeps over the vacant bar cart and the bookshelf adorned with black spines, but the Lord is nowhere to be found.

The room remains sealed. There's no other exit, nowhere else he could have gone.

Willa tugs on the leash and climbs onto a nearby loveseat, emitting a contented sigh. At least one of us has found a place to rest. I look around again, but still can see no clue to where he could have gone.

Well, if he's not here, then I can claim this room as my own until he tells me otherwise. I collapse next to Willa, half-expecting a cloud of dust to bloom up around me, but the material appears pristine, the cushion firm beneath me, as if untouched by time.

I pull Willa onto my lap and dig my fingers into her wiry black hair, wishing I could bury my face in her. Her dark coat perfectly matches this place, and she seems content to make it her home, at least when the Lord isn't around. I wish I fit in as well, but even the purple of my dress fails to match the right shade, making me look like spring flowers left on an abandoned grave.

"Stop moping."

I say the words aloud as though that will give them more power and lift my sinking spirits. It doesn't help.

I lean back against the couch, trying to get as comfortable as I can, even as my corset digs into the tender spaces of my flesh. The floor squeaks behind me and I spin around, expecting to find the Lord standing there. The space remains empty. I'm alone.

This is it, then. The culmination of years of training, all

for a man who clearly doesn't desire my presence in a castle that seems on the verge of rejecting me as well.

I sink back into the cushions and sigh. Death may not have accepted my earlier invitation, but I have no doubt it will arrive in this place soon enough.

Two

A GLIMMER of sunlight disrupts the oppressive darkness, tugging me from the clutches of dreams filled with shadowed figures. Willa senses my stirring, her tail wagging eagerly against my leg.

My surroundings gradually come into focus, a crack in the curtain revealing a room adorned not only in blacks and greys but also full of maroon and muted jewel tones. The room has far more elegance than I gave it credit for yesterday. And not a hint of dust touches any surface.

My scrutiny intensifies as I notice all the hints of servants being around even though I haven't seen a single one. The Lord wouldn't be in here dusting, so who does it?

"Good morning."

The sturdy boning of my corset keeps me from leaping out of my skin at the Lord's silky voice. He sits in the wing-back chair opposite me, one leg casually draped over the other as he regards me with a gaze as cold and beautiful as his face. In the rays of light coming through the window, I can finally see his features clearly. He's a sculpture of sharp lines and alert grey eyes that match the silver of his hair. It's a face that could be marble, especially as his expression doesn't change as he continues watching me.

My hands long to check my hair, to travel over my dress and make sure I'm still decent, but I'll do none of those things while he watches me. Instead, I sit up straighter, with all the haughtiness I can come with after just waking up.

"Good morning."

It feels ridiculous to respond to him, but years of training win out. Plus, what would giving him the silent treatment get me? I'm already drowning in the silence of this house and I won't drive away the only other living person I've seen since I've been here.

"Did you not wish for better accommodations?" His tone carries a lightness as if posing an actual question. Does he really think I chose to sleep on his couch instead of in a bed?

"Nothing else was offered." Not even this was offered. If I hadn't tried to follow him, I would have ended up sleeping on the cold tile floor.

He shifts in his seat. "Jameson should have helped you."

"This is the first I'm hearing that anyone else even lives here." The break in decorum feels like a sharp crack in the air. I could just melt into the floor and die. But I won't. I refuse to show that I know I shouldn't talk like that to this man who abandoned me here after forcing me to come. Still, he watches me with wide eyes like he's never been talked to like this. Maybe he hasn't.

"You couldn't possibly think I live here alone. That would be preposterous."

"Preposterous though it may be, I have yet to see anyone else." I lean forward, a wicked glint flashing in my eyes. "Why did you bring me here? Obviously you don't have any use for me."

His hand gripping the armrest goes white-knuckled as he stares at me. "You're not like other women, are you?"

My face flushes even though he says it in more of a question than an accusation. The question brings flashes of other moments of my life crashing against my mind and I'm forced to live through each moment before I'm released. Moments with my father, with Nanny, with the girls in my finishing class, with boys at the town picnic. I want to shake my head to clear them away, but I can't, not in front of the Lord.

"No, I suppose I'm not."

He grins, his teeth flashing in the morning light. It's the first real expression I've ever seen on his face. It's gorgeous and terrifying, like a wolf.

"Good. You may just survive this after all."

He stands, smoothing out his black jacket. He crosses the room in a few quick strides, going back through the curtain blocking the room off. I struggle to follow him, my legs tangling in my skirts after sleeping in them. I can't let him out of my sight though. That's how he disappeared yesterday and I'm not ready to be left alone with no answers and no purpose again.

I pull the curtain aside. "What did you mean by that? What do you mean I might survive this?"

The Lord stands halfway up the stairs, his hand resting against the banister. "My dear girl, no one survives this castle for long."

He turns and continues his ascent. I hesitate only a moment before following him. It's beyond rude to go uninvited into someone's private area, but I won't spend the rest of my life confined to the foyer and the sitting room either.

Lifting my skirts that might be wrinkled beyond repair, (Nanny would be furious,) I take the stairs as quickly as I can. Willa gives a sharp bark as she stumbles up after me.

"Wait a moment," I call after him when he doesn't seem to notice or care that I'm following him.

He stops but doesn't turn all the way around; instead, he only shifts his head to give me a sidelong glance. "Yes?"

"Wh-what..." I take a breath before I continue, my face turning red and hot. "What am I supposed to be doing here? Surely you can't expect me to hang around in the foyer like some kind of seasonal bouquet. That can't be why you forced me to come here."

He chuckles, the sound dark as it trickles along my spine. "You think *I* am the reason you were brought here?"

"Well, that was your agreement with my father. It certainly wasn't my idea." I brace a hand against my hip as though that will give me any sort of dignity.

He shakes his head, silver hair falling over his forehead. "Believe me, your presence here was not my idea, my intention, or my desire. I don't care what you do here."

He continues up the stairs and my body freezes, unable to follow him. I'm stuck, suspended halfway up the stairs as he continues up and out of sight.

* * *

Willa's needs are the only things that keep me focused. I take her back outside through the lobby and front doors, trying my best to ignore the cold trickle along my spine constantly telling me I'm not wanted here.

My fingers freeze, turning purple then white as I hold the leash for Willa to do her business. The sky above the castle stretches bleak and grey, making the world around me look all the same as the frost from yesterday still coats and crusts the ground. It feels so different from the home I just left, that it makes me wonder just how far I had to come to get here. Surely I couldn't be *that* far north. I was able to get to the Lord's castle in only day. Could the world between us really be so different?

And yet there can be no denying the full winter that envelopes this place, and I am completely unprepared.

I might have something better in my trunk, but that was left in the carriage. There's absolutely no way I could have carried it on my own. And now the carriage is nowhere to be found.

At least it gives me a reason to complain to the Lord the next time I see him.

Not that I don't have a million other things to bother him with. The evasive Jameson still hasn't shown up to help me, and I've yet to have anything close to a meal here.

"Come on Willa." My breath clouds in front of me and my shoulders shake in the frigid air.

Willa growls low in her chest as she finishes her business and I'm not sure if it's because something is endangering us or if she just didn't appreciate being rushed. I look up just in case, but the courtyard stands walled in, and the iron gate firmly closed. The closed gate feels ironic because the Lord said he didn't care where I went, but he obviously doesn't want me to leave. The whole situation feels pointless. *Why bring me here if he didn't have any plans for me? Why not let my father be free of the contract?*

If only my father had told me more about the contract, he had entered into with the Lord. He never said much about it, only that they had found a compromise with me. Some compromise that was. How wonderful that they could find common ground by involving someone who hadn't initially been involved at all. I never did anything to the Lord. Why should I be forced to pay, presumably, my father's debts? But every time I asked Nanny about it, she told me to leave men's business to the men. Easy for her to say. She still gets to live at home.

I tug on Willa's leash and bring her back into the castle. The inside feels barely warmer than the outside. The fireplace grates are empty and with no servants around to take care of them, I don't imagine fires will be lit any time soon.

This punishment exceeds what I should endure. Am I really expected to both starve and freeze to death at the same time?

I lean over to pet Willa, hoping to absorb some of her heat.

"Miss?"

From my position on the floor, I can see shining black shoes as they approach me. My stomach feels sick and my heart rate quickens, but I pull myself to standing and do my best to hide my feelings behind a stony face.

"You must be Jameson."

I expected someone old. Most butlers I've met are old enough to have gathered more than a few grey hairs, they need the time to have learned enough to earn the station. This man however, doesn't look much older than me. He has a slight frame and night-black hair. His fingers twitch as he watches me, and he looks like one word from me will cause him to flinch and run away.

"Y-yes Miss." He scratches behind his ear. "I was told you needed assistance?"

Yet another reason why an older man usually does this job. He wouldn't need to be told that guests need rooms and announcements for meals. This *boy* though... I'm obviously going to be on my own.

"Yes. I have already been forced to sleep on a *couch* of all things, my belongings have not been brought in, and I have not received a single meal yet. I don't know how you usually deal with guests, but this is absurd." I keep my voice haughty, like Nanny's. It seems to have an effect because Jameson cowers under my gaze.

"The Lord told me you were not a guest, Miss. I didn't assume you would need my help or direction." He tugs on his gloves, revealing just how poorly fitted they are to him.

I want to argue with him. To push him to see the ridiculousness of thinking someone who had never been to this house wouldn't need even a little bit of help, but such a conversation wouldn't do either of us any good. He wouldn't listen to me, and I would just get angry. Not that I'm not close to it now. This boy feels easier to let my anger out on than the Lord. He'd make far too easy of a target.

"Be that as it may, I still need my belongings brought in and I would like to have a room. Can you also tell me when I might expect breakfast?" I stick to my basic needs. He doesn't seem like he can handle any more than that.

"The Lord doesn't usually take his meals here." Jameson doesn't bring his grey eyes up to meet mine. "And as for rooms, I'm sure you can have any one you want. The Lord doesn't usually have visitors."

"If the Lord doesn't eat here, then where does he eat?"

Jameson shrugs and I just want to shake him by his narrow shoulders. *What does he expect me to do?*

Instead, I try to remember my lessons. As much as I hated them, they would be useful with this boy. I square my shoulders and tilt my head so that I'm looking down on him.

"You *will* take me to a room, you *will* bring my belongings to me, and you *will* ensure that I am brought breakfast. Have I made myself clear?" I try not to flinch away from my voice like Jameson did. I sound exactly like Nanny.

"I'll see what I can do." He tilts his body, attempting what seems to be a bow before scurrying away.

If this is what I have to look forward to during my time here, it's going to be exhausting.

* * *

With Jameson taken care of, my mind wanders toward the mystery of the rest of the castle. *Where is everyone and where does the Lord keep going? More importantly, why am I here?*

I march back into the parlor, ready to find some answers. I throw the heavy curtains covering the windows open, hoping that will bring in a little more light. However, the grey light from outside does little to illuminate anything. Instead, it spreads across the floor like a smear.

I shake my head, dark curls bouncing against my shoulders. If this represents the best I have to work with, then I'll have to make do.

The starched material of my sleeves resists my desire to push my sleeves up and get to work. It's just as well anyway. If the Lord showed up and saw the scars on my arms from my repeated escape attempts, I would have no appropriate answers for him.

I march to the bookshelf. If I've learned anything in my life, it would be that books hold the unanswered truths of our minds.

The Lord doesn't have many in here, which isn't surprising. The entire room gives the impression that he rarely uses it, especially considering the empty bar cart. Still, I'll find a way to use what books he has to my advantage.

Reaching for a thick volume with black binding off the shelf, I take a deep breath to prepare myself for investigating. But the preparation does little to help me when I open it only to discover writing in a different language. My gaze travels over the words over and over again, willing the strange symbols to turn into something I can decipher. But nothing changes and I'm left shoving the book back onto the shelf with more force than necessary.

I try the next book, but the writing is the same. Books aren't going to help me today.

Unless the writing itself is a clue.

By coming to the Lord's house, have I left behind the safety of my own country? With no windows in the carriage, I had no idea where I was traveling to. Anything is possible. Anything within a day's ride that is.

I try not to shift on my feet just thinking of the carriage that brought me here without horses. Strange magic manifests here. Stranger than I initially realized.

My gaze combs through the shelves, looking for knick-knacks or anything that might tell me more about the Lord. But there's nothing. No little trinkets from travels, no pictures of loved ones in gilt frames, nothing to suggest anyone lives here at all. It looks like a model house. Or a doll house made life-size.

My nose wrinkles. There has to be something around here. I refuse to believe this house has no answers for me. It might just be time to let go of propriety altogether and delve into deeper snooping.

Willa tugs on her leash, pulling me towards the stairs. There are more rooms on this floor I haven't looked at, but I can't deny that I'm also curious about what lies on the upper levels. After all, I last saw the Lord going up. But that also means he's far more likely to catch me delving into his secrets if I follow him.

My stomach clenches as I place a booted foot on the first step. Willa has no such hesitation and runs ahead of me, her tiny legs stumbling up the steps as she refuses to break stride.

"Willa, slow down." I try to keep my voice low and not draw attention to us while still making sure Willa can hear me. But if she really can, she has no interest in following my directions.

"Willa!" I hiss when she reaches the landing and starts sniffing at the chairs and small table set up there.

She pays me no heed, her tail wagging happily back and forth as she continues her examination. I stumble up after her, feeling about ready to collapse into the chair. The first-floor ceiling exceeds ten feet in height, which leads to a lot of stairs to get to the next level.

Willa doesn't wait for me to recover before she heads up the next set. The stairwell twists after the landing, giving me my first glimpse of the second floor.

This floor seems even darker than the first. Dark, twisting shapes cover the floor, and no light from any windows permeates the space. I wish I had my notebook to start sketching the rooms and the layout of the castle. At least some of my lessons with Nanny should come in handy here.

Willa whimpers as she reaches the top. Even she isn't brave enough to take the final step of the stairs.

I hesitate beside her. But it can't actually be dangerous. How could it be? The Lord just came up here.

But he never came back down.

I shake my head again. This is all ridiculous. It's just a house. A weird house for certain, but one that he lives in. Jameson lives here too. There are people here. I'm not about to be eaten up by shadows.

The hair on my arms stands up as I step onto the second floor, the feeling of magic rippling over my skin. I tug the leash to get Willa to follow me as she hesitates, the traitor.

The air feels thick in my lungs as I breathe it in, and so much warmer than the first floor. Everything feels still, waiting. But waiting for what, I don't know.

The shadows along the floor dissipate and draw back, giving us room to walk. Without them clouding the space, it doesn't feel half as scary anymore. I can do this.

I steel my spine and head towards the first door, the handle cold under my palm. Willa presses against my leg as I turn the handle, her small body shaking so hard my dress rustles with it.

The door swings open on silent hinges. My breath stops as I peer into the darkness inside.

"Can I help you with something?"

I choke on my spit, tripping over Willa as I turn to face the Lord. He stands with his arms crossed over his chest, watching me with a raised brow. He wears black pants, a shirt, a cravat, and a jacket, like he just came from somewhere even though he's only been upstairs all this time.

"Jameson said it was okay to be up here." I swallow the sigh of relief that wants to come out as easily as the lie did.

"Did he now?" The side of his mouth quirks in what might be close to a smile.

I turn my back on the dark room, quelling my curiosity for now. "I didn't think I was going to be kept downstairs until our contract ran out."

His eyes narrow. "You believe the contract will expire?"

"How could it not? My father wouldn't just give away my whole life without my consent."

I hate the way he looks at me. So much pity exudes from his narrowed eyes. They make my body feel tight. All I want to do is run away from them.

He taps a finger against his jaw. "In the future, I would prefer if you didn't wander around on your own. This castle can be a dangerous place for the unprepared."

"What am I supposed to do? I've been alone almost constantly since I arrived." Even when I arrived. *Why didn't he greet me? How could he just leave me in the carriage?*

His jaw grows tight. "Be that as it may, the rule stands."

"How about you give me a tour of where I'm allowed to be and then I *might* agree to follow your rule." I cross my arms over my chest to cover the shaking growing in my arms. It doesn't matter that this shouldn't be allowed or that I'm acting out of line. I need to do this. If I don't make a stand for myself now... what kind of life will I be destined to lead?

"A tour..." he tests the word in his mouth. "I suppose that isn't too far outside of the expected."

It's not outside reasonable expectations at all. "You must not get many guests."

"Not any who stay."

He smiles at me, the expression chilling me to the bone. He reaches behind me to close the door still hanging open, his body far too close to mine than what propriety allows. My breath catches in my throat, and I don't know whether to lean closer or further away. He smells like ice, and fire, and earth.

I step back before he can see my indecision. With the door closed, he extends his arm to me, and I take it, his body cold beneath my fingers.

"Let me show you my home."

Three

THE LORD LEADS ME DOWNSTAIRS, and I try not to crane my neck to see the second floor it took me so long to get to. What answers could be hiding up there? If he notices me looking though, he doesn't say anything about it.

"The parlor you've seen already," he says as we reach the bottom of the stairs. I half-expect him to lead me inside it anyway, but I'm pleasantly surprised when he guides me towards the room across the foyer instead.

He parts the curtains keeping the room closed off with a long arm, ushering me inside. The room is dimly lit with candles spread sparsely throughout the space. *Does Jameson habitually hide here, lighting candles for empty rooms?* He still hasn't come back with any news on when I'll be fed. My stomach grumbles its disgust and the Lord gives me a sidelong glance.

The room itself proves pleasant enough. It has black embossed wallpaper over its dark wood wainscoting and a fireplace sits against the far wall. The layout is similar to the one across the hall, but with more of the personal touches I was looking for before. This room has far more books and has a more 'used' feeling with cushions on the couch out of place and a book laid open on the coffee table. An empty cup sits on the window ledge, a black grand piano sits open on a black rug that's flipped up in the corner. *Is this where the Lord disappears to?*

I peek at his face as he takes in the room as well, a frown creasing his mouth. So not the Lord then. But who else would it be? Jameson? He runs a finger down the piano keys, the sound sending a chill down my spine.

"Well," he grunts. "You've seen the study now."

He takes me back through the curtain divider without letting me see anything else. My shoes clip along the wood floor as he leads me through the foyer, but his are as silent as the grave. Everything he does remains silent and cold. Will I become this way if I stay here? Is that what he meant about surviving being in the castle? Perhaps I will spend enough days alone and cold until it becomes a part of who I am, just like him.

"Would you like to see anything else on this level?" He asks it like he can't think of any other rooms on this floor. Or perhaps he worries I'll see more disheveled places.

I guess it's a good thing he doesn't want me to see them. It means I probably won't be reduced to a maid while I'm here. Small blessings, I guess.

"I'm sure you have a dining room," I prompt. "Maybe a kitchen?"

He sighs but takes me further down the hallway. The same dark wallpaper lines the walls, with paintings hung at even intervals that are just as black. I've never seen anything like it before. And without any lights lit through the hallway, I can't even pretend to see what lurks in the black paintings. It feels like walking into a cave. A beautifully done cave, but a cave, nonetheless.

The Lord stops and pulls open a set of pocket doors on

the right side of the hallway, sending in a little light peeking through the curtains in the other room. I peer around him, taking in a long narrow table set for twelve.

"This is the dining room." He gestures with his hand toward the room like I might not know. "It is doubtful you will ever use it. We only have formal meals here when forced to."

A frown prickles my forehead. "Then where should I eat? What is the point of having such a nice room if you refuse to use it?"

The muscles in his neck tighten. "I don't see the need for formal dining. This room is here because the house was built this way."

An answer that isn't an answer. How quaint.

"Would it offend you if I began taking my meals here?" Just because he lives like an animal doesn't mean I will. Plus, I need to give Jameson a place to start setting my meals for me. Otherwise, I might just starve to death in this place.

The Lord opens his mouth like he wants to refuse me but instead closes it again and shakes his head. "That is your choice."

Excellent. If he doesn't want to live by decorum and routine, I will instate it anyway. I was raised to be the picture of perfection. While I might not be keeping all of the rules that have governed me, I know peace in schedules and I'm not willing to toss that away yet. Not completely.

He slams the doors closed again, the wood clacking against itself as it threatens to burst open again under his force. I can't tell if he hates the room itself or my request. Either way, I'm not taking it back.

"The kitchen is this way," he says through gritted teeth.

He doesn't offer me his arm this time and I'm glad. I wouldn't want to take it. Maybe that would be too much to say, but I don't feel like leaning on a man who can't control his anger long enough to even close a door with politeness.

The kitchen door sits at the end of the hallway. Its squat compared to all the others and the Lord has to stoop to open it. I doubt he goes directly to the kitchen for his meals.

He pushes it open with a grunt, revealing the most brightly lit space I've seen since coming here. The back hosts a wall of windows with no curtains to block any of the hazy light coming in. The light, dim and pale in comparison to home, but I've been in the dark so long that I just stand there for a moment and bask in it with my eyes closed.

"Wh-what are you doing?"

I glance at the Lord, and he watches me with his head tilted, his eyes narrowed.

"Don't you enjoy feeling sunshine on your skin?"

He frowns. "That's what you're doing?"

"Your home is..." I can't find nice words that convey what the castle has been like in the one day I've been here.

"It's cold," he whispers.

"Yes." *All the black doesn't help*, I want to add but keep it to myself.

He looks at the window like he's never seen it before. He braces his hand against the dark wood countertop, looking at the light play against his knuckles.

"I'm sorry you had to come here." His words are quiet, and he keeps his gaze down. "I'm sorry this castle isn't a home."

"Have you lived here long?" Propriety dictates that I try to keep the conversation moving and away from hard subjects. I still haven't broken that habit completely. Plus, he wasn't going to explain the contract to me anyway.

His smile has no humor in it. "Long enough."

I lean against the counter, my back to the window. On a small table in the middle of the room, a pile of croissants sits waiting on a white plate. My stomach rumbles and I think about asking the Lord if I can have one before quickly changing my mind. I won't ask. If I live here now, I can't ask every time I want to eat.

The rich croissant coats my fingers in butter grease just from touching it. I don't bother looking to see if the Lord watches me before tearing off a piece and shoving it into my mouth. Not lady-like, but then again, I guess I'm not going to be a lady after all. Nanny had really hoped... it doesn't matter now.

The buttery bread tastes like heaven after so long and I struggle hard not to reach over and grab another one. I slow down to listen to my stomach. If I keep stuffing it, it will never have a chance to say anything to me.

"So how long is 'long enough'?" Without Nanny here to scold me, I lick the butter residue off my fingers, saying goodbye to the decadent treat with each taste. Manners nearly forgotten; I study his face. As Lord, he should be old, and if he is the same man who made a deal with my father many years ago, he should be wrinkled.

"Are you trying to determine my age? To see if I am as old as your father?"

I ignore the question. Admitting it would be improper, as would lying.

He stares at my hands. "Time doesn't exist the same here. It wouldn't make sense if it did because of the work that needs to be done." His attention shifts to my face. "It would be much more accurate to say that I'm closer to your age than your father's." My face screws up as I try to make sense of his words.

"Would you like another?" he asks.

I glance at the Lord, not sure if I should let my smile show or feel guilty for enjoying the experience too much. His face doesn't reveal any direction, so I put my arms behind my back.

"No, thank you. One was just perfect."

"It looked perfect."

I look into his face, noting the way his gaze has traveled to my lips. His eyes are dark, almost black, but with glimmers shooting through them the longer he looks at me. I resist the urge to lick my lips, certain I've left some crumbs behind. Something about the way he looks at me says that wouldn't be a good idea.

"Would you care for one?" My heart beats hard against my chest and I delve back into decorum, always a good idea when discomfort takes over. I grab the plate, placing it between us.

"Maybe later." He smiles and glances away. Instantly I feel better, and my heart rate returns to normal. "Would you like to see the rest of the house?"

I have a hard time swallowing. "I think I would like to rest. Can you show me to my room?"

Half-expecting a denial, memories of previous refusals flicker through my mind. I wait for him to tell me that Jameson will help me, wherever that little traitor has gone. Instead, he just tilts his head toward me in a slight nod and sweeps past me into the hall.

He doesn't wait for me to follow him as he heads straight for the stairs. Willa bounds after him, oblivious to the undercurrents that still ripple through my body. At this moment I wish we could switch places.

I've never had a man look at me like that before. Though my exposure to men has been limited, none have looked at me as if I were... something to devour.

The thought sends shivers down my spine, and I keep my gaze fixed on the ground as I come closer to him. Heat blooms in my cheeks as he offers his hand to assist me up the stairs. I can't take it. I can't even look at him. *Does he know what I'm thinking? Do I even know?*

He says nothing about my coloring and follows my brisk

pace up the stairs. The sooner we can get away from each other, the better. I just need to be in my room, safe and settled. That will help me figure all this out and find my balance.

Maybe that's what the problem is. I'm reading too much into what the Lord does because I've gone too long without sleep and food and normality. I'm just a little off right now. It's a good thing I've figured that out before I did something I would regret later. Not that I know what I would do, or even what I thought he wanted me to do.

Light flashes at the corner of my eyes, a headache announcing its coming presence. Too much has happened in the last day, I would have been surprised if I *hadn't* had one of my signature headaches, but that doesn't mean I like it.

"Is everything all right?" the Lord asks when we reach the top of the stairs, and I don't let go of his hand.

"Y-yes." I wrench myself away from him, even as it makes me nauseous to stay standing. "Sorry, I'm just not feeling well all of a sudden."

I try to look at him, but everything feels fuzzy and out of focus.

"Nothing a little rest won't help, I'm sure." He sounds so confident like he finds it normal to encounter weak and swooning women. I hope he doesn't think that's what I am.

"If you would?" I wave him forward. I just need to be alone in my room, why does that feel like too much to ask?

He takes me by the elbow, guiding me forward when my eyes fail me. We pass several heavy-looking wooden doors before he stops in front of one and wrests it open.

"I would warn you," he says as he moves me inside. "To stay away in your room. It would be unfortunate if an accident were to befall you so quickly after your arrival."

In my foggy state, I'm not sure whether to hear a warning or a promise in his voice. Possibly both. All I know is that ahead of me in the darkness lies a bed, and that's the only thing that matters right now.

I push myself forward until I hit the edge of the bed, the comfort of the blankets wrapping around my legs. I fall forward onto it, giving in to the headache before I can even check to make sure that he left and closed the door behind him.

THERE'S a stillness to the castle that bleeds into my soul, making me want to be content where I am. Unfortunately, that was never going to last. The longer I do nothing, the more I feel like I need to do *something*.

The Lord told me not to leave my room. He said it was dangerous to move around the castle. Of course, he would say something like that. I'm a prisoner of my father's bargain, the Lord wouldn't want me to leave when I belong to him.

I struggle to move through the mist that fills the hallway outside my door, but I force myself to do it anyway. Willa refuses to follow me. She sits in the doorway, tail tucked under her body. She cocks her head at me as I move away from her, a small whine building in her throat. For a moment I consider picking her up and carrying her with me, just so I won't be alone, but her stout body bears so much heaviness and I'm already uneasy enough about being out here that I don't want to be off balance holding her. Plus, this makes sure that she stays safe. She has more sense of self-preservation than I do, so she should be the one to survive.

The pervasive dark presses against my skin as I close the

door to my bedroom. The light remains the same here. Never getting brighter, never getting darker as the sconces keep everything in the same dusky twilight.

My feet feel numb as I move through the hallway. I'm not sure where I'm going, but I must go *somewhere*. I can't sit around pretending everything is okay when it isn't. My father may have made this bargain to bring me here, but nothing says I must *stay*. There must be another way out of here. I don't think I could manage the Lord's magic carriage on my own.

I can't say there wasn't magic in my town. I'd felt it on occasion. It existed but was reserved for the rich. They got to experience the conveniences that magic could bring while the rest of us continued. They got their horseless carriages and we had to maintain our horses to go anywhere. They got to have limitless lights and we had to ration our candles. There were moments before Father made his bargain with the Lord that we had no candles at all, and I got to watch through my dark window as the townhouse across from us remained bright with magic all through the night.

I wasn't surprised when the magic carriage came for me. No, it made sense that the man who had bested my father would be one of the lucky ones. One of the privileged ones I had wished to be on so many dark nights.

If he keeps a horse around here though, even though he doesn't strictly need it, I could find my way out of here. I could choose to go somewhere new. I could forget my past altogether.

As I move through the hallway, whispers seem to come from behind the doors. I hear my name so faintly that for a moment I convince myself that I heard nothing at all.

"Cora..."

It comes again, louder this time. My hands feel clammy and the warnings of the Lord press against my mind.

I clench my fists and keep moving. If danger lurks behind

those doors, then I'm grateful for the panels of wood between us. If a way existed for whatever hides behind them to escape, I'm sure it would have already occurred. I'm safe... enough.

I haven't even made it to the staircase yet when I feel something moving behind me. Turning slowly, I try to make out what could be out there without being too obvious. I can't see anything through all the mist filling the hallway. There could be someone right next to me and I wouldn't even know until it was too late.

My chest feels heavy, my breathing labored as I rotate, trying to make out something real. The mist moves and swirls, but I can't see anything else.

A low growl sounds close to my ear, and it takes every ounce of courage I have to stay standing. This is different than the whispers. Different than my name. This doesn't sound like it could be coming from behind a door at all.

"J-Jameson?" It's a baseless hope that it would be him. Why would he be out here growling? Still, I wait, hoping I've misunderstood the sound and that it's actually him despite the lack of response.

"Not Jameson," a deep, gravelly voice says right beside my ear.

A shriek explodes from my chest, finally waking my body and getting me to move again. I stumble over my dress as I turn, my feet moving faster than the rest of my body. My breath comes in tight gasps as I run toward the stairs that I know must be waiting somewhere ahead.

Heavy footsteps pound the ground behind me, rattling my bones with each step. I glance behind me once and make out the curl of a silver horn through the mist, its height almost at the ceiling. A monster stands behind me.

There were rumors of monsters in the forest around my town, but I always took them to just be rumors. Monsters were more likely to be men in the flesh. My father taught me that. But this...this is real.

Something sharp trails down my back in a feather-soft movement that arches my spine and slows me down just as I can finally make out the banister curling ahead of me.

"Don't go," the voice says.

My back tingles as I brace myself for more. I put a hand on the banister, letting it hold me up as I wait for the monster to finish what he started.

The mist thins by the stairs, exposing the monster. He stands like a man, his pale silver body lithe and muscled. Horns sprout from his head and long silver hair curls down his shoulders. His hands and feet have long talons and my spine itches with the memory of being touched by him. His face, resembling a mask, exhibits nothing but teeth and hard planes.

I keep my gaze focused on him as I move down a few steps, putting as much distance between us as I can without him coming closer.

The Lord told me there were monsters here, and I should have believed him. My fingers dig into the wood of the banister as I try to not let fear get the better of me.

The creature moves closer, its footsteps heavy enough to rattle the paintings hanging on the wall. I attempt to match its steps, maintaining the same distance between us. However, this only ensures it towers over me as it reaches the top of the stairs.

In that moment, I know I must run, even if it isn't the smartest thing to do with an animal. I can't keep standing here hoping it will lose interest when it obviously won't.

I turn, hating the feeling of turning my back to the monster as I sprint down the stairs. The front door looms ahead of me taunting me with its closeness as the creature bellows its displeasure behind me.

I'm not dressed for the cold I know waits for me, but I would rather take the risk of freezing in the elements than being torn to shreds on the stairs. The doorknob, as cold as ice, defies my attempts to clench my hand enough to turn it. Panic finally compels me to do it successfully just as the creature reaches the bottom of the stairs behind me.

My heart feels like it will burst out of its chest as I fling open the door, desperate for my freedom. I make it down the front steps, then almost lose my balance on the cobblestones. Ravens watch from their post along the wall, their black eyes glinting as the monster enters the courtyard with me.

I want to scream. I want to beg for help, but no one here can help me. Jameson won't notice I'm gone, and the Lord already warned me about wandering around and I didn't listen. Why would he choose to help me now?

The black carriage that brought me here is nowhere to be found. There's nothing out here but me and the monster and the gate that encloses the whole property. If I can make it to the gate before the monster and close it behind me, I might have a chance. Not only of surviving this but of surviving my father's contract as well.

The creature runs faster, his breathing heavy as he makes up the distance between us. I can't breathe, even as I try to move quicker. Black spots sparkle in my vision and my dress feels far too tight. My ankle twists on the uneven stones and only sheer force of will keeps me from hitting the ground. I must stay upright. If I fall now, it's over. There will be no way to survive this. And if there's one thing, I've learned in all my attempts to escape this horrible fate, this horrible future, deep down, I really want to live.

At the very least, I know that I don't want to die at the hands of a monster.

The gate sits just in front of me. Its black metal finish

shines in the murky light that permeates this place. I reach out a hand, eager to grip it.

My breath fogs in front of me, the chill settling into my skin in bright red lines. It hurts to move, hurts to breathe, but I force myself to keep going. If I don't, the hurt will be much worse.

The creature roars as my fingers close around the gate. I don't even stop to let the sound rattling my ears sink in and scare me. I can't stop now.

The ground shakes behind me, almost knocking me off my feet. My back tenses, waiting for the claw I know is coming for me. I struggle with the lock on the gate as my mind fills me with images of blood blooming across the slick cobblestones.

"Let me in! Open the lock!" My fingers slip on the cold metal of the lock, and I tug at it with no key to grant me access to the outside.

Outside the gate, the world looks brighter, with no hint of the chill that soaks into this land. Everything looks...normal... out there. It makes me tug harder, wanting more than anything to be outside. To be free of this place.

The lock creaks like it might open, and that renews my focus. I put all my weight into tugging the lock, into making it let me out of this awful place.

A howl comes from the other side of the gate as though answering the creature's roar. I still, waiting for the creator of the sound to reveal itself.

A pack of wolves moves along the wall, their jaws snapping close enough to the gate that I have to jump back or face losing fingers. They circle, watching me with raised hackles.

I have no way out, not through this gate unless I want to face the same fate I do on this side. At least behind me, there is only one monster instead of a whole pack to tear at me.

My chest caves in, a tear slipping down my cheek. This is how it ends then.

I should have listened to the Lord. If I hadn't been so eager to figure things out and find a way out myself, I would still be safe in my room with Willa.

Willa.

I hope the Lord takes care of her. I hope he doesn't hold her accountable for my sins. I hope someone keeps her safe and maybe even sends her home. She's too good of a girl to be left to rot in a place like this.

"Cora, time to go."

The voice, strikingly familiar, momentarily steals my breath anew. Not the voice of a monster...but...

"Cora." An all too human-looking hand reaches for me at the side of my peripheral. "You're safe now."

I wish I could believe that. But I can't believe anything. Can't trust anything. Not as I turn around and see the Lord standing in the courtyard with me, with no hint of the monster I was running from moments earlier.

"Wh-where did it go?" My gaze roams around the court-yard, desperate to find my enemy before he can find me.

The Lord grabs me by the wrist when I still don't take his hand. "It's gone. You may come back inside now."

My body freezes, unable to move both from the chill and the events of the last few minutes. He tugs gently on my arm but I still can't move. I can't do anything but stare at him in his black suit as he watches me with dark eyes that spark with light that swirl in a mesmerizing spiral.

"Cora. You're safe now." His tone grows softer but my shoulders still shake.

I don't even know what safe would be anymore. If he can think having a monster around like that will ever be safe, then we are two very different people.

His hand loosens on my wrist and slides down to my hand, wrapping around my fingers. "Let's go back inside now. It's far too cold for you out here."

I think I nod, but the cold makes it hard to tell. Shivers wrack my body and shock still keeps me in its firm grip. He gives me a grim smile and leads me back to the castle. He holds open the door for me and my body crumbles when the lock clicks behind me.

I cannot run away from this place.

Five

IT TAKES FAR LONGER than it should to figure out where I am when I finally wake up After being left in my room, the night was filled with hours of tossing and turning in darkness until the pain finally receded and life felt possible again. Willa kept me company with a warm lick from where she'd climbed onto the bed, which kept me from worrying that something had happened to her.

All through the night, all I could think of when coherent thoughts were possible was the Lord's warning and the monster in the castle. My headache came on strong when I got to bed and refused to leave in part because of the fear that kept my pulse racing. What else was sharing this floor with me?

Opening my eyes to the weak streams of daylight coming through the cracked curtain is too much for me to take without pangs of sorrow entering my heart. The coffered ceiling with the dangling chandelier felt too unfamiliar after years of sleeping in the same bed.

"Willa?"

I wait for her reassuring presence, wanting her warm body to give me the semblance of home.

"Willa?"

My movements are hesitant, not wanting to tempt my headache into a reappearance. Willa stays always by my side. For her to not answer...

I take a deep breath before my heart can race and my head can renew its pounding. Willa must be fine. She's a smart dog. She probably just...

My view zeros in on the open doorway.

Instantly the fears that kept me up before, flare up and nothing I can do will stop them. Where could Willa have gone? Did someone come in and take her? I think of the hallway full of closed doors we passed. *Could one of those hidden fears have taken her?*

"Willa!" I stumble off the bed, nearly tripping on my trunks that have been brought in and left in front of the bed and knocking over the tray set with tea and croissants resting atop them. The hot water scalds my feet but I barely pay them any notice as I run.

As I stand in the doorway, the hallway seems longer than ever. The mist that coated the second floor when I came up by myself has returned and I can't see the floor. Willa wouldn't have dared run through this, would she? I know I don't want to. My feet won't move no matter how hard I try to press them to.

"You will do this. You will find Willa before she can find trouble." I try not to dwell on whatever that trouble could be.

Peeking my head out the door, I almost imagine the other rooms in the hallway open, beckoning me in. But a shake of the head dispels the image and sends me back to normal.

Head safe, I finally get my feet to follow. As soon as my toes touch the mist, it shifts and backs away, revealing the black damask rug running across the wooden floor. My breath comes quickly and I brace myself against the wall. Sticking to the side feels safer, even though I know Willa wouldn't have done the same. I'm sure she ran right down the middle, right into whatever waiting trap the Lord left for her.

No, the Lord wouldn't do that. He never said a word about Willa, never even acknowledged her existence. He wouldn't have cared enough to have stolen her while I was sleeping.

"Jameson? Willa?" My voice lilts halting and quiet as I work my way to the stairwell. A whole other side of the hallway runs beyond it, but I can't bring myself to go there. Instead, I follow the wall until a banister replaces it and I use it to guide me down the stairs.

Just leaving the second floor helps me find steadier footing, my shoulders straightening the smallest fraction. I can't get too comfortable though. I may be safe now, but I have no guarantee of Willa's well-being.

A quick peek into the rooms the Lord showed me before, reveal no evidence of Willa passing through. I don't even bother opening the dining room doors. They're closed the way the Lord left them, and nothing could have coerced her to try and force them open with her small black nose.

The kitchen door at the end of the hall hangs slightly ajar, with the sound of muted voices coming through the gap. I inch my way closer, sticking to the side of the wall again as my heartbeat threatens to overwhelm the sound the voices make.

Willa's growl echoes through the hallway and I rush forward, pushing the door open with a bang. My gaze scans over the room in quick succession, only searching for Willa. She sits on the floor, a large bone still coated in meaty remains lies in front of her. I fall to my knees and scoop her into my arms. I breathe in the smell of her coat and ignore her grumbly protests.

"Willa, where did you go, you silly girl? You scared me." I squeeze her tighter, feeling her breath on my face.

"Can I offer you anything, Miss?"

I release Willa enough to see Jameson standing red-faced by the counter. Keeping a grip on Willa, I rise from the floor. My body shakes as I point a slender finger at him.

"Did you take her? Did you come into my room and take her from me?"

"N-no, Miss, I only—"

"Did you tempt her away so you could get rid of her?" I step closer to him. "You never should have touched her. She's —she's the only thing I have left." My words hitch in a sob, and once they find that crack, the sobs don't stop.

I stand shaking and blubbering while Willa works on the bone at our feet.

"I assure you. I didn't touch her. And I only wanted to help. She came to me." Jameson reaches a hand toward me then removes it just as quickly. "I never would have hurt her."

His voice stays sincere as he stares at me with big eyes, but I still can't stop crying. I've been doing my best to be strong, but without Willa...I can't do it without her. And even though the threat wasn't real, it felt real to me.

"Jameson?" The Lord stands stooped in the doorway, his attention fixed on me as a frown grows across his pale face.

Jameson shakes almost as hard as I do. "I swear sir, I didn't do anything to her. I saw the dog and wanted to help. I never thought she would react like this."

Of course, he wouldn't. He has no idea what the Lord told me last night.

The Lord looks down at where Willa happily laps at her bone. My hand remains still wrenched in her collar and I don't know if I can ever let her go.

The Lord's severe frown loosens as he looks at me. Not by much. I would have missed it if I hadn't been watching him. I sniff and use my sleeves to mop up my tears from where they've stuck to my face. In the list of worst-case scenarios I could have come up with, this definitely would rank higher than others. He must think I'm such a baby. But even knowing that doesn't stop another fat tear from slipping down my cheek.

"Come." He extends a hand to me.

I wish I could move. I wish I could take it and pretend everything is all right. But my body won't do it. Even after a long night's sleep, I'm exhausted. I can't take any more. Maybe I was never as strong as I thought I was.

I expect him to sigh, to become frustrated, to storm away from the mess I've made of myself, but he doesn't. He steps further into the kitchen and takes my arm with a gentle grip that sends a chill through my body.

"Send up more tea."

More tea. The tray. There was a tray waiting for me. In my haste to save Willa from herself, I didn't spare a thought for the tray that had been left. To the croissants that had been delivered to me.

The only person who knows I like them is the Lord.

My body feels tingly as he leads me back to my room. Willa struggles after us, carrying the bone in her mouth and growling at Jameson as she passes him.

"I apologize for this morning. If I had guessed you would react this way, I never would have..."

I shift so I can see his face where he towers above me. "Would have what?"

He shakes his head. "Never mind."

My room remains the only one with the door open, making it easy to spot. Tea spreads across the rug, and all the croissants are left in a flaky mess on the floor. Something about it makes me want to cry again. I'm saved from the embarrassment by my lack of ability. All my tears have been left behind in the kitchen.

"Would you like to rest here? I can have a bath brought

up." The Lord looks at the mess I've made of the room, avoiding eye contact with me.

"That would be wonderful. Thank you." *For everything.* But I can't say that. I can hardly say anything to this man I don't know. I don't even know his name for goodness sakes.

He gives me a curt bow and exits the room. Willa gives him a low growl before going back to her bone. Her stupid bone that caused all this trouble. I want to grab it and throw it out the window, but I know it isn't her fault what happened downstairs. That was all me. Maybe not all me. My headache played a big part in that. If I had slept better, I definitely would have been able to find more manners. I could have kept my tears a secret like I'm supposed to. Wouldn't Nanny be proud? Horrified more like with the rules I've decided to keep and the rules I've been more than happy to throw away.

I grab the tray and start replacing the items. Willa eyes the croissants, but I don't throw one her way. If I can't have them, she can't either. We're at least in *that* together.

With the tray fixed, I can do nothing about the wet mess, but I've done my best to right what I could.

I run my hand along my trunk, feeling the few days before when we packed it. Everything precious from my old life sits in here. I'm torn between wanting to fling it open and keeping it closed forever. It doesn't feel right to expose my things to this weird and empty world I've been left in. That's not where they belong. Not where I belong.

"Your tub."

A hiccup catches in my chest as I spin around. The Lord stands next to a gleaming copper tub set in front of the fire-place where a crackling fire now sits.

He just used magic like it didn't mean anything. He used it for a *tub*, a tub for *me.*

"Is this why you don't have many servants?" The question

flies out before I can stop it and I decided to just live in this one. No apologies, no trying to take it back.

"Is what why?" he asks with a raised brow.

"If you have the magic to do it yourself, why would you need anyone else." He obviously doesn't care for people, that eliminates that reason.

He stares into the flames. "That would make sense."

But my logic apparently isn't the reason why this castle is so empty.

He gives me a nod and moves to leave. I stay frozen beside my trunk, watching him go.

"Thank you." The words barely squeak past my lips, but I can tell by the way he hesitates that he heard me.

He closes the door behind him, leaving Willa and I alone again. It takes only seconds to strip down and sink into the tub. I submerge myself beneath the water and pray for the strength to survive the rest of my time here.

* * *

The water grows cold and I remain in the tub. Willa lays stretched out beside me, her belly warming from the fire that has continued to crackle away without needing any attention.

I still can't believe I made such a fool of myself. I've never felt so weak before, so out of control. But I don't know what I would have done if something had actually happened to Willa.

Rolling on my side, I eye my bed and my trunks. At some point while I was gone, the bed has been remade. The pillows are fluffed and the dark blankets have once again been pulled tight. The tray of ruined food has been taken away and in its place sits a single pot of tea with a teacup etched with fine delicate lines.

I turn away before I feel like crying again.

I don't understand why he's chosen now to act so

thoughtful and so kind. If this was who he really is he would have been this way from the beginning. If he were kind I never would have been in this situation. A thoughtful and kind man wouldn't sign a contract to take away another man's daughter, even if he offered her.

It still doesn't make sense that my father would have offered me at all. What kind of trouble could he have possibly been in that would have made him want to give away his only child?

For fear of crying again, I pull myself out of the tub. Water drips in heavy streams down my legs and I swat Willa away as she tries to lick them, her tail wagging back and forth.

Opening the wardrobe instead of going right for my trunks, I find an assortment of items inside, including a purple bathrobe so dark it's almost black with butterflies embroidered on the sleeves. I wrap myself up in it, smelling the collar as I'm enveloped in cedar wood and spices. It soothes me even though I know it was probably just a mixture used to keep moths away. Still, it's warm and nice and eases my nerves as I sit on my trunk beside the tea Jameson made.

I pour myself a cup, eyeing the details on the China. They're covered in paintings of a tree, heavy with some sort of red fruit I've never seen before. The beautiful design feels just as unsettling as everything else in this castle. I take a sip, enjoying the fruity blend, sweet but also spicy.

In many ways, even though things are so odd here, I feel better cared for tonight than I ever did at home. At least, since the monster chased me outside. My father never would have worried over me the way the Lord just did. He never thought to send me tea or make up a bath. And Nanny never would have done that. She would have thought it would have coddled me and made me unfit for the task ahead. If only she had known just how much of that task she had gotten wrong.

I wasn't traded here to become a bride. Thinking on it

now, perceive the absurdity of that thought. Why would a great Lord have wanted a nothing daughter of a man who couldn't control his finances? He would have had his pick of any ladies. I'm sure he still does. No, I really must only be here because my father wanted it. The Lord never asked for me.

If I could I would feel ridiculous, but I didn't make this deal. I have nothing to regret.

Willa's ears prick up before a soft knock comes from the door. She pads over and whines, pressing her face into the floor so she can smell through the gap between the door and the floor.

I don't have to guess who stands there. I know of only two people living here with me and if either of them were a threat, Willa would know. She wouldn't be eager for the door to open for any of the dangers the Lord said lived here.

"Come in." I straighten my back and keep my voice even. I want to erase any memory of the monster chasing me outside or the terror I unabashedly displayed thinking Willa was gone forever.

The door opens slowly as though the Lord still isn't sure he even wants to be here. He peeks around the frame, his silver hair glinting in the firelight.

"I wanted to make sure you were all right." He looks around the room, keeping his gaze from landing on me.

I pull the robe tighter at my throat. "I'm much improved. Thank you for your assistance."

He nods as Willa rolls at his feet, belly up and ready for scratches. "I apologize for the way things have been. I should have been better prepared to receive you. I have been remiss in my duties as your caretaker."

Caretaker. Something about that word makes me feel like I'm something special, like a work of art that needs to be protected and preserved. I take a sip of my tea to distract me from the heat I feel blooming in my chest.

"That being said, I wanted to warn you that there are other guests on their way to the castle." He crosses his arms over his chest and I feel my mouth drop open. "They are here for business matters and shouldn't interfere with you. However, if they do become a problem, be sure to let me know and I will take care of it."

Guests. He will host other guests. *Does that mean this place will become full of regular people to talk to?* Even though it's only been a few days, I already long for the normality of the regular movements of people in the house. I can't help the smile that spreads across my face. His head tilts as he notices it, his attention caught on the movement despite how hard he's been trying not to look at me.

"This pleases you?"

"Well..." I try not to be rude. "It's rather quiet around here."

His eyes narrow as he looks around the room as though trying to see it how I see it. "Yes, I suppose."

My chest tightens. He clearly loves the solitude or he wouldn't keep his castle this way. It was the nicest way I could say it. I'm not trying to hurt him.

Even though we don't know each other well, I know that his feelings matter to me for more than just propriety's sake. He may be cold, physically and emotionally, but he has a soft edge to him that I'm just beginning to discover.

"What kind of business will you be discussing?" I try to land somewhere safe, but the tension in the corner of my eye tells me I've chosen wrong.

"Unfortunately they are matters I cannot discuss with you. Very few are privy to the work I do here." He glances back at the fire and the flames shrink under his gaze.

I cross my leg over my knee, being careful to make sure the robe doesn't slip. "Does my father know what you do here?"

"If he did, he never would have sent you here," he says coldly.

He paces towards the door, hands curled into fists. I set my tea down and follow after him, taking his hand in mine. He looks back at me, his brow raised and body stiff, but he stops moving.

"I didn't mean to offend you." I squeeze his hand as though that will help convey my apology. "I know my questions are hard for you. This place...it's such a mystery and I want to know more."

He can't possibly blame me for that. If he were in my position, I'm sure he would feel the same way. Although, if we had traded places, he would have been sent to my father's house where more than enough servants are willing to trade gossip for favors. I have had no such luck here.

His eyes grow pained as he looks over the eagerness on my face. "This place better remains a mystery. Please try to enjoy your time here and avoid trouble. That is the best I can offer you. And when my guests come, it would be best if you tried to avoid them altogether. They don't know you're here and I would rather it stayed that way."

My forehead crinkles into a frown and he pulls away from me, closing the door behind him.

Six

I WAIT by the window in my room, watching the empty courtyard and waiting for the Lord's guests. He doesn't want them to see me so I'm not sure where else to be in the castle besides my room. I just have to hope that someone remembers I'm here long enough to keep me fed or I'll be forced to venture out despite his wishes.

It doesn't make sense to me that he would be so concerned with hiding my presence. Often, castles play host to many different guests. The fact that I'm not here of my own accord could have been something he asked me not to mention and I would have kept that secret. It's not exactly flattering to me either.

Despite how much I wanted to keep my home separate from this place, I'm forced to open one of my trunks to get dressed. I can't live in a bathrobe and the same dress that has been wrinkled beyond repair during my time here. Still, it feels weird to put on the trappings of my old life and be doing it all by myself. I always had someone to help me with buttons and other trappings each of my dresses requires. I pick the simplest one among my things, a hard task in and of itself when Nanny was the one that did my packing. Its plain brown coloring with a simple cream overlay contrasts with the heavy black of the castle, but how was I supposed to know the Lord's home would be completely black?

I struggle in front of the mirror with the neat row of tiny buttons traveling up my spine, and I still can't get all of them done. The Lord shouldn't have worried at all about me embarrassing him in front of his guests. I can't even leave my room like this.

I want to slump down on the floor in defeat, but that would only encourage Willa to jump into my lap and I don't need another outfit ruined. Besides, then I won't know if the Lord's guests are here or not, making it hard for me to even avoid them.

The window ledge spreads wide enough to serve as a seat, even with my fuller dress on. I nestle in as best I can, making myself comfortable. I don't know how long I'll be waiting. I don't even know *if* I should be waiting. Perhaps it would have been smarter to head to the kitchen and stock up first. Maybe I should have told Jameson to make sure I was taken care of. Either way, it feels like if I leave now, I'll get caught downstairs and I want the Lord to trust me.

I'd say it was a stupid wish if not for the fact that we're stuck together. No matter that he's cold and distant, he remains my only human interaction around here, whether either of us likes it. I cannot be blamed for wanting the only human around to trust me. That's just a normal and realistic thing.

If I push that edge of it, then maybe I won't be able to think about what Nanny wanted for me or the kindness I see in him myself. There could be more there than he'd like me to see and given long enough, I know I'll grow to like him in spite of himself. Maybe never the way Nanny wanted, but at least as a friend.

A friend wouldn't be so bad in this frozen prison.

Willa licks my ankle, reminding me of her presence.

"You're always my number one friend, don't you worry girl." I give her a reassuring pat on the head and she lolls her tongue out at me. "I don't know what I'd do without you."

Voices echo through the hallway, slinking under my door. I whip my head from the door to the window and back again. This couldn't be the Lord's visitors. No one came into the house. Not that I saw.

I drop off the window seat and move for the door, crouching down as I press my ear into the gap to hear what's going on. I try to block out the images of having some terrible creature stick a long talon through the gap and into my ear. I wish the Lord had never warned me about this place. I have no idea if he even meant it literally or figuratively. I'm not actually prepared in any way for whatever he wanted to protect me from. Instead, I just feel jumpy and paranoid for no reason.

Still, I swallow my irrational fears and keep listening, waiting for clues as to who the Lord's guests may be.

"Must it be so cold here?" a female voice asks, her tone tinged with disgust. "Some of this proves a choice right?"

Another man laughs. "It wouldn't be Aidoneus if it wasn't miserable around here. Right brother?"

"This remains the land you gifted me. You can hardly be surprised at what it's like here," the Lord says, his voice bored.

Aidoneus; the name feels weird in my brain. I've been calling him 'the Lord' for so long. I never asked for his name, and he never felt prompted to tell me.

Aidoneus.

It would be weird to call him that now. Too personal almost. Too...intimate to use his first name.

"If it has to be an extreme, why pick this one?" The

woman's voice itches against my brain. "Why choose for it to be cold when you could just as easily choose a hot climate?"

"Because then it wouldn't match Aidoneus anymore. Come, you must agree, it aligns perfectly with what you imagined for him." The man laughs again.

"Can I show you to your rooms?" The Lord, Aidoneus, asks. His voice sounds bored, but I can hear an edge to it.

Maybe the reason he didn't want them to know I was here has nothing to do with how they would respond to *me* and everything to do with his dislike of *them*.

"I'm not sure how long I can stay here." The woman's voice becomes more of a whine. "It's too cold for me. I'm sure I'll turn into ice overnight."

"Don't be so dramatic," Aidoneus says. "After all, my dear brother has had me down here for years without once checking on me and I never turned to ice."

"I can't believe you're still sore about that." The laughter has evaporated from the other man's voice. "I hadn't much of a choice either. Someone had to take care of business here."

"Yes, that sounds like me, nothing but sore for no reason."

I find it hard to stay on my side of the door when all I want is to see the Lord's face and know what he's thinking. Not that I know him terribly well for that yet, but I would know more than I would in my bedroom.

Willa whines from her spot on the floor next to me, blowing out a moist breath that doesn't make it all the way through the crack beneath the door and instead hits me in the face.

"What am I going to do with you?" I whisper to her, torn between feeling disgusted and wanting to squish her in my arms.

"What was that?" Aidoneus's brother asks. The footsteps that had been coming down the hall halt.

"What was what?" Aidoneus's voice stays carefully bored. "There are many creatures around here, as well you know."

"No," his brother says and I can feel the smile creeping across his face. "This definitely isn't a creature."

I grab Willa's collar and pull her back from the door with me. My breath grows shallow as my legs hit the side of the bed. Willa growls low in her throat at the door. I can't hear them moving in the hallway, but I can *feel* their presence on the other side.

The Lord asked me not to let his guests know I was here, and I've done that. I haven't left my room. Why did he bring them up here if he didn't want them to discover me?

Why did I open my stupid mouth?

Never in my life would I have expected them to hear me. By all accounts, they shouldn't have. I was being quiet. No *normal* person would have heard me.

The doorknob rattles and my knees go weak.

I don't know why I'm afraid of them. Sure they sound rude, but *afraid*? I'm having such an illogical response that it has me questioning my sanity. Nothing has been normal for me since I came to the castle, and I've never wanted to be back home more than I do now.

From the other side of the door, I can hear the Lord say something, but I can't make it out. I wonder if he'll tell them I'm one of the awful monsters I've thought live behind the other doors. I'm sure in some ways he believes that. He doesn't want me here and I can't leave. That could be considered awful.

The doorknob jiggles again, the metal knocking against the wooden door. Willa growls for so long that I'm sure she'll bark. And then...silence.

Willa stays alert for a few more minutes and then relaxes, rubbing her back along the carpet with her paws in the air. I wish I could relax so easily.

I watch the door for a long time, my heart rate easing down slowly.

That was close. I have no idea what the Lord said, but I can feel in my bones that he saved me.

The Lord. Do I dare call him Aidoneus, even in the dark recesses my mind? Why does that feel so disrespectful...so intimate? He didn't give me his name and I never asked, but now that I know it, I still don't know if I want to use it.

The funny name feels odd in my mouth even without saying it out loud. It feels like another reminder of how far from home I am. Not that a regular name would suit him. I can't imagine him as a Walter or a Robert. No, Aidoneus suits him somehow, despite its oddity.

I'll get used to it.

I sink to the floor with Willa, letting her roll onto my legs. Petting her belly brings my heart rate back to normal. I just hope his guests aren't staying long.

* * *

Jameson brings me up a tray at what I assume is dinner time. The sun never gets bright and never moves in the sky, at least from what I can tell, which makes tracking the time feel impossible.

Still, I'm grateful to not be forgotten. This time he even brings a small foldable table that he places the tray on. No more precarious trunk sitting.

"What are the Lord's guests doing here?" I ask him as he keeps his face turned away from me.

"What do you mean?"

"If the Lord doesn't want to have guests, why are they here? What are they doing?" I pry from my place on the bed.

"The Lord must do as his brother commands. That is the nature of being the younger brother." Jameson lifts the lid off the tray, revealing succulent meat in a warm brown sauce.

Younger brother. That makes more sense, especially considering what they were saying. The Lord doesn't want to be here, but this is the part of the estate that was given to him. That's not that out of the ordinary. Why would the oldest brother give something he could want, away? It definitely makes sense on his end to get rid of the parts he might see as 'undesirable'.

"Does his brother visit often?"

Jameson grimaces. "More than the Lord would like, but not often, no. Their relationship has proved complicated."

"Who is the woman with them?" I know I'm pushing my luck here, but I can't help it. I have to know what's going on.

Jameson glances at me, his eyes animalistic in the firelight. "If the Lord wants you to know, he will tell you."

"That would be assuming he comes around to check on me." I sink further into the bed.

"I'm sure he will." Jameson sets the metal lid down with a clang. "Now, eat up. Enjoy yourself. Take advantage of the quiet."

I probably would if it didn't seem like a threat that every day would be like this. There's not so much enjoyment in something forced.

I stare up at the ceiling, listening to Jameson's footsteps across the floor and the click of the door as he leaves. I don't want to run into the Lord's brother, I really don't, but I also don't want to sit up here letting the mystery pass me by either. If Jameson is wrong and Aidoneus doesn't come around to check on me, there will be no way to get any answers. Which would be tragic considering this marks the first interesting thing that has happened since I came here.

Grabbing the tray, I move it into the bed with me. The meat is soft and warm and perfectly seasoned. I'm being fed better than I usually am at home. Although, there I at least got every meal and here it can be hit or miss. I can't win them all.

At least I know that even with everyone here, I haven't been forgotten. Jameson showed that by nature of this meal, and Aidoneus perhaps because he was forced to by his brother. But forced may prove better than nothing. If I'm stuck here thinking of him, then I want him forced to think of me just a little bit.

Seven

IT TAKES LESS than half a day for me to become too bored with sitting in my room to stand it anymore. Willa agrees with me, although her need to use the bathroom probably serves as the biggest driving force for her. She could probably stare at the same walls for the rest of her life and never complain as long as she's with the right person.

Maybe I could be like that too but I just haven't met the right person.

Still, I can't just stay here and I'm sure somewhere exists where I wouldn't get in the way of anyone. Like the kitchen. My stomach growls, reminding me that I've missed breakfast. I can't imagine that Aidoneus and his brother would be in the kitchen. That could be a safe place to be. Plus, Jameson might be there and that would give me someone other than Willa to talk to, even if he doesn't like my questions very much.

It takes me a few tries to get up and reach the door. Even though I don't want to stay here, I *really* don't want to run into Aidoneus's brother. There's something about him that feels... different. And not like Aidoneus is different. There's an... aura there that I want to avoid. But if I can make it out the door and down the stairs, I should be good. The stairs that worry me the most. If they see me there, I'll have nowhere to go. I'll be stuck, discovered, and Aidoneus will be furious.

Willa's leash clenches tight in my hand as I finally muster the courage to open the door. The hallway sits quiet and empty. Not even the fog that has covered the floor in the past is there. Everything hides from Aidoneus's brother.

I give Willa a stern look as though that could keep her from barking if she sees someone. It may be a long shot, but it's worth a try. She gives me a tiny huff which I like to believe means she knows what I'm asking for and takes offense that I even feel the need to ask.

The rug running along the length of the hallway muffles our footsteps as we creep closer to the stairs. I want to cling to the side of the wall, but I don't want to get any closer to the other doors. I still don't know what lurks inside those rooms and I don't want today to be the day I find out.

The sconces lining the wall have been lit. I never even noticed them before in the near darkness, but now they emit a bright blue flame that curls and twists, bringing light to the hallway without leaving a trace of smoke on the ceiling. It's a nice touch even if this isn't when I needed the light. The shadows that permeated this place would have been a nice touch to keep me moderately hidden as I crept to the kitchen.

Willa's tail wags back and forth as she pulls me closer to the stairs. The silence settles on me like a thick blanket. I can hear nothing but the ringing in my ears. Not even the flames make a noise as they guide our way. But maybe that will be helpful. Maybe it will mean we'll hear Aidoneus's guests long before they can hear us.

I grab the stair rail with shaking hands. With every step, my heart rate has increased. This was beyond stupid. There's no way I won't get caught. I have to keep going though. I tell myself that I'm doing all of this for Willa. She needs to go out or else she'll eventually have an accident. That's just facts. Facts Aidoneus didn't think of when he told me to stay hidden. This isn't *really* my fault.

I find it pathetic how hard I'll push that as though I'm just ready to get caught.

Willa pulls me down the stairs before I'm ready, leaving me stumbling after her. My footsteps are louder than before, practically clattering in the silence. If anyone resides in the two main rooms downstairs, they'll know I'm here and catch me before I can even get to the bottom.

I tug her leash, forcing her to wait for me. My breathing sounds louder than my heartbeat as I stand halfway down the stairs for a few minutes. It may be risky, I need to compose myself before I can keep going. Willa whines but I give her a look that shushes her. She slumps onto the stairs, her tail wagging as she watches me. I wish I could be more like her. Nothing gets her down. Not even being forced to move here and hide upstairs for an eternity. I do like to think that she would have been devastated if I'd left without her though. It's a long shot as she probably would have just shifted her affections to someone else. But I like the idea of it just the same.

When I feel like I can breathe normally again, I give Willa a gentle nudge and we move down the stairs together this time. Her nails clack against the hardwood as I move us along at a quick pace, hoping that if we can just make it to the kitchen, everything will be okay.

I practically run off the end of the stairs and whip around to the hallway. We move past the dining room doors, open this time with the table set for three. The curious part of me feels tempted to stop and see what Aidoneus and his guests will eat, but that's an incredibly quick way to get caught. Instead I take the last few steps to the kitchen door, gently swinging it open and ushering Willa through before she can change her mind.

Chaos reigns in the kitchen. Food covers every inch of the kitchen counters, filling the room with mad preparations. Flour hangs heavy in the air, making the room feel just as dark as the other areas of the castle.

"Jameson?" I can see no obvious cook in the room, but he must be around here somewhere. I won't complain though because no one else happens to be in the kitchen either. Better to have no one than to have Aidoneus's brother.

I grab a few meat scraps off the counter to give Willa who continues to sniff around the room while her tail goes crazy. A bowl of whipped cream sits under the window, and I use a spoon to lift off a small serving to taste.

"What do you think you're doing in here?"

The spoon clatters to the ground as I slowly turn to face the wide-open kitchen door. A woman stands there, her curly grey hair spiking out in a million different directions. Flour coats her from head to toe, making her look like a ghost. I lick my lips to make sure none of the offending whipped cream still sits there.

"Sorry, I didn't realize anyone was here."

"And that makes going through the belongings of someone else, okay?" She braces a hand against her wide hip as she stares at me. Behind her, the door still hangs open and I offer a silent prayer that no one decides to come down for their dinner right now.

"Of course not, I was just looking for Jameson. I thought he was the cook here." I thought he did everything here. After days of seeing no one else, I almost can't believe this woman exists.

"Jameson the cook?" She laughs. "That poor boy couldn't boil eggs."

So Jameson doesn't cook anything. I file that bit of information away. No wonder why he never brought me meals like I told him to. So what does he do then?

"I'm Cora." I hold out a hand to her.

She raises her hands, covered in a thick layer of flour, and shrugs before lowering them back down without accepting my offer. "I know who you are. You're the girl forced upon the Lord."

I feel myself start to babble, my lips moving without any words behind them.

"Are you stupid too?" the woman asks as she comes deeper into the kitchen and the door finally swings closed. She picks up a wooden spoon and a bowl and starts mixing.

"No, of course not." I try to straighten my spine and wipe the stupid look off my face. "I've just never encountered someone so..."

"Honest?" she supplies with a smile. "Don't worry about that. You'll learn that we don't stand on much ceremony here."

I still don't know what to do with her. No one back home would have talked like this and I met plenty of people that didn't live completely by propriety. I mean, Nanny often had words with me that she would never dream of for anyone else.

"What else do you know about me?" I lean against the counter, using it for extra strength.

She glances at me for a second before continuing her mixing. "Just what I needed to. You're another one sent to pay off another's debts."

Another one?

"There have been others?" My voice is so quiet that for a second I'm sure she doesn't hear me.

"More than I would like to count. They come, they wither, and then we never see them again. There are not many that could survive here long."

"So I've heard."

My fingers grip the table harder. Could that be what Aidoneus meant when he gave me his warning before? There are no monsters around here. I'm just going to collapse into nothingness and wither away. I bite my tongue to bring myself back into focus.

"Is that why no one else is around?"

She glances at me with a smile. "Not many *could* be here. We're just the lucky ones."

She slaps the mixture she's been working on with a heavy *thunk* into a tray that makes me jump as she casually pops it into the oven.

"This doesn't bother you at all?"

"Why should it? It's always been this way."

My forehead wrinkles as I try to understand this woman. "There are many things that have always been a certain way and they still manage to bother me."

"And in that we are different. I do not strive above my station. I do not try to alter my present. This is my life and I am grateful for it. It could always be worse."

Not exactly a ringing endorsement of living here. I want more from my life than that it 'could be worse'.

It feels as if my life insists on never truly beginning. I've moved from one limbo of waiting to another. And the worst part is that no one even seems to care. Not my father, not Aidoneus, not the cook. Everyone else seems content with how things are. Only I feel like there should be more.

Maybe my father was right when he told me I was the problem.

"Don't look so blue." The woman pauses to wash something in the sink, her hair sticking to the side of her face as the room heats up. "I'm sure you'll do just fine here."

Not like the others Aidoneus mentioned.

I'm not sure if I feel sick or faint. My legs threaten to give out on me, but I don't want to sink to the floor in front of this woman. She seems far too strong and capable for me to be so weak in front of.

Willa nudges my legs, reminding me that her needs are what helped force me down here in the first place.

"Do you have a back door in here? I need to take her out."

The woman peers over the counter at Willa as though seeing her for the first time. "Yeah, right through there." She points at the back corner of the kitchen where a small door with a glass window set in it waits for us.

"Thank you." Just because she doesn't have many manners doesn't mean I'll abandon mine altogether.

I grab Willa and head for the door, bracing myself against the cold waiting for me. She doesn't seem to care as I open the door and she races out with wild abandon.

The chill air races into my lungs, burning into me almost instantly. I don't even have my gloves this time to pretend to be prepared for this place. But even so, being outside feels better than being in the kitchen with the cook.

Something about her just got under my skin in a way no one else here has. Sure I was worried about what Aidoneus said to me, but it didn't have the same backing to it. It was fear without basis. Now I feel like I have basis and I don't like it.

Willa and I take the wooden stairs down to a stone court-yard that mimics the one we arrived in. Except instead of seeing a fence at the back, there are other outbuildings. I'm sure the carriage went there, and the horses if he even has them. He certainly doesn't need them like the rest of us do.

Willa whines as she searches for a patch to do her business in, but she won't find one. I haven't seen a single green thing in the whole time I've been here.

I glance at her with a sad smile. "You're just going to have to learn to make do."

"As do we all," a low voice adds in.

I jump closer to Willa as Aidoneus's brother comes

around the corner of the house. He doesn't wear gloves or a jacket either, but he seems fine even as his breath billows out before him.

Creeping toward the wall, I keep an eye on him even as my heart rate skyrockets. I should have just stayed in the kitchen with the cook. If I can just back up a bit, I might be able to find the stairs and make a run for it.

"So you're my brother's secret." He watches me shift, blue eyes flashing in the dim light. "No wonder he didn't want me snooping around. He sent me outside to get me far away from you."

I cringe. That makes sense and I appreciate the gesture. Something about his brother makes me feel unsafe. Something lingers in the air like when a predator hunts. I've felt it before at home with wolves but Aidoneus's brother looms far larger and feels far more dangerous.

"So where did he collect you?" He gets closer to me but stays far enough away that I shouldn't feel like running. It doesn't work.

"He didn't collect me. I came on my own." Kind of a stretch, but one that feels important as his eyes widen.

"You came here all on your own? You wanted to be here? Surely it wasn't for my brother. There's a reason he was sent here. No one wants to be with him."

I'm glad Aidoneus isn't here to hear him. He may be cold and odd, but he's still a person. If my father had talked about me that way...it would have been devastating. It gives me the courage I've felt slowly fading in the face of this man.

"Maybe you don't know your brother very well." I straighten my spine and tighten my lips.

"Is that so?" he grins, and I feel his desire to come closer to me, like a jungle cat testing its prey. The hair on the back of my neck raises up. "And you do?"

"I know as much as I need to."

He laughs. "This is perfect! What a funny twist to come upon. And I thought when I came here to inspect what Aidoneus had been up to that it would be boring. That couldn't have been farther from the truth. You, my lady, are a delight."

He tips his head toward me and continues walking. His laughter fills the courtyard and I feel like I can't move until I can no longer hear it. But the silence almost worsens the situation as my knees turn to jelly and I sink into the freezing stone.

My heart hammers. I can't breathe. Closer. He steps closer.

I did the one thing Aidoneus asked me not to do. Sure it was on accident, but I don't think that will make it better. Aidoneus's brother exudes danger, and he wanted me hidden from him with good reason. *What will happen now? Will The Lord defend me the way I defended him?* Somehow I don't know.

It's cold. So cold here. It pierces through my skin and into my bones.

Willa licks my hand, giving me just enough courage to do what my brain and heart are screaming to me.

Escape. Flee. Run, run, run for your life.

Scooping up a protesting Willa, I run for the door. The cook tries to say something to me, but I just keep running. I breeze past the dining room and up the stairs to the hallway where the misty second floor looks thicker than ever as though trying to make up for not being there before. I don't even care. None of this compares to the fear waiting for me outside. I push through the fog, forcing it out of my way whether it wants to move or not. I won't be taking orders from it today. Not when it stands in the way of the only place of safety I have in this castle.

Willa struggles out of my arms and hits the ground with a

heavy *thunk*. She doesn't seem to care though as she runs for our room too, making it there before I do.

I open the door and let us in. I don't feel safe even with the door closed. Leaning against it, I take ragged breaths, bracing myself against the door.

What happened down there feels like only the beginning.

Eight

I SPEND all night waiting for Aidoneus to come and rage at me for doing the one thing he asked me not to do. I try to sleep, but my racing heart won't let me calm down enough. Willa has no such problems and lounges at the end of the bed, feet up and belly exposed as she finds complete peace.

She's so perfect and I love her so much even as I wish I could ease and find rest myself. Then again, when Aidoneus does eventually come, it won't be Willa who finds trouble. That will be saved for me.

The thing that really keeps me from sleeping is just not knowing what he will say to me. *How angry will he be? What will his brother say to him about me?* I have no control over any of that. I thought I had no control in my father's home, but that was nothing compared to being here. This cold, dark castle has tested my limits of self-control and autonomy.

When the grey light of dawn comes in through the window, I stop pretending that I'm going to find sleep. It's not like it matters anyway. I have nothing to do here so I can rest *after* Aidoneus undoubtedly yells at me.

Digging through my trunk, I try to find simple clothes to

wear, but Nanny didn't pack it that way. Some of these gowns I might as well throw out the window. There's no way to wear them with their complicated buttons and clasps without another person to assist me. And having met the only other woman in the castle, she would be the last person I would ask for help with this. I can only imagine what she would say about the intricacies of garments meant to entice a man to marriage. The whole idea remains ridiculous, and I'm embarrassed enough on my own without including her in it too.

I grab a light pink dress and shimmy into it as best I can, leaving buttons and clasps already done up. It squeezes against my body and traps me in the material, almost making me panic as I stop making progress for a minute. But then I'm free and the fabric slides into place like it should.

A sly, happy grin sneaks its way across my face as I brace my hands on my hips in victory. I did it. I did it all on my own.

Soft knocking comes from my bedroom door and the smile vanishes from my face. My hands feel clammy, and I struggle not to give in to the urge to wipe them on my skirts, but this material would be unforgiving so there's no option than to just let them be. They slip on the lock as I unlock it.

"C-come in."

I hold my hands behind my back and straighten my spine as though that will make everything better. At least no one else has to know how badly they're shaking.

The door cracks open slowly, as though whoever waits on the other side has just as much apprehension about this as I do. The hinges creak and Willa jumps off the bed to get closer. Her tail slowly wags at whatever lingers on the other side, so at least not someone dangerous. Probably.

"You broke your word." The door finally finishes opening, revealing Aidoneus on the other side. In some ways, I find relief that he's finally come. Let's get this over with.

"I assure you, it wasn't my intention. Willa needed to go out. I had no idea he would be out there."

Aidoneus's face resembles stone as he watches me. His hands are tucked into his jacket pocket and halts in the doorway.

"I thought outside the castle would keep Canaean a safe distance away. Apparently, there is no safe distance away from you. Is it your mission to find trouble?"

My brow furrows as I bite my lip. "Actually, this marks the first time we've had trouble since I've been here. That doesn't sound too bad considering what I could have gotten up to."

He looks away from me, his frown growing, but breaking eye contact says to me that I'm winning this one.

"Why aren't I allowed to meet your guests anyway? One of them is your *brother*, so they're not random people. Plus, I saw that you use the dining room for them. Am I not a guest deserving of the dining room too?" At least if we ate there it would give me something to do around here.

"I would be less likely to hide you away for a stranger than I am for my brother. My brother..." He grimaces. "It would have been better for all of us if he didn't know you were here. But the damage is done now and nothing we can do to change it."

"You guys aren't close then I take it."

Aidoneus glances at me, his eyes narrowed. "No. We aren't."

I wish I could melt into the floor to get away from my stupid question, but now that I've said it, I might as well continue. "What happened?"

He stares at the fire crackling in the grate, the frown growing deep lines on his face. "He sent me here."

It's a simple statement, but one that holds so much meaning behind it. I glance at the room around me with new eyes. While not as bad as the rest of the castle, it's still dark and cold and lonely. It makes sense that he wouldn't have chosen this for himself. Who would? It feels awful here like the hope has been sucked out of this place.

What could Aidoneus have done to get him sent to a place like this?

"I'm sorry."

He glances at me, humor dancing in his eyes. "Are you now? And what exactly are you sorry for? Have the accommodations not been to your liking?"

I can't tell if he's teasing or genuinely annoyed, but something about the way he looks at me prompts me to be honest. "No."

His eyes grow wide and he tilts his head as though seeing me for the first time. "No?"

"I'm sure you know what it's like to live in a normal home. You know what normal expectations are. Do you pride yourself in subverting them?"

"I haven't—"

"But you have. Where are the servants to keep such a fine castle? Where might the lady's maid be to help me dress? You don't even keep regular mealtimes with me and then expect me to be fed some other way which I'm forced to discover myself. Your castle feels cold and empty. This shouldn't be the way anyone lives."

His eyes narrow as I finish and he looks away from me again. "This is not a place made for the living."

I fight the urge to roll my eyes at his dramatics. "You only feel this way because you look at this place as a punishment."

I'm just guessing now, but his jaw tightens and I must be close to the right track. My hands feel less sweaty now and I take the risk of relaxing them by my side.

"This place *is* a punishment. How else am I supposed to look at it?"

I take a step closer to him. "Perhaps as an opportunity."

He raises a brow, his face incredulous as he looks at me. "An opportunity for what?"

"You said your brother seldom comes here. Doesn't that mean you can turn it into whatever you want? Does it really have to be cold and sad here all the time? I'm sure no one forces it to be so empty. These are all choices that only *you* can make."

"No one would want to join me here."

"Maybe it isn't all about you." I brace a hand on my hip. "Maybe they want to come and join me. Plus, it mustn't be all or nothing, now and forever, maybe they just come for a visit."

Aidoneus laughs. "A visit? Impossible."

"Why not?" I can't help but frown, the attitude bleeding into my voice. "Your brother and a lady are here right now. Why are they the only ones who can visit?" I keep myself out of it. I'm still hoping this isn't permanent but obviously, we have different ideas about what happens at the castle.

"It constitutes one of the conditions of being here."

I flinch. If he notices, he doesn't say anything. No wonder why we have different ideas. If I want to ever go home again, he will be the one I'll work on first.

"Have you ever thought about giving it up?"

He glances at me sharply. "Give it up?"

"Just because your brother gave you this castle doesn't mean you have to live in it. You could start over on your own and do something else."

The humor comes back to his face and I can't help but smile at him too. I don't know anyone who would give up a castle or a family title just because they didn't like it. Even not liking a castle would be miles better than living on the streets and trying to learn a trade you were never brought up for. This likely comprises all he knows: managing an estate. Not that there can be much of one to manage.

He sighs. "I couldn't leave even if I wanted to. There are

some things you could never understand, and it's better for you that way. I appreciate your desire to help me, but some of this proves necessary."

"Including your misery?"

He looks at me and I can see it so clearly in his eyes. How does everyone else not see it? He's suffering here.

"Including that."

He turns around and grabs the doorknob, his back tight under his black suit jacket. "I appreciate your help, but there truly remains nothing you can do. This must be. Don't worry yourself about me."

Thrusting the door open, he slams it shut as soon as he exits the room, leaving me alone once more.

He didn't yell. He barely scolded me. My surprise nearly outweighs my relief.

* * *

I go back and forth on what I want to do with the rest of my day. I don't have a ton of options, but I do have a few and they either agree with what Aidoneus wants or go directly against him. Still, the decision feels harder than it should.

In the end, it really comes down to a war between pleasing myself, Aidoneus, and my fear of his brother. But his brother knows I'm here now, no matter what I do. So in that way hiding doesn't make any sense. The only thing it does is please Aidoneus and then I'm stuck in this room. But staying in this room also means not having to see his brother again, which I also prefer. Everything points to staying here where I'm safe but it's just too boring and I can't do it. Apparently, I'm willing to throw away my safety if it means not staring at the same four walls forever. Plus, my belly lets out a loud rumble, reminding me that it should be dinnertime by now and breakfast was never brought up. Dinner may never be brought up either unless I do something. So really, leaving serves my best interest because it will help keep me alive. I'm not *that* stupid.

Still, Willa whines as I try to go out the bedroom door.

This has become ridiculous. Why must my bedroom be my only sanctuary? It's always so hard to leave it. I just want a normal life in a normal castle where dinner gets served at normal times and I'm expected to be there and maybe even given someone to help me dress.

Given the circumstances, I know the dresses I can manage on my own are nothing close to what would be considered evening wear. Still, there's nothing I can do about that, and dressed remains better than the alternative.

I hold my hand up for Willa to stay and head into the hallway with a straight spine and a determined focus. The fog isn't waiting for me, and something about that feels like a victory. It won't intimidate me anymore. I'm mastering this odd castle. One step at a time.

I keep no hint of hesitation in my steps even as I descend the stairs. My body stands strong, and my legs are steady. I don't need to show his brother that he scares me. That's information that only I need to know.

At the bottom of the stairs, I can hear the clink of silver against China and it makes me hesitate. Being late to a meal was something Nanny would never have allowed. There were a few meals at home I missed entirely because I hadn't shown up when dinner was served. Nights spent crying with an empty belly cured me of my tardiness, just like Nanny said it would.

At home it would be impossible to go into that room, but here? Here I'm already not allowed so what does it matter? Either way, Aidoneus will be upset and his brother will be just as creepy. Maybe I'm a little more of a target than I would have been if I had been on time, but I was going to be a target tonight either way.

The starched layers of my dress rustle along the hallway

and my shoes clack on the wood floor. If Aidoneus wants to stop me, he only has to be paying attention a little bit to know I'm coming.

I pass the parlor and take a deep breath before moving into the open doorway of the dining room. The low hum of conversation stops and all eyes turn to me. Aidoneus sits to the right of his brother who has taken the head of the table, with the lady who came with him sitting on the other side. Aidoneus scowls at me, but his brother has a wide grin. Slowly, Aidoneus rises from his seat, giving me the courtesy due me for being a lady, and his brother follows suit.

"I did not think you would be joining us," Aidoneus says through clenched teeth.

"I know, I just thought—"

"Surely enough room exists at the table." His brother gestures to the many empty seats. "Why shouldn't she be invited to dine with us? She seems like most diverting company." He smiles in what should be a charming way, but all I can see are his teeth.

Aidoneus swallows and looks down at his clenched hands. "Would you care to join us?"

I nod and Jameson appears, seemingly out of nowhere, to pull out a chair for me next to the other lady. She doesn't look at me as I settle in next to her, keeping her focus on Aidoneus's brother.

"What a pleasure it was to meet you outside, if only for a moment," his brother says as he sinks back into his chair. "You ran away before we could become better acquainted."

I don't ever want to be more acquainted than we are right now. Dining companions represent the farthest I want to go. And for a moment, it all feels worth it as Jameson dishes me a steaming bowl of soup. I steady myself, giving myself a quick reminder of my manners as I dip my spoon into the rich broth and give it a gentle blow before I can swallow it.

"So," his brother says when I've had time to swallow. "What brought you to this unfortunate castle?"

His eyes dance in the candlelight as he watches me, but there are no sparks to light them up like Aidoneus's and I find myself missing the brightness.

"That feels like an interesting question coming from someone also staying here." I dab at my lips with a napkin.

He waves away my distraction. "I would not be here if I didn't have to be, as I'm sure is the case for you as well. Business requires attention. Debts need paying."

I glance at Aidoneus but he still won't look at me. It seems my father isn't the only one who can get himself into trouble. At least Aidoneus seems to be more of a man than my father and will take care of his debts himself instead of foisting them onto some unsuspecting innocent.

His brother leans over his bowl, smiling at me. "Are you also here because of debts?"

"My presence here is my own business."

He explodes with laughter falling back into his chair. "Aidoneus, you should have guests every time I come to visit. I demand it. She proves so much more fun than you."

I focus on not frowning by remembering how many wrinkles doing so could form. Plus, if I truly show his brother that I am affected, then he will only find more fun in messing with me. I can feel it.

"Enough Canaean," Aidoneus growls. "She does not serve as your toy, and you do not get to treat her as such."

Canaean's head whips toward Aidoneus, his smile growing even wider. "Is she your toy then? Is that why she is here?"

"You bore me." The woman beside me puts her spoon down with a clang. "Surely this mousy girl is not so entirely riveting that she will take over the entire meal."

"Teleia, you cannot possibly be jealous of this one."

Canaean seems to be having the time of his life as even the lady he came with becomes disgruntled. "Am I not permitted any fun at all?"

"Not of this sort." She flings her napkin onto the table and stomps out of the room, light purple skirts swishing behind her.

"You must forgive her." Canaean leans toward me conspiratorially. "You see, we're under contract to be married and that makes any woman a little more volatile. Wouldn't you agree?"

Jameson steps forward to remove my barely touched soup.

"I believe that a woman you are about to marry deserves your respect." I'm not sure what exists between them, but I wouldn't like it if my betrothed was eying another in front of me either.

Aidoneus jerks his head toward me, his narrowed eyes pleading with me to stop.

"It seems, Aidoneus, like we have only continued to gather women determined to bring chaos into our lives." Canaean sighs. "It was too much to hope for that there would be one woman in this house who would understand my predicament."

"And what predicament do you mean?" I ask dryly.

This wouldn't be the first time a man has insinuated that I'm crazy and I'm sure it won't be the last. If I fell to pieces any time that happened, then what they said about me would be true. I would never allow that.

"This predicament was foisted upon me by others due to a few missteps. I'm sure you of all people believe that our lives should not be ruled by a few moments." He takes a sip of the red liquid filling his goblet.

My fingers dig into the napkin on my lap. "Why do you think this would be something I would agree with?"

"Isn't that what happened to you?" His eyes twinkle, but no magic exists behind it. "A few moments you wish you could take back and then you wouldn't be forced to live in this place despite your delightful dining companions."

I bristle. "You know nothing about why I'm here."

Jameson sets down the main course in front of Canaean, meat covered in a sauce filled with little mushrooms fills the plate. Canaean spears a mushroom and tilts his head at me.

"Regardless of how much you wish it wasn't so, because this was a domain of mine that I have given Aidoneus, I know more about it than you. I know you couldn't have possibly shown up here just because you wanted to, no matter how much nicer of a story that would be. Something has led you here, and I'm willing to bet you wish you could take it back, just as I wish that about a few things that happened with our dear Teleia."

I wish I could stand and leave the table just like dear Teleia, but she's already used that move for power. It wouldn't have the same effect if I used it now. I'm going to finish this dinner if I want to leave with my head held high.

"I think you talk too much," Aidoneus says, coming to my rescue. "Are you trying to scare her away?"

"If she were so easily scared, she wouldn't have ventured in, in the first place." Canaean's smile turns feral as he shifts his attention to Aidoneus.

"Regardless, I need you to not scare my guests away. A moment of entertaining conversation can't be near as pleasant as several encounters. If you continue to act thus, I cannot guarantee she'll be willing to join us again." Aidoneus cuts into his meat with a bored stroke, but I can see the tension in his neck. I'm sure Canaean can too. There can be no fooling him, no matter how much we both want to try.

"I'm sure you couldn't keep her from me if you tried." Canaean keeps eating, his attention never wavering from Aidoneus. "What makes you eager to protect this one?"

I feel Aidoneus wanting to look at me, but he keeps his

focus on his brother. "I've seen what you've done with others who have come through here. This may be the domain *you* have given me, but this remains *my* house. I get to say what happens to those under my care."

A tickle of a smile wants to prick at my lips, but I know it will only fuel Canaean more, so I don't let it come out. However, not letting it out on my face only lets it travel and bloom as warmth in my chest.

I glance at him, but he focuses on his plate, silver hair falling in front of his face. He doesn't look much like his brother, with his skin still bearing the bloom of sunshine. His hair is blonde, and his face is lively, but Aidoneus captures my attention. It's his cold and calculating face that makes me want to find out what he could be thinking. It's the distant way that he carries himself while still finding ways to take care of me that has me coming back for more. And something about his cold features drives my focus. He's beautiful like the sun reflecting off frozen branches in the winter. His skin is all smooth planes, untouched by time.

Dragging my focus back to my plate, I dig in with larger bites than ladylike manners would indicate, to keep my emotions tamped down. Any more thinking about him and I would definitely end up betraying myself.

The rest of the meal stays silent, each of us deep in our thoughts. As soon as Jameson takes the last plate, I move from the table as gracefully as I can. I make it into the hallway before I break into a run.

If only my bedroom were a safe place to hide from myself.

Nine

NOW THAT I'VE gone to a meal, Aidoneus can't hide me away like he was hoping to. However, when we meet again for breakfast, Canaean doesn't drill me with any more personal questions. I'm not sure what Aidoneus said to him, but the reprieve allows me to behave as a lady, something that acts as a shield of protection between me and the rest of them. I keep myself under control and all my emotions safely tucked away. I didn't realize before how much I needed that wall.

Teleia comes to meals just as quietly as I do, but her eyes are busy. She watches Canaean with an intensity that makes me wish I could leave the room. Whatever happened between the two of them remains far from over.

The castle has become more interesting than before they were here, but I'm not sure I like it any better. I know that Aidoneus doesn't. Each day we meet for meals, he looks more and more like a shadow of himself. Dark circles grow around his eyes. He keeps his shoulders back, but he says almost nothing at the table, except when Canaean forces him to.

After a light breakfast of toast and fruit, Aidoneus and I

are the first to leave. I knock my shoulder into him in the hallway, the sausage I grabbed for Willa falling on the floor.

"Sorry." I stand aside as he stoops over to retrieve the fallen treat.

"No trouble." He plucks the sausage from the black runner that fills the hallway between his thumb and pointer finger. "I hope this wasn't intended for you."

"Maybe I would have done something like that last week when I wasn't sure when I would eat again, but not right now." I smile like we're sharing a joke between us, but he doesn't return the motion.

"You don't mind our guests?" He glances at me, his eyes sparking with an inner light.

I shrug. "They're not who I would pick to stay in my home, but they make for entertaining company."

"Entertaining." He laughs. "I suppose that could be a good way to look at it."

Better than being miserable about it. Which he obviously feels. He wasn't a big smiler before, but I haven't seen anything close to one from him in days. I'm not sure what he does with his brother all day, but he clearly doesn't enjoy it.

"Will your guests be staying with us much longer?" I'm not sure of the politeness of the question, but I want to know regardless.

"I'm not sure. Canaean seems to do whatever he wants, like being here right now."

"But why?" The question bursts from my mouth and I let it. Aidoneus doesn't seem to care how proper I am and I want to know. "Why does he stay when he doesn't like it here either?"

Aidoneus smiles at me, but it feels bleak. "He finds fun in making me miserable. He must visit to make sure his punishment does its intended work."

"Is being here really so bad?"

"You would understand if you had seen where I come from."

Images of my own home waft through my mind like smoke. "I'm sure you can visit though. If Canaean can come here, why can't you go there? Bother him on his own turf."

"For me to go there, I would need an invitation." He glances at the floor. "One I've never been given."

Perhaps we have more in common than I thought. Both of us are trapped here with slim chances of ever going home again. I reach for his hand, surprising us both as his wide eyes watch my movement. His hand sits cold in mine, but I don't recoil. I squeeze it, trying to transfer some of my life to it and bolster him up.

He looks at me, the sparks in his eyes swirling faster. He leans closer and I'm paralyzed, unable to move away even if I wanted to.

"I know you're not here of your own free will, but I am glad you came." His voice is quiet, barely traveling across the space between us.

I open my mouth to say something back, but Canaean and Teleia enter the hallway before I can. Aidoneus rips his hand away from me, his eyes shuttering back into their gloom from earlier.

"You guys looked like you were having an interesting conversation," Canaean says. "Please don't stop on our account."

"We were just finished." Aidoneus doesn't even look at me.

"Too bad." Canaean looks at me with a dark smile. "We'll try again next time."

The three of them continue down the hallway to whatever work they do during the day. I stand in place, watching them go. My hand still tingles from where it held Aidoneus's. The chill of his hand sunk in deep, and I can only hope that he still carries the warmth of mine with him.

* * *

I return to my room, giving Willa her sausage. One of my trunks was full of books, and it's this one that I turn my attention to. I dig around in it until I find something interesting enough. I've already been through a few of them during my time here. If I had known how much time I would spend alone here, I definitely would have tried to bring more. Not that Nanny was eager for me even to have these. She always felt like reading was a waste of time when there were other things for a young lady to do. Plus, she thought reading would give me squinty eyes and wrinkles. Time will only tell for those.

I can't focus on the words today. I try a different book, but it stays the same. All I can think about is Aidoneus. *Was he being honest that he's glad I'm here?* I can see how much he hates having his brother here, but I didn't think it was possible he liked my presence. I figured I was just another annoyance for him. An inconvenient guest in his castle he could do nothing about.

The book slips from my fingers and falls onto the bed. I do the same, flopping onto the heavy blanket. If I can't focus, there will be no point in pretending.

A soft knocking comes from the door. Willa stands, growling softly as she waits for me to decide what threat level to expect. There aren't many options and one of them could be considered even close to okay.

I smooth my skirts back out, the few seconds I laid on the bed already leaving wrinkles behind. Taking a moment, I fluff my hair back up and pinch my cheeks. No matter who stands on the other side, looking my best will help me handle it better.

The knocking comes again as I cross the floor. Throwing open the door, Aidoneus stands there, his fist still hovering where the door used to be.

My tongue feels like it grows in my mouth and a small smile flitters across my face. He looks at me then glances away. I wait for him to say something but he hesitates long enough that standing here feels awkward.

"Would you like to walk with me?" he finally asks.

"Walk with you?" From what I've seen of the grounds they're nothing but cold and gloomy. Nothing exists out there to see besides the birds and even they left when I arrived.

He clears his throat. "There are some gardens behind the castle if you would care to see them."

My chest feels tight. It would be interesting to see more of the castle and to spend more time with Aidoneus, but I have no winter things. Those are all still packed safely at home, as Nanny didn't expect the weather to be any different here than it was at home. What she packed for me should have been good for at least a few months. After that, I'm not sure what her plan was.

"I would love to accompany you, however, I have nothing suitable for the weather."

A frown flashes across his face as he looks at the trunks still sitting on the floor behind me. "You brought no coat amongst your things?"

I shake my head. He grumbles something under his breath that I can't make out.

I know I wasn't worried about winter things because I was hoping to be home by then. Nanny wanted me married off though. She thought that was the obvious outcome of Father's deal. It makes no sense that she wasn't interested in packing the rest of my things then.

"I'm sure my father would send the rest of my things if I asked." I've thought about writing him a letter so many times. Never to ask for things though, only to ask for answers.

His hand tightens into a fist. "That won't be necessary. I'm sure I have plenty of winter coats. You may keep whatever you like."

A shy smile plucks at the side of my mouth. "Thank you, sir."

He looks at me, eyes flashing. "I think at this point we can dispose of some of our formalities. I know you have been made aware of my name. I give you permission to use it."

"Thank you...Aidoneus." The name feels weird in my mouth as I say it out loud for the first time. Some of the tightness leaves his body though as he hears it.

"You're most welcome, Cora."

A tingle runs down my spine as his deep voice says my name. "I didn't know you knew my name."

"How could I have a contract involving you and not know your name?" He offers me his arm.

I take it, feeling a bit silly. Of course, he would know. I'm sure my father was all too eager to write my name down in place of his. Still, something feels different between us as I nestle my hand in the crook of his arm, the chill of his skin reaching me even through his suit jacket.

Instead of heading right for the stairs like I expect, he takes us further down the hallway. Willa follows after us, snapping at the hem of my dress until I give her a firm glance to stop.

Aidoneus throws open the last door on the left, revealing a bedroom wreathed in gloom and darkness. Shadowy shapes fill the inside and if I wasn't attached to Aidoneus's arm, I don't know that I could have remained standing so close to it.

"We store odds and ends here. A castle collects a lot of things over time," he says by way of explanation.

The thought of him squirreling things away makes me smile. Nanny never would have allowed that to happen in our home. Everything had a place and anything extra was removed from the premises.

"Where did it all come from?"

As we step into the room, it fills with a faint glow, illuminating wooden crates stacked in lopsided piles and furniture covered in sheets. Barely enough room has been left to walk through it all, but Aidoneus moves with confidence like these items were placed here only days ago, even though the layer of dust bellies that belief.

"Some come from people who have stayed here." He lifts a crate off the top of one pile and moves it to another. "Others even I don't know. This castle has been around longer than even me."

His comment makes me think he's as old as some of the layers of dust, but his behavior seems nearly boyish.

I release his arm as he works on the wooden planks holding the crate he's revealed closed. No tools are waiting around, so he can only use his hands to pry it open, a task I would find impossible. He has no trouble with it at all though as the strange magic of this place seems to flow through him and the plank comes off with minimal effort.

Dust floats through the air, causing Willa and I to sneeze. Aidoneus appears unaffected as he digs through the crate. He lifts out heavy cloaks, fur-lined hats, and assorted mittens and puts them on top of another stack of crates. I reach for one of them and he shakes his head at me. Instead, he lifts out from the bottom a red cloak that is so dark it is almost black with a black damask pattern over the top of it. Black fur rings the neckline of it and its silver clasp winks in the dim light.

He hands it to me, his body relaxed and casual while his eyes watch me closely. I run my hand over the fur. It must be rabbit by its softness, while the rest of the cloak feels like velvet with a wool lining. It will definitely be warm. I place it around my shoulders, letting the material pool around my legs.

"Thank you." My voice comes out as a whisper even though we're alone with no need to be so quiet.

"You're welcome," he whispers back, his voice soft in the stillness.

He steps away from the crate and comes closer to me. "May I?"

I nod, not sure what he's even asking to do. He reaches out to me with slender fingers and grabs the clasp and pins it to the other side, enveloping me in the heavy warmth of the cloak. His fingers brush my throat as he adjusts the neckline and for a second I can't breathe. His gaze shifts to my face, searching for the problem there.

We're so close to each other. I didn't notice until he actually touched me, his body only inches from mine. If I looked up at him, our breaths would mingle. I keep my gaze on his chest. It rises and lowers a little too quickly to be casual as if he too, has just noticed our proximity.

I take a step back and he lets his hands lower to his side. The tightness in my body ebbs away as I have space to breathe again. He offers me his arm, and it feels even more dangerous than before. I know I can trust myself to touch him. I won't do anything improper. But what will it make me feel?

Still, I can't refuse the offer, especially when it will make it so much easier for him to guide me on our walk. I swallow down the lump in my throat before I place my hand on his arm. Even then I find it hard not to close my eyes as I feel his chill penetrate me.

"I forgot," he says quietly, almost to himself.

He reaches back into the box and pulls out matching mittens, dark red with a fur-lined opening. He tilts his head at me, eyes waiting for permission. I feel frozen for a second before I can give him a nod. He slips the gloves onto my hands with expert precision, his skin never touching mine despite the opportunities to do so. I'm relieved and not all at the same time.

"I think you're ready for that walk now." He smiles at me and I take his arm once more. The gloves are so warm that I can't feel him anymore. I suppose that means they will work excellently for outside as well.

I expect him to take me down the hallway to the front door, or even back through the kitchen like where I take Willa, but he does none of those. Instead, he leads me deeper through the castle, passing rooms I've never seen before with doors firmly shut. Dark portraits hang on the wall, their occupants seeming to look at me as we pass by.

"This wasn't part of the tour," I point out as he stops in front of a large door and fumbles in his pocket for the key.

"This is more of a private space. It wouldn't be placed on *any* tour." He pulls a large black key from his pocket with a smile of victory and twists it in the keyhole.

"But you're showing me now."

He stops, his hand on the doorknob, and gives me a smile. "Yes, I'm showing you now."

Twisting the knob, he pushes the door open, revealing a world much different than the one I'm used to seeing out the windows. Winter still sits heavy on the ground, but out here skeletal trees twist around white stone walkways. Rose bushes line the space between them, their delicate leaves covered in a frosty film that makes them look like glass as the pale light dances along their edges. Even without being in full bloom, his garden is beautiful.

"Do you like it?" he asks.

I glance up at him, a blush coating my cheeks as I realize he's been watching me. "It's incredible."

He looks over the garden as though trying to see it for the first time himself. "It's one of my favorite places here."

"I can see why."

He smiles but doesn't look at me. It's not one meant for me. The smile seems self-satisfied without being prideful. Just...happy.

For some reason that makes me want to smile too.

The white stones crunch under our feet as he leads me into the garden. A breeze floats through, making the leaves tinkle as they brush each other. On the rose bush closest to me, sits a single red bloom trapped within the ice. I long to touch it, to feel this beauty that also became trapped here.

"I come here a lot," Aidoneus says, looking at the curling branches of the trees reaching above us. "Sometimes as a reward, and far more often as an escape."

"Do you feel a lot that you need to escape inside?" The only thing I've noticed would be his brother and his brother's fiancée. Other than that, the castle doesn't seem so bad.

"The duties that have been assigned to me can feel like a heavy burden sometimes."

I glance at his solemn face with a wry smile. Obviously, I don't know everything that happens in the castle, but I feel like it can't be much. He has maybe two servants and two guests. With winter upon us, he wouldn't be worried about farming or whatever else his land might be good for. It looks like a pretty cushy gig.

"What did your brother assign you to do here?" The issues he has probably have more to do with that than with the actual workload.

His arm grows tight under my hand and his eyes narrow. "Unfortunately, part of the burden stipulates that I must carry it alone."

I let the conversation lag after that. We walk through the garden, each of us lost in our own thoughts.

It just doesn't seem right that Canaean has forced Aidoneus to be alone out here. I wonder what it would look like if he felt like he could have the proper amount of servants and people to confide in. I'm sure Aidoneus would be like a whole new man. Perhaps that's why it's not allowed. If Canaean wants to punish him for something, then loneliness is an easy way for the punishment to be perpetual.

"I'm sorry." Aidoneus sighs and puts his hand over mine. "I meant for this to be an enjoyable experience and I've ruined it with my own brand of melancholy."

I smile at him brighter than what I'm actually feeling. "You haven't ruined anything. Your garden is lovely."

"And my company?"

I trip, shocked by the directness of his question. He pulls me up with the arm I'm holding easily, as though I weigh no more than a feather. His dark eyes watch me, waiting for an answer I don't have.

My hesitation lasts too long and he shakes his head and keeps walking, releasing me from his gaze. His gait is longer and quicker as he moves through the garden. My legs burn as I struggle to keep up.

It's not that I don't have an answer. I've just never been asked something like that before. It wouldn't be considered proper. How can we be coy if we ask questions that cut directly to the matter? It just isn't done. As such, I've never had to actually form concise words for my feelings before. And I think that may be where his question was leading.

"I want you to know," I say, my words coming out in little gasps as I try to keep up with him. "That I enjoy your company more than anyone else in the castle."

His steps slow and relief courses through my system. I didn't say anything hard or even untrue. I haven't met many people in the castle, so easily he's my favorite one. He certainly intrigues me the most.

"Are you sure about that? I know my brother can be quite charming." Aidoneus practically grinds his teeth at the word.

It feels hard to conceal my scowl. "I cannot find someone

charming who openly seeks for a new partner despite being already engaged."

"Ah, well, that relationship is a complicated one." The smile that flits across his face is practically gleeful. "If he could find a way out of it, he probably would."

"Still, regardless of how you feel about the arrangement, you should have respect enough for your partner to not flirt with the only other woman in the house." The whole thing makes me sick for Teleia, not that she's been very kind to me, but I don't know if I could be kind either under the circumstances.

He pats my hand. "You're probably right."

He leaves his hand there, covering mine. A shiver runs down my spine, tingles running into my toes.

"You must be cold. I should get you back in the house."

I open my mouth to protest, but words fail me. The only thing I can think about is how close I am to this man, and the last thing I want to do is say *anything* about that.

Instead, I'm forced to give him a brisk nod as he turns us back to the castle. I'm sure there will be other moments in this garden. I'll just try to be less foolish next time.

Ten

I DON'T SEE Aidoneus again until dinner. He remains bumped from his seat at the head of the table by Canaean who watches him with a catlike grin as he goes through some papers.

"Bringing work to dinner?" Canaean asks. "Couldn't find a partner instead?"

"If I am busy with work, it is only because of you," Aidoneus says in a low voice as he flips to another page.

I settle into the seat next to him, hoping to catch a glimpse of whatever he brought to read. I don't know if I'll ever figure this place out. After another check of his books, I was disappointed to learn that none of them were in English. In fact, I have no idea what language they're in. I thought earlier about asking Aidoneus, but I don't want him to think I was snooping, even though I obviously was.

Canaean turns his attention to me as Jameson brings in our first course, making it harder to casually look at the papers in Aidoneus's hands.

"Are you enjoying your time here, Cora?" Canaean picks

up his napkin and drops it in his lap. Teleia watches him with narrowed eyes as she eats her soup, her gaze never straying.

"There are far worse ways to spend my days." I don't look at him. I keep my attention on the area in front of me, as though that will make him lose interest.

Canaean laughs. "That may be true. However, there are far better options as well. How would you like to come with us when we leave the castle? I could show you what it's like where life flourishes, unlike this drab wasteland."

"You forget, I have not always been at the castle. I know what life outside the walls is like." I take a delicate sip of my soup.

Teleia's spoon clatters against the table. "You also forget that we will have work to do when we get home that does not involve babysitting."

I can feel my face wanting to turn red, but I don't let it. I take a few deep breaths and remember that her words have nothing to do with me and everything to do with Canaean. I'm not the one in trouble here, although she seems willing to let me take some damage on his behalf.

Canaean sighs. "There will always be work to be done. That doesn't mean I shouldn't be allowed to have a little fun."

"I could name several other reasons why it would be inappropriate if you like." Teleia's voice grows louder.

Aidoneus slams his papers down and I lean over to get a better look at them, but they're in the same language as the books in the parlor. "If you insist on us eating together, the least you could do is consider some manners."

Canaean smirks. "I believe the only one who doesn't enjoy our meals would be you, brother."

I would like to disagree with him, but the meals together are so much better than being alone. Plus, this schedule means I'm not forgotten either. Weirdly, it's become a win-win for me. Less so when they're fighting, but even that can be interesting.

"Unlike you, I have a lot of work to do." Aidoneus shakes the papers at Canaean. "I don't have time for all your little pleasantries."

"The dead can wait." Canaean pushes his soup forward. "They have nothing but time now."

Aidoneus looks like he wants to say more but clamps his mouth shut instead. He picks up his papers and ignores his meal, making little marks next to the strange symbols with a black pen.

The dead can wait.

What kind of business could Aidoneus be running? I've never heard of anyone working with the dead making any real sort of money. Plus, my father would have had no reason to trade me for his debts if Aidoneus was in the business of death. Unless perhaps, he wanted someone killed. But that remains unlike the kind of man my father has proven to be, and I can think of no one who would have wronged him enough for that kind of action to be taken.

I just wish I could read Aidoneus's work. It sits right there right next to me, but I can't read it.

"Spoken as someone who cannot experience a pile up in his home if his own work sits neglected." Aidoneus's tone grows bored as he reads over his pages.

Teleia grimaces. "Leave him alone, Canaean. The last thing I want is to be exposed to any of that mess while I'm forced to be here."

"I think forced would be an overstatement." Canaean leans forward, his grin stretching wide. "You were the one who insisted on coming."

"Only because you're the fiancé I cannot trust."

He dismissively waves his hand. "You knew what you were getting into when you made the deal, my dear."

"I—I thought..." Unshed tears gleam in her eyes and her small hands curl into fists as she tries to maintain her control.

"I have never hid who I am. It is you who decided to ignore my nature and believe I was something different."

Even I flinch back at his heartless words. Aidoneus watches me from behind his papers where Canaean can't see him. His jaw grows tight, and his eyes are sad. He doesn't agree with any of this either.

Tears slip down Teleia's cheeks, her pale complexion still immaculate in a way mine could never be while crying. She holds her chin high even as her shoulders shake.

"You should be ashamed of yourself. I have done nothing but love you. It is you who have spurned my efforts and looked for new meat while I was right beside you. There are not the actions of a man but of a spoiled child."

She doesn't wait for Canaean to respond before she scrapes her chair across the floor and sweeps from the room, skirts rustling behind her.

Canaean's face turns red. His large hands curl into fists. He jerks his head at Aidoneus, looking for a new target.

"You dare to sit here and complain of your work to me? Without me, you would be nothing, and here you are a god. You should be thanking me!" he roars.

Aidoneus doesn't even look up from his paper. "Thank you, brother, for giving me such exhilarating work and forcing me to live in this wasteland."

Canaean's chest rises higher as his breathing puffs in and out. "This is a privilege. One I did not have to give you."

"I'm sure you'll do whatever you find to be right," Aidoneus tells him, his voice distracted.

Canaean's gaze sweeps the table and I wish I could run away like Teleia. I'm the only one left for him to snag his nastiness on.

"Cora, it seems our host has forgotten all his manners."

He tries to give me an easy smile, but the edges of it are too forced and his face looks crazy. "I apologize that you have been forced to see any of this, and indeed forced to be here at all."

"On the contrary, I'm growing used to our meals together." I take another sip of my soup to further my image of nonchalance.

Aidoneus watches me, his brow furrowed.

"Still, such things should not have to be gotten used to by a lady," Canaean presses.

"And yet you keep fostering them anyway."

The papers crinkle in Aidoneus's hands. Canaean's jaw hangs as he watches me. This would be the perfect moment for my own sweep from the room if Teleia hadn't already taken that exit. Instead, I finish my soup in silence while the men watch me.

I wait for Canaean to say something. I wait for him to express his displeasure, but Jameson serves the main course and still nothing has been said. Aidoneus doesn't pick his papers back up either. My words seem to have broken something.

By the time we're finishing the meal, I feel relatively powerful. My words created this situation. I reversed what Canaean was trying to do.

I place my napkin on the table, a slight smile perking up the side of my mouth. Aidoneus follows suit despite the half-full plate in front of him.

My skirts rustle as I leave the table with my head held high. Canaean says nothing, but I hear the scrape of a chair as Aidoneus follows me. He waits until we're up the stairs before he says anything, as though needing to be farther away from Canaean.

"You really shouldn't rile him up like that," Aidoneus whispers as I reach the second floor.

The smile slips off my face, revealing the stress I've been

carrying underneath. "He has poked and prodded and instigated and *I* have acted out of line?"

"I can understand how you feel that way." He takes a deep breath. "But my brother can be dangerous. I don't want you to get hurt."

"Your brother is dangerous, this castle is dangerous. What around here isn't going to hurt me in some way?" I pause for him to answer, but he only frowns. "I cannot live out this contract cowed by everything around me. If I am to be here, it will be on my terms."

I owe that much to myself. I didn't get to choose coming here so I might as well get to be in charge of how I act. In some ways, it feels as though my father sent me to the lion's den. But I will not cry. I will not show weakness.

"I don't want you to get hurt." Aidoneus reaches halfway for my hand before changing his mind. "I don't want him to hurt you."

"If that is his wish, I think he will do it regardless of what you like." I square my shoulders before I turn the conversation. "What did Canaean mean when he said the dead can wait?"

Aidoneus goes stock still. His eyes seem to stare through me. "There are things I'm not allowed to say."

I take a step closer to him. "Will you not tell me anyway? It must be such a burden. Let me help you with it."

I'm not sure if he would consider it a burden or not, but I know he's tired of carrying it. He hates his job and this castle, and his brother for sending him here. I should hate my father like that. I should loathe him for what he's done to me, and yet...when I'm standing here with Aidoneus, it doesn't seem so bad.

Aidoneus shakes his head, slipping a hand into his jacket pocket. "It remains impossible to tell you. It is better this way though. You are better for it. Enough exists to be afraid of around here without needing to know what lurks around the corner."

"When you describe your home like that, I beg to differ. I would rather know what is waiting for me than let it surprise me."

Aidoneus smiles. "I have things under control. Nothing will surprise you as long as you stay where you're supposed to be."

But that remains part of the problem. I can't live the rest of my life in my bedroom and the dining room. Especially when Canaean will eventually leave and then the meals in the dining room will cease and I'll have nothing to break up my time again. The endless nothing will end up driving me mad, I can feel it.

"How long will that last though?" I don't even know what I should be afraid of, but I know that if my safety rests on his remaining in control, it can't possibly last. Everyone slips eventually.

"Don't you worry about that." He rests his hand on the banister next to mine, his gaze following the curve of my fingers. "I will do anything to protect you."

"But why?" It doesn't make sense. I'm nothing but a nuisance here. He has to work harder to keep his secrets while still maintaining an air of normality. He could be done with me and it would be so much easier on him.

He smiles and my chest grows tight. "I like having you here."

"You do?"

How surprising when he's made it very clear how much he doesn't like company.

"How could I not? You're passionate and bold. I never know what you're going to say. Closeness to you feels akin to resting beside the source of life itself," he murmurs.

Flattery makes my cheeks flush, but I keep a hold of

myself. I'm not a simple girl who can be taken in by easy words.

"Could you not also say the same of your brother?"

He scowls. "My brother may be the sun, but getting too close to him would not be the same as basking in the warmth. All who get too close to him get burned. There are no exceptions."

I think of Teleia and the hurt she experiences at almost every meal. He knows she cares for him but he can't seem to treat her with any dignity, despite the closeness of their relationship. Being engaged should make her feel like she has won, and yet it seems like it has only revealed more chinks in her armor.

"Is that what happened to you? How you got sent here?"

Aidoneus looks away from me. "That constitutes part of it. Just trust me when I say to leave him be. Everyone will be happier for it."

* * *

Sleep refuses to find me that night and I find myself staring at the ceiling instead. Nothing about this family could be described as normal. Nothing about Aidoneus or my situation feels normal.

The dead can wait.

What is Aidoneus doing here? No kind of work that I know of dealing with the dead can afford such a lifestyle as he lives. There's no answer for it.

Unless he works in history. Perhaps those documents are from a civilization long dead and that could be why I don't recognize the writing. That makes more sense. It's not an occupation, it's a hobby. One done by a gentleman who doesn't need to work because of his family estate. Still, that doesn't seem like the kind of work that would create such animosity in him towards others.

I roll in the bed, burying my face under my pillow. Frustration builds in my chest and I want to scream. Canaean knew what he was doing when he planted that little seed. He must have. I don't want to admit how much it's grating on me. I don't want to admit the kind of power his words have had over me. He doesn't deserve that.

To make matters worse, if I wasn't such a coward, I could have pressed Aidoneus to tell me when I asked him about it. But I already know he hates his work here and I don't want to be the one that hurts him more over it. I don't want to be the reason his face gets twisty and sad. Not even to resolve my own curiosity.

My body feels too tight to keep lying in bed. I fling the blankets off and slide into the slippers left at the edge of the bed. A matching robe lays across the back of the accent chair and I grab that too. Willa whines at me from the end of the bed but doesn't get up to join me.

I don't know what I'm going to do, but I can't just lay around here. That will be the surest way to drive me crazy.

THE HALLWAY HOLDS the same eerie dimness, yet not dark that it has remained since I got here despite the late hour. My steps are sure as I walk across the black runner, passing firmly closed doors that only a few weeks ago would have frightened me just to be next to. I don't know if it's just that I have that much trust for Aidoneus now or if I've been exposed to them too much to be scared. Whatever lurks behind them obviously isn't interested in me, regardless of Aidoneus's warning.

If I had grabbed a coat and Willa, I might have been tempted to try and find the entrance to the garden that Aidoneus took me to before. But if it was cold during the day, I can only imagine what it would be like now. Unfortunately, I'm attached to *all* my limbs and digits, so I'll be staying inside the house. Inside, and as far away from Canaean as I can get while still listening to Aidoneus's warning about what lurks behind these doors.

Silence fills the castle as I follow the hallway and take the stairs. Maybe I just need a little tea to help me sleep. A quick stop in the kitchen won't hurt anyone, not even the cranky woman who apparently works there.

The curtain covering the parlor rests partially open, a slender sliver of light poking into the vestibule. I hesitate at the bottom of the stairs as men's voices travel through the hole. Their words are too indistinct for me to understand from this far away. Getting close to the doorway seems like the wrong choice, but I feel myself inching closer anyway. My slippers are quiet on the stone tiles, and I barely breathe as I ease closer to the opening while making sure I can't be seen by whoever waits inside.

"It is none of your business what I choose to do here. You sent me here. Let me live my exile in peace." Aidoneus's voice grows sharp and tight, and it makes me clench my own fists.

"You keep calling this an exile, that was never what this was intended to be. Someone needed to run things here and I needed someone I could trust." Canaean sounds more earnest than I have ever heard him before.

"It's not that you could trust me. I was the one you didn't mind not having around anymore. I didn't fit into your entourage."

A thump sounds as someone throws themselves onto the couch.

Canaean's voice remains steady. "Maybe you should have thought about that then. You made it clear you weren't going to be part of the group. It made sending you here an easy decision."

"Why are you really here, Canaean? You know you don't need to check up on me. I always make sure to do my job." Aidoneus sounds tired and I can easily imagine that he's the one who decided to sit down.

"I heard you had a guest." A smile creeps into Canaean's voice. I don't even have to be in the room to feel it. "I had to know what you'd done to convince someone to join you here."

"That is also none of your business."

I creep closer to the edge of the curtain, hoping I can see them inside. It doesn't make sense that Canaean would come here for me. I'm not the first guest Aidoneus has had, and this castle is made for guests. Why would having one be strange enough for Canaean to want to come and see me like a monkey in the zoo?

I can just make out Aidoneus's black shoes next to the couch, proving my point that he sat down. From my little vantage point, I can't see Canaean at all.

"In a way it is," Canaean says. "For you see, I am responsible for whatever happens to her here."

"How so? This domain belongs to me, along with my problems."

"Your domain is merely a small portion of my kingdom. Everything resides under me. Your decisions affect me."

Aidoneus's foot taps against the rug. "One girl cannot be a big enough issue to distract you from your own work, oh mighty one."

Canaean doesn't seem to notice the sarcasm. "You might think that, but there's something different about this one. *You're* different with this one."

"Absolutely not. She will meet the same fate as the rest. It's what's required of those who come here." Aidoneus's foot stills.

Canaean steps closer, his shoe almost touching Aidoneus's. "And that makes this so interesting. I can feel how much you don't want that to happen to her. What makes this one so different?"

"She will follow the same path as the rest." Aidoneus stands and moves away from his brother's looming presence. "You have nothing to concern yourself with."

"Would you really not consider letting me buy her

contract? You know it would save you both a lot of heartache."

Canaean knows about the contract? If that proves to be the case, then he shouldn't have pressed me to confirm it. Many consider it rude to discuss such matters, regardless of how much power he thinks he has. This was between Aidoneus and my father. Not even I get to talk about it.

"I think you have more than enough on your plate right now." Aidoneus does his best to sound bored, but it doesn't work, not for me.

"Do you mean Teleia?" Canaean laughs. "That will all sort itself out. I'm not concerned about it."

"Maybe you should be more concerned. It would be in your best interest to cultivate that relationship and leave the rest of us alone."

"As much as you would love that, being here with you is much more fun."

Footsteps come closer to the opening and I scramble backwards. My heel catches in my dress, sending me tumbling to the floor. I wait for a second for one of them to peek through the curtain and catch me, my heart beating hard against my chest. A second passes and no one comes through. I pick up my skirts and struggle to my feet. Keeping my slippers on the hallway runner to make sure they stay quiet, I make my way down the hallway and away from the door, just in case.

The kitchen beckons me, drawing me in with the allure of safety. At least it has a door to hide behind. I'd rather be caught by the cook right now than either of the men.

I burst into the room, shutting the door quickly behind me. Leaning against the frame, I breathe slowly to force my heartbeat back to its normal rhythm.

"Was there something you needed or are you just playing games?" the cook asks. She stands with her back to me as she washes dishes in the sink, but I know that she knows that I'm the one standing here.

It takes me a moment to remember why I ever left my room in the first place, aside from boredom. "T—tea please."

She turns around and gives me a crisp nod as she wipes her hands on her apron. "Any particular type?"

I shake my head, my hands twisting behind my back. She reaches into an open cupboard and pulls out a metal tin, placing it on the counter. I stand there, unsure where I should be as she grabs a teapot and fills it with water before putting it on the stove.

"Having a hard time sleeping?"

I shrug.

"You're not the only one who has a hard time in this place. It's an odd house but can be gotten used to. If you're here long enough." I can feel a threat in her words.

"It seems I'll be here for a long time." My throat feels tight but I force the words out anyway. I should be glad I'm going to be here. It would have been miserable for Aidoneus to trade me to Canaean like I'm nothing more than a horse or a piece of furniture. And to constantly be put in a place where I'm making Teleia upset? No thank you.

"Well." The pot whistles and she moves it from off the stove and onto the counter. "That should make him a little happier. It's not often he has a guest that can stand on her own."

"What do you mean by that?"

She gets a cup and saucer out of the cupboard and puts something from the metal tin in the cup before pouring boiling water over it. The steam curls around the edges of the China as she slides the saucer toward me.

"There are not many that come here that are strong that don't hate him. I'm sure you've seen that with his own brother." She adds the pot to her dishes by the sink. "It can be isolating to only have staff to talk to, and not many of us anymore at that."

Leaning forward, I curl my hand around the cup, enjoying the warm leeching from the porcelain. "Where have all the staff gone? It seems impossible for an estate of this size to run with only two of you working."

She waves a hand at me, her joint swollen from years of kneading bread. "We do just fine. You'd be surprised how little there can be to do sometimes. But the others...there were far more of us a long time ago. There would have been enough help to make sure you were well dressed." She nods toward me, and I resist the urge to reach back and check that all my buttons are done up right.

"So what happened to them?"

"Their time came and they left." She puts away the tin and moves back to the sink.

"What do you mean they left?" Perhaps they were here under contract as well. If I can figure out how they ended theirs, there might be hope for me too. Then I would never have to worry about Aidoneus trading me. He can't give to someone else what doesn't belong to him at all.

She hums to herself. "It was just their time."

And maybe she won't say anything useful at all and I'll be in the predicament I was in before. At least this time I get tea. The steam has evaporated enough that I feel safe to take a sip. Splashes of orange and ginger dance around my tongue and the warmth of it feels like it melting into my bones. I sag against the counter with a small smile.

"There you go. I thought that would be just the thing for you." She turns from the sink and gives me a nod. "Something cheerful. Everyone who comes here needs a little more of that."

Now that she mentions it, I do feel more cheerful. Well, maybe not cheerful, but a quiet hope sinks into my belly that feels almost like cheer. I curl my fingers tighter around my cup.

She and Jameson are still here, so their contract must not be up. What will happen when that time comes? Aidoneus can't just let all his staff go and never hire any new ones. That would be insane. He can't possibly think that he could just take over all of their work. Imagining him in an apron making dinner makes me smile and I hide it behind a sip of my tea.

"Thank you." I set my empty cup on the saucer on the counter. "I feel much improved."

She smiles at me, the first time I've seen her do that. "I'm glad to have been of service."

I don't hesitate as I move past the parlor door on my way back. The low sounds of men's voices still come through the curtain, but I've learned enough for tonight. The last thing I need is to be caught listening and forced into Canaean's proposed trade.

No, in a weird way being here feels a little more like home, and I'm not ready to give that up yet.

Twelve

DESPITE NOT WANTING to get involved, and I really don't, I can't help but wonder about the issues between the brothers. Something happened to them to tear them apart this way. I don't believe they were small children together like this. Aidoneus must have done *something* to get him exiled out here. That must also be why he doesn't enjoy taking care of the castle as well. It would be hard to love something that was forced on you and talked of like a burden.

I can relate. I felt that way about coming here.

At least once I got here, life improved for me. Maybe it was because my father and Nanny weren't here to constantly remind me of my job and purpose anymore. No, in a way finally making it here was an easing that allowed me to fully breathe again.

I glance down at the scars on my arms, barely peeking out above the lace cuffs of my nightgown. I spent so much of my time at home trying to avoid ever having to come here. It's a little humorous to me now that I thought escaping and risking death would provide a better alternative. Maybe all I really needed was the freedom to leave my father's house.

A knock pounds on my bedroom door and I pull my sleeves down to cover my wrists. "Yes?"

Aidoneus opens the door so slowly that it emits a long squeak. It's hard not to smile at it and he seems to share the same thought because even his lips quirk up at sides.

"I wanted to see how you were doing." He hesitates, hand on the doorknob as though unsure whether he should leave it open or close it behind him.

"I couldn't sleep earlier, but I got some tea and feel much better." I watch his eyes, looking for any hint that he knows I am listening, but they remain impassive.

He nods. "Excellent. I'm glad we had something that could help you with what you needed."

After what he said to his brother, I'm sure it's more than a relief that I am comfortable here, even if that isn't the question he's asking.

"Yes, your cook is an interesting woman."

Now the smile he wears feels completely real as it grows. "She certainly is. I'm lucky to have her."

This is it, my moment to ask him about what he'll do when her contract expires and why he didn't replace the other servants, but the words get stuck in my mouth, and I can't do it. Something about the way he looks at me makes me want to keep my more interfering thoughts to myself and leave him in peace. As much peace as he has anyway. I'll figure things out at another time. Maybe after he's grumpy from fighting with Canaean. I don't mind making a grumpy person grumpier, but I don't like taking away from the peace of someone else.

"You're settling in here well, though?" Something in the tone of his voice makes him feel younger, more eager than I've seen in the past.

It makes me want to reassure him. "You have a fine castle here. I've been here long enough that sometimes it feels a little like I'm home."

His eyebrows almost touch his hairline. "Like home?"

I grin, sitting up in the bed and pulling the covers over my chest. "Well, you have to understand that home wasn't exactly the warmest place to start with. This wouldn't be hard to compete with it."

"Having met your father, I can understand that." His face grows darker as the shadows of past memories flit across it. "I did not enjoy the time I spent with him, and it was short. I can only imagine what a whole lifetime would be like."

"Well," I correct him. "Not *whole* anymore. Now I've spent part of it here."

He jerks his head toward me, his jaw softening. "Yes, you have. And you like it?"

I could think about the moments when I've felt trapped here or the strange fog that like to live on the second floor, or the odd warnings even he has given me about this house, but honestly, when he looks at me like that, none of those things seem that bad. "I've found peace here."

Something inside him seems to bloom and I know I've said the right thing. A silly smile wants to force its way out, but I hold it back. He would just look at me and think I'm being self-serving or childish, and I don't want to do anything to change the way he looks at me right now. His dark eyes linger on me, his mouth quirked up in a side smile, and his shoulders relax in a way I've never seen them do before.

"You don't know how glad that makes me," he whispers. His words can barely be heard over the crackle of the fire, but they pierce me anyway.

"And you don't mind having me here? I know your feelings on company." It would be hard not to with the way he glares at Canaean every time he sees him.

He moves closer to me, his steps silent against the rug. My throat goes tight but I don't tell him to move back. His eyes are warm as he watches me.

"Maybe I don't consider you company."

I disregard the way my cheeks heat. "Ignoring it doesn't make it true."

Despite how he may feel, I know I don't belong here. I may like it, but that doesn't mean I actually *belong*. I don't know that I could when I'm here because of a contract and not out of choice. But if I could choose... I'm not sure what I would do.

He reaches over and touches my hair where it escapes my bun. I can't breathe.

"Company means you'll leave." His voice grows sad. "And that's something that will never happen for you."

He curls a finger through a ringlet. His words crack open a hole in my chest. My eyes burn and I want to cry.

"You'll never let me go?"

He shakes his head. "I couldn't even if I wanted to."

"But you don't want to?" I bite my lip and he releases his hair, his hand trailing back to his side.

"Can you blame me?" He gives me a crooked smile. "You see the kinds of people I get to spend my time with here. Why would I give up someone I actually like being with?"

It's wrong. All of it feels wrong. I shouldn't like the way he talks about being with me. I shouldn't like that he doesn't want me to go home. But something about it warms my chest and makes me want to lean closer to him.

"You are a breath of fresh air in this sad castle. You bring life in a way that hasn't been done before. And the way that you talk to my brother..." He laughs. "I would want you here for that alone."

"How long will he be staying?" This feels like safer territory than going back to how much he likes having *me* in the castle.

Aidoneus steps back and shrugs. "I'm not sure. He comes at his own discretion. Honestly, having you here might make him want to stay longer. He enjoys picking at people, especially me."

"Has it always been this way?"

He nods.

"But surely when you were small there must have been moments when you got along." I don't have any siblings, but I'd like to think it would have been fun to have someone to talk to about Father or Nanny. Someone who would understand how hard they could be while still loving them like I do.

He shakes his head. "Canaean and I were never close. He saw me as competition."

"Competition for what?"

"Attention, power. Anything he could have. Canaean doesn't exactly share."

"But he expects Teleia to." My tone grows bitter.

If a man should be lucky enough to get a good woman to be his wife, he should treat her well. No scenario exists where it is okay to start looking for another partner when he already has one.

Aidoneus grimaces. "Canaean is *complicated*."

"Complicated?" That just sounds like a more thoughtful way to say selfish.

"Much about him that isn't great. I will agree with you all day about that. But a lot of his life he hasn't gotten to choose, and that has only made him act out more than he would have ordinarily, I think."

"Teleia deserves better."

"Yes." He nods. "She does. But she has problems of her own. In a way, they seem to complement each other."

"I guess you would know that better than me." I can't think of a meal I've been to where she hasn't left early. We're not exactly friends. It could have been nice to have someone else in the castle to talk to though.

"I've known both for a long, long time. Believe me, Teleia

can hold her own against my brother." Aidoneus smiles but there isn't much humor in it.

The whole thing makes me laugh and the light comes back to his eyes with the sound. His lips twitch, a smile almost touching the corners.

"So, we're probably stuck with them for a while." I grin at him.

He sighs melodramatically. "I suppose so."

"I guess we'll have to be each other's support, in this trying time," I declare.

He smiles. "It may be the only way we'll survive it."

"Canaean won't like it." I try to stop smiling and be more serious, but I can't. My cheeks hurt with how big my smile grows.

"He definitely won't, but it could be good for him to not always get what he wants." Aidoneus reaches for me again then stops, his hand falling back at his side.

I don't know what I want. I don't know if I want him to touch me again or leave me alone. I shouldn't like him. There's no reason I should. He's not friendly and he hasn't been overly welcoming. His house can be a little scary and he doesn't stand up for me to Canaean. But worst of all, is that he agreed to my father's deal. He let my father trade me like I meant nothing. He didn't hold him accountable for whatever he did that got me in this mess in the first place.

Tears burn at the side of my eyes. No one has ever treated me like I'm worth something all on my own. Aidoneus doesn't do anything, one way or another. He doesn't use me and he doesn't need me. Maybe that makes being with him better, more comfortable. He feels safe in a way I haven't felt from anyone else before.

His jaw tightens and his hand closes into a fist. He turns from me, his back taut in his jacket. I want to call him back and tell him that it's okay, but we both know it isn't. No matter how strange this place can be, there are some rules that shouldn't be broken. Some rules that I'm not sure I'll ever feel okay with breaking.

He moves towards the door, his motion fluid despite the agitation I can feel rolling off him.

"Thank you."

He pauses and turns his head just a little bit. "For what?"

"For coming to check on me."

He nods and lets himself out of the room.

I lay back against my pillows and stare at the ceiling for a long time. Sleep refuses to claim me, as my mind swirls with the day. Even pushing my face into the pillows doesn't help. I want the sweet oblivion of sleep, not to have to think about every moment with Aidoneus and how I should process it.

But my mind finds it so much more delicious to linger on Aidoneus than to drift into sleep. He came up to check on me. That counts for something. He said he wouldn't let me go even if he could. That's something else. Definitely something I should be upset about. So why does it make me feel warm inside instead? Nothing he does should have that effect on me. I should be immune to his charms. It must just be that this house is strange and everyone in it is strange, so now I'm becoming strange too.

Willa jumps onto the bed and makes her way to my face on her short legs. She curls up into my spine like she knows I'm never going to find sleep without help.

I roll over and wrap my arm around her thick waist, pulling her closer. She grumbles but lets me do it. With her face close to mine, she licks me with her warm tongue.

"What am I going to do, Willa?" That question holds so much more ambiguity than it used to. It used to be about how I would get home, but now...now I don't know if I ever even want to go home. I *feel* more at home than I ever did with Nanny or my father when I'm with Aidoneus.

It's strange, and I know it's wrong. But I couldn't change it even if I tried.

Thirteen

THE TURBULENCE of not knowing what I should feel about Aidoneus persists into the morning. It makes my fingers feel numb as I attempt to put on my fancy dresses and do up the little buttons on my shoes. Willa watches me with her dark eyes as though she knows why I'm having all the troubles I am and judges me a little for it.

I take her with me when I start downstairs, despite it being later than usual and knowing that breakfast will already be on the table. I'll just have to skip the group meal this time. I'm sure Aidoneus will understand.

The traitorous part of me hopes he'll seek me out and wonder why I wasn't there.

I take Willa out the front door so I don't have to worry about seeing any of them or passing the dining room at all. It feels childish to be so afraid of what they'll say, but I'm giving into the childishness at least this once.

Willa bounds ahead of me, her tail wagging back and forth without a care in the world. Sometimes I wish we could trade places. She can struggle through everything it takes to be human and I'll exist just to wonder when I'll be fed and when

I'll be taken out. I won't need to think about Aidoneus anymore.

The air around the castle remains cold and dark. The whole place has been wrapped up in the same temperature bubble the whole time I've been here. It's strange. Especially since it wasn't even close to being winter at home.

My fingers hurt and I debate writing home to have them send more of my things, but I just can't do it. It would be one thing to admit to myself that I like being here and don't necessarily want to go home. It would be another thing entirely to have to admit that to someone else, especially my father. Nanny would be all too happy if things worked out here and all that she had strove for my whole life came true.

The scars on my wrist itch at the thought, the same way my body seemed to itch every time she described the future she wanted for me. I was never going to be one of those girls who only wanted to grow up and get married. I'm not sure what I want, but it wasn't that. If she had just left me alone, I might not have had so many...extreme...moments at home. Things that I would never want to explain to someone else, and definitely would if all Nanny's dreams come true. Be that as it may, I'm a little glad there's been no one to help me dress, because then it would be someone around here that knew. That knew about me in a way I don't want. I don't want Aidoneus to look at me the way everyone does when they find out about what I've done, what measures I'd stooped to in an effort to escape this fate. No, I like him thinking of me as strong and capable.

He never said what he thinks of me, but until he says anything, I can insert exactly what I want.

"Come on, Willa. I'm too cold to stay outside any longer."

She looks back at me with a long whine. She loves being outside despite the weather, just another point for being a dog instead of a lady.

"Come on. If we stay out here, I'll lose my fingers, and then how will I get you breakfast?"

Her tail waves back and forth slowly like she's thinking. Then her black face splits into what could be considered a grin and her tongue lolls out as she trots back to me.

I pat her little head and she leans into me. "I don't know how I would have survived here without you," I whisper into her neck.

"Good morning."

The Lord's voice causes me to still completely. Willa licks my neck, looking for more pets. I look up to see him coming from around the corner. His long legs make his fast approach look like an easy stride. My body freezes for a moment as I watch him.

"I see you're out enjoying the day as well," he says, looking around the dour courtyard.

"Willa needed to go out."

He glances down at Willa where she sits next to me, tongue hanging out. "I see."

"You're outside early though." I'm not sure what I'm doing, but I don't want him to leave yet.

He shrugs in his dress coat like he can't feel the cold at all. "There was work to be done this morning."

"Are you sure you're not just avoiding a certain 'friend' of ours?" My mouth stretches into a grin.

"It's true that he doesn't enjoy being outside, not around the castle at least." He returns the smile, his hands slipping into his pockets. "But I did have work to do."

"Of course, me too." I point to Willa.

"You weren't hungry then?" he asks. I shake my head even as my stomach growls. "They'll be wondering where we've run off to together."

"You mean to say that you expected me to be at breakfast

with your family without you?" I place a hand on my hip in indignation and to cover my shivering.

He looks at the heavy double doors behind me. "I only thought about how I could not bear it myself this morning."

His words create a pain in my chest. He didn't think of me at all. He was just running away himself. I can only imagine how horrible breakfast would have been if it was just the three of us, and he never once thought of that. My fingers dig into my waist, creating a pulsing of pain to distract me.

"I should probably take her back inside." I turn to go, tugging the door open with a blast of warmer air.

Aidoneus follows behind me. "I've done something wrong, haven't I?"

I grind my teeth. "No, everything is fine."

He holds onto the door as I pass through. "If that were the case, your shoulders wouldn't be so tight and you wouldn't be holding your head so high."

He follows me into the foyer and closes the door behind us. My shoes clip across the floor as I march for the stairs.

"Would you just let me—"

"I need to be alone right now." I rest my hand on the stair banister, as though that will make me look more regal and less like I'm running away. Willa follows me, her black tail wagging like nothing is happening.

Aidoneus's face grows stony. "If I have done something to offend you, I would like the opportunity to make amends."

"Don't worry about it." I try to stretch my face into a smile, but the movement pains me. "I'm fine. I just want to be alone."

He frowns, but doesn't follow me as I make my way back upstairs. Maybe he's right and he deserves a chance to explain himself, but I don't want to have to hear him say directly that I don't mean anything. That he enjoys having me here more than other people but that still doesn't mean he wants to spend much time with me.

I drift back to my bedroom and rest my head against the wooden door. It's so stupid. I shouldn't be so upset that he didn't think of what I would have to deal with at breakfast. We're not even really friends. I'm just someone he got stuck with because of a contract. Just because he doesn't hate me like he does his brother doesn't mean he *cares* about me. That's a big next step.

Something in the way he talks to me that made me think that maybe...but obviously not.

I steel my jaw and let myself into the bedroom. This will be better for all of us. Of course there should be boundaries between us. I'm not a real guest. It was good for that reminder and I'm sure that's what he would have said too if I had given him the chance.

I'm nothing here. I'm nothing anywhere.

* * *

I choose not to go down for any of the meals. I don't want to see Aidoneus and I don't want to be caught at a meal without him either. I don't want his brother's all-knowing eyes following my movements while I try to sustain myself. No, it would be better to starve.

But that doesn't become an option either.

At dinner time, a soft knock comes from the door, and Jameson lets himself in with a large silver tray. I sit up from where I've flopped onto the bed to watch him.

"The Lord thought you might be hungry," he says by way of explanation before setting the tray down on the table and exiting the room.

The smells of roast and vegetables fill the room and my stomach groans. My chest does too, but not out of hunger.

Maybe I was too quick to dismiss Aidoneus...but no, it doesn't matter if I was or not because there's nothing to dismiss. And if he thought of me to take care of me now, then it was probably out of a sense of burden. I belong to him in a way. If he wanted, he could replace a missing servant with me and there would be nothing I could do but what he wanted me to.

I need to keep myself grounded in knowing that I'm lucky just to be given 'guest' status. I don't need anything else. I certainly don't need him.

Sliding out of bed, I can't wait any longer to eat. It doesn't matter what my inner thoughts are while I eat. Aidoneus won't know them anyway. And he won't know how long I hold out before eating either. All of this serves my personal benefit.

I start on the roast, which is smothered in gravy, and so tender I almost don't have to chew. It explodes across my taste-buds and only heightens my hunger. Digging into the vegetables, I can't stop to even taste them, my body feeling ravenous. Carrots and potatoes disappear with my quick fork. I clear the plate in quick succession, but my hunger doesn't fade. If anything, it seems to grow.

My mouth salivates, gravy dripping down my chin. My gaze sweeps the room, looking for more. Willa whines at my feet, but I ignore her. If there's not enough for me, then there's certainly nothing there for her.

I dig through trunks, overturn the table, and press on, looking for more. The need seizes me and won't let me go.

Lunging for the door, I swing it wide open. Willa runs through my feet and takes off down the hallway. I don't know where she's going, I don't care where she's going. I'm finding something to eat.

My steps are uneven and sloppy as I make my way downstairs. The hunger driving me feels like a hole in my stomach.

Everything hurts and I can only focus on my need to eat. My stomach growls and my hands are white-knuckled on the banister by the time I reach the first floor.

My back hunches as the ache in my stomach grows. I stumble towards the kitchen, the smell of dinner still wafting through the air, leading me forward.

I hesitate as the pain becomes too much and I don't know if I can continue. Wrapping my arms around my belly, I sink to my knees. I let out a soft keening sound that feels more like an animal than a noise I could make.

The sound of a fork hitting the table stops me instantly. My head jerks toward the dining room. The table in there still holds dinner, plates full of unfinished items waiting for Jameson to take them away.

I move on all fours, my knees catching in my dress and slowing me down as I struggle to move faster. I reach for the cream tablecloth, my fingers gripping it with a strength I don't recognize. Pulling at it, I wait on my knees on the floor for it all to come tumbling down for me. Silver gleams at the edge of the table and my mouth waters so much at the sight that it dribbles out the corner of my mouth.

"What is happening here?"

I don't stop to answer Aidoneus as he stands in the doorway behind me. I tug harder at the cloth, wanting to get the food before he can do anything to stop me.

"Neither of you showed up for meals today. I had to do something more to entice you," Canaean says from the head of the table. He watches me, eyes gleaming as the first plate clatters to the ground beside me.

I drop the tablecloth and move to the plate face first. I don't bother with silverware; I have no time for something like that with my overwhelming pain. Meat and saliva mix together as I hover over the plate like a dog.

"Stop this." I don't know if Aidoneus is talking to me or Canaean, but either way, I don't even hesitate. "Release her."

"I don't think I will." Canaean's voice plays at coy as I reach up to drag another plate off the table, this one licked clean.

Aidoneus steps forward and grabs me by the back of my dress. He tries to haul me back, but I'm stronger in my desperation. Gravy stains the front of my dress as he pulls me to my feet. I make it two steps forward, my fingers grazing the next plate that teeters on the edge.

"This isn't right. She's done nothing to you," Aidoneus pleads.

"Done nothing?" Canaean pounds his fist on the table. "If only that were the case. She has insulted me time and time again and then refused to even sit in my presence. You call that nothing?"

"I call it self-preservation," Aidoneus grumbles.

I make it forward another step and grab a roll from the table, shoving it into my face. But still, the ache grows.

"You're going to kill her." Aidoneus stops being delicate with me and wraps his arms around my waist to pull me back.

Canaean shrugs, his golden hair falling into his face. "If that must happen, then that will be."

"If that must happen...what do you mean? Release her!"

My fingers dig into the table as I try to get closer, my fingernails pulling as he moves me a step back.

"This feels like a fair punishment. Neither of you will dine with me, and while I can do nothing to you at this point, plenty can be done to her. Now she will do nothing but dine. It will be a funny addition to the room, don't you think?" Canaean smiles as he watches me. As he watches me use every ounce of strength I have to pull another roll from the table.

"Your 'funny addition' won't last the day at this rate. How

long do you think she can maintain eating like this?" Aidoneus points out.

Canaean shrugs. "I've seen many eat more and for longer."

"But you've not seen anyone *like her* do that. I'm telling you, she can't maintain it."

"Good," Canaean shouts, standing so quickly that his chair clatters to the floor behind him. "Then the deed will have been done and she will have fulfilled what would eventually happen anyway. No one who comes here will escape that fate, no matter how much you baby them."

Aidoneus's grip on me grows tighter. "This domain belongs to me, and it will abide by my laws. You have no say here."

"Wrong!" Canaean stabs his fork into the table. "You rule under my jurisdiction. You have gone on too long here alone if you think that you are the only one with power here. It proves fortunate I came when I did."

I can't move anymore, Aidoneus holds me anchored too far away. With a growl, I shift my attention from the table to his hands, my teeth bared. Drool drips from my lips, landing on the back of his hand. It's the only warning he gets before I drop with my mouth open, teeth ready to sink into his skin.

He moves his hands, my teeth just skimming them. He tries to get another hold on me, but I rush to the table, shoving anything I can get into my mouth.

Canaean laughs. "Isn't it delightful? Like bringing an animal inside."

Aidoneus doesn't try to grab me again. He turns his attention to Canaean. "Stop this. You've made your point. Release her."

"Have I though?" Canaean steeples his fingers, resting his chin on them. "What will stop you from disrespecting me again? I'll leave this place and you'll go right back to your ways. I can't risk it. This is a necessary lesson for you I think."

I shove roll after roll down my throat as Aidoneus's jaw tightens.

"You want a deal then?"

"It seems only fitting that I should get one. Isn't that what you offer everyone else? Even though forbidden. You and that big heart of yours." Canaean sighs. "What are we going to do with you?"

"I won't make the contracts anymore."

Canaean tuts at him. "That won't be enough anymore."

"What then?" Aidoneus steps forward and puts a hand on my back. "What do you want from me? Do you want this castle? You can have it! And all the responsibility that comes with it."

Canaean scowls. "Why would I want this place? No, I think it fits you perfectly. I want you to stay right here."

"Then what?" I feel his hand tighten on me as I move toward the roast in the center of the table. "What could I possibly offer you? I have nothing. You know that. You made sure of that."

"Oh, Aidoneus, always so dramatic. You were not left here powerless."

Aidoneus's hand grows limp. "If you take my power, then how will I do my job?"

Canaean smiles. "I don't need to take it. I want control over it."

"Is it not enough that you have control over everything else?" Aidoneus's tone grows bitter. "This was the one thing left to me, and you need it too?"

"The power of life, the power of death. It would make me pretty formidable." Canaean muses as he watches me consume the roast with my bare hands. "Beware of time running out though. How much longer do you think she can go on like this? I've heard the stomach can explode inside the body and I've always been fascinated by that."

Aidoneus grabs me, trying to make me stop, but the magic gives me strength I shouldn't have and I break free of his hold. "You've made your point. I'll bow down."

"No!" Canaean slams his fist on the table. "You should have done that from the beginning. I should never have had to force you. It was my right by nature of my position."

"The position you were given." The words seem to slip out before Aidoneus can stop them, but he doesn't try to take them back. Instead, he grabs a tray from the table and throws it across the room before I can start eating off it.

Canaean's smile grows dangerous. "I see. That's what lies at the heart of it then. The reason why your respect has always been lacking. Simply, jealousy isn't enough for our dear Aidoneus. That is what I assumed it was after all. But no. Not jealousy at all. You think I haven't *earned* my place."

"Can you tell me that you have?"

Tightness grows in my belly as my dress tries to hold all of me in place. My stomach becomes a round bulge that is hard to the touch. I want to slow down, but I have no choice but to keep eating at the same ferocious pace. Even my teeth begin to hurt.

"It was given to me for a reason. If you can't see that, that's not my fault." Spit flies from Canaean's mouth and sprays across the table.

Aidoneus's hand returns to his side. "There are many at fault here. Myself included."

"Yes. At least you know that you are a problem." Canaean walks around the table. "But you *will* submit to me now."

"You have given me no choice." Aidoneus's voice grows quiet.

The sounds of my eating fill the silence between them. I slurp down the carrots, not even needing to chew them at this point. My stomach aches but I can't stop eating.

"Good." Canaean watches me, his face still. "It is better

this way. We all need to be reminded of our places in life sometimes."

"Your warning would be sufficient." Aidoneus doesn't even look at me.

Canaean picks a fork up from the table. "No, it isn't. That's why we're here today. But you'll remember long after I leave what I do today."

My gut clenches and food does its best to move back up my throat, but Canaean's magic won't let it.

"You will relinquish your magic to me. I will let you use it as I deem fit." He smiles as Aidoneus's shoulders sag. "And in two weeks, you will step down entirely. I will find someone new to take over your work. It shouldn't be hard. I needed someone new down here anyway. After the last few years, I knew I could never trust you again."

"Then why bother coming here at all?" Aidoneus asks through gritted teeth. "You could have made your decision and left it at that."

Canaean stabs the fork into the table. "Where would the fun be in that? No, it was much better this way. Plus, it gave you the opportunity to show me your loyalty. An opportunity you never took, I might add."

Aidoneus's eyes dim as he sees the visit for what it truly has been this whole time: a trick.

"Don't look so sad, brother. Everyone gets bested occasionally. This was your moment. It was always going to be this way."

"I agree with your terms. Now release her." Defeat tinges his voice, but he still holds his head high.

"I'm glad we were able to come to an agreement. The contract stands." Canaean gives him a smile. "Enjoy your last few weeks."

The magic holding me up disappears and I collapse against

the table. My stomach heaves and Aidoneus turns his back on Canaean to help me. I'm too exhausted to be angry with him anymore, especially not after he made an agreement with his brother to save me. I lean into Aidoneus's touch as he helps me out of the room. Canaean watches us go, eyes gleaming.

Fourteen

WITH THE CONTRACT AGREED UPON, Canaean doesn't linger at the castle. His work accomplished, he and Teleia leave first thing in the morning, the former with a big grin on his face.

Even with them gone, the mood in the castle doesn't improve. How could it, with Aidoneus's deadline hanging over all of us? I'm unsure what his agreement will mean for me, and I'm afraid to find out. There wouldn't be much Canaean can't do when he has control over Aidoneus's assets, which will include me.

I expect life to go back to how it was before their visit, but Aidoneus keeps the meal routine the same. He doesn't take the head of the table and instead keeps his seat and motions for me to sit opposite him.

His face stays empty and dark, as Jameson serves us. The only noise in the room remains the persistent clanging of silverware against the China plates. Canaean's presence lingers in the room with us, watching us and waiting to tear us down with what we care about most. But as far as it concerns Aidoneus, he's already done that. Maybe he didn't enjoy being the master of the castle as much as he should have, but I firmly believed there was a part of him that enjoyed it. Now that's been ripped away.

I try to focus on the soup in front of me. It's a warm, clear broth that I wish was more distracting. Aidoneus picks up his spoon but doesn't even try to eat. This meal feels pointless for both of us.

"I hope you know…" He looks up at me, his eyes dancing with the swirling sparks inside. "That if there was a way to get you out of here, I would do it. As it is, I'm trying to find a way for you to be free of my brother's control…after."

I give him a small smile. "Because you're an honorable man."

"You're wrong." He drops his spoon and it clatters against the table as he rises. "If I were an honorable man, I never would have taken your father's deal in the first place. He would have paid his price years ago and this never would have been your problem."

"I'm sure you had your reasons." I try to take a sip of my soup like everything is normal.

He runs his hand through his silver hair, causing pieces to come loose and fall into his face. "All of my reasons were selfish. I should have left you out of this. If I could go back in time, I would hold your father accountable and Canaean would never have had the chance to see you."

"I don't care about Canaean." The statement feels less powerful without him actually being here, but that feels like the positive of it. It doesn't have to be true right now. I can say whatever I want to. "I'm glad I got to come here."

He glances sharply at me. "You are?"

"Absolutely. All I have ever wanted was to get out of my father's house." True. There was never a lot of love lost there. Before the contract and Nanny's obsession, I drifted through that place like I meant nothing. Even with the contract I meant nothing to him. I was a convenient way to get out of something.

"Your father..." Aidoneus hesitates like he wants to say something but doesn't want to embarrass me. "I didn't know what to expect from you after meeting him. You are nothing like him."

"Thank you."

He slowly sits back in his seat. "I'm sorry you have been caught between my brother and me. I wish I could tell you things will work out, but I'm not sure what will happen now."

"Where will you go after this?" *Is there a way for me to go with you?*

"Most likely into the darkness. There is a chance however, that he might bring me to his castle to prod at me and make fun of me to his court. Canaean loves being able to control the laughter." He scowls and I can't help but think of all the times Canaean tried to get me to laugh at Aidoneus with him. It never worked.

"Perhaps he will take me there too." A tinge too much like hope colors my voice, making Aidoneus tilt his head as he watches me.

His hands rest against the side of the table, his fingers pressing into the wood. "I hope for your sake that he does no such thing."

"Well," I try to be jovial. "If he leaves me in the castle alone, I'm likely to starve to death. You have no idea how difficult the food situation was before we established mealtimes."

Aidoneus doesn't even smile. "The suffering you would feel here would be short in comparison to Canaean's domain. You have no idea what Teleia can do when she has her own power back."

"Back? Is she not still the fiancée of your brother and powerful no matter where she goes?"

His eyes grow dark. "Not when in my domain. Maybe if

they were already married, but I doubt my brother will ever let that happen. He may have been tricked into a betrothal with her, but he won't submit to her, not until that's precisely what he wants."

"How horrible."

He shrugs. "They are both manipulative, tricky. They deserve each other. Don't feel bad for her. If she wanted out, she would find a way."

He talks about Teleia, but I feel like he could be talking about me. If I wanted out, wouldn't I have tried harder to leave once I'd arrived? I was concerned with that in the beginning, but then I grew complacent as I got to know Aidoneus better. If I had figured out how to get out of my father's contract, then I wouldn't have to worry about Canaean taking it over now.

"Still, even they deserve love."

Aidoneus snorts. "Canaean has more of that than he knows what to do with."

"But maybe not from the people that matter to him the most."

This is not the direction I wanted this conversation to go. Aidoneus leans back in his seat, studying the flower design on the rim of his bowl.

I want to reassure him, but the words won't come. I don't know how to fix family relationships. My hands grow moist. If I knew how to fix things, I wouldn't be stuck in my current situation. I would have found a way to talk to my father. But I never did that. I never found the words and now I'm under contract to Aidoneus I thought, but maybe not. Maybe it was to the house itself.

He rises from his chair, soup untouched. "I apologize for what has transpired here. I can only hope that things will turn out for the best for you."

"For both of us."

He glances at me sharply, the sparks in his eyes resurfacing. He gives me a curt nod then breezes from the room without a second glance back.

I stare at my half-eaten soup. It feels cold now, just like my chest. Jameson comes in bearing a heavy tray laden with the main course but stops short when he sees Aidoneus missing.

He sighs, setting the tray down on the table so roughly that the glasses shift and threaten to tip over.

"I didn't mean to do anything." I don't know why I'm telling Jameson anything. He never says much to me and doesn't seem to care what I do anyway, but I feel like I must say it out loud to someone. Releasing those words means something different than keeping them inside.

Jameson shakes his head and leans against the table. "This was bound to happen no matter what. Your presence here was more likely a catalyst than a cause."

"They really seem to hate each other."

A wry grin spreads across his face, the most emotion I've ever seen from him. "It was inevitable. Their father pitted them against each other. Made them struggle for everything. We all knew Canaean was going to be victorious. Despite his father's games, it was obvious he was the favorite. So when he succeeded...he made sure to give Aidoneus a job that would put him in his place."

"Is it really so bad here?" Sure the castle isn't the warmest and he warned me that there was danger here, but I've yet to see it.

The smile drops from his face as he picks up Aidoneus's forgotten bowl. "You wouldn't even ask that if you knew what he had to do here."

"What is his job then?" I've yet to see anyone actually do anything. I doubt there's something so bad that Aidoneus has to do that takes up so little of his time.

"That wouldn't be for me to say." He places the bowl on the now-empty tray and takes it back to the kitchen.

I debate dishing myself some of the roast chicken that he brought in, but the idea of it turns my stomach enough that I know I'm done. I can't keep eating when I know I've brought him so much pain.

I can't eat, but I also don't want to just sit in my room. With Canaean gone, there doesn't seem to be a reason enough to have to hide. Plus, if I can find Aidoneus in the house, then maybe I can find a way to apologize. There has to be some word I can find that will make this better.

My shoes click against the floor as I move toward the hallway. Everything feels darker than it has in days, the scones on the wall burning low enough that I can't make out the pictures on the wall anymore. Willa stays close to me, growling at every dark corner we pass.

Her temper might almost be enough to get me to go back to my room, almost. Aidoneus is out here somewhere and he isn't afraid, so I don't have to be either. If something lurks out here, he'll protect me from it. I know it.

The main floor of the castle spreads out farther in either direction than I've ever been before. I've never needed to look through any of the other rooms, especially not with Aidoneus's company around. But now... I make my way around to the parlor and keep walking through the darkened hall that leads from it.

The doors on all sides are closed, with no hint of shadowy daylight to give me even a glimpse of light outside of the dark sconces. Willa sits in the parlor as I walk further and whines.

"Are you coming or not?" I keep my voice low. Just because I'm not scared doesn't mean I'm stupid. She scoots back further, black eyes begging me to stay. "I *have* to find him. What you do remains up to you."

She barks as I keep walking. I pick up my pace to get away

from her. If she wants to act like a decoy, I'll let her. I can't stick around just because my dog feels scared. I'm definitely stronger than that.

But Willa never led me astray before either.

My stomach churns, making me feel sick. Without Willa by my side, the walls feel like they're looming closer to me. Tingles run from my neck down my spine. I glance back for Willa to call her closer, but I can't see her anymore.

Breathing comes harder and it takes focus to remember to exhale. Everything in my body begs me to go back. But I can't, not when Aidoneus could be down here hurting. Hurting because of me. I won't let it happen.

I take fistfuls of my skirts to hide the shaking of my hands and keep moving. Every step comes hard but I don't let it get to me. This is a weird house, Aidoneus said so. I'm not going to let it get to me anymore. I would be a fool to let this building get to me when I've already survived so much.

No sound permeates this part of the castle and barely any light streams in. If Aidoneus did come down here, he wanted to be left alone.

The thought almost makes me turn back, but I can't now, not after I've come this far. He deserves to hear my apology. I don't want him wallowing in this darkness when he doesn't have to.

A slight scratching comes from under one of the doors ahead of me. I move quickly to get to the sound before it goes away. Placing my hand on it, it feels like a thick solid wood like the door to my bedroom. It wouldn't be easy to make a noise that would travel through that thickness to be heard in the hallway. My chest aches and I'm sure that he's making that noise because of me.

I press my face against the narrow gap in the door. "Aidoneus?"

The scratching stops. I wait a moment longer but he doesn't say anything.

"Aidoneus, I need to talk to you about earlier." My throat feels thick, and I still find it difficult to find the words I want to use. "Would you please come out?"

If I keep talking to a door, I won't know if he really heard and understood me. I'll just continue standing here, feeling ridiculous.

I move closer to the door. "Aidoneus, please let me apologize to you." I ensure my voice sounds louder this time and I can hear shuffling from behind the door that says he's still here. "I didn't mean to be rude at breakfast. I'd like to apologize but I want to do it face to face. Will you please let me in?"

The sound moves away from the door. I lean my forehead against the wood and take a deep breath to keep from feeling annoyed.

"I didn't mean to imply that you owe your brother anything. That was wrong of me. I don't understand your history together. I know that. It makes me an unfair judge and I should have kept my opinions to myself." I brace my hand on the handle of the door. "Please let me see your face while I say these things."

I pause but now I hear no sound at all. He really won't let me say I'm sorry to his face. I knew I hurt him, but I didn't think I'd said anything to warrant this level of reaction.

A wave of hurt breaks into me and my grip on the doorknob gets tight. He really must want to see the worst in me to not allow me to talk to him and explain. I don't understand why he would want to hold onto his hurt when I'm here to take it away.

Maybe I've been wrong about things this whole time. I thought we were at least friends, but maybe that was just a daydream. He doesn't want to be my friend. Enjoying my company more than he enjoys his brother's probably doesn't mean a thing to him. It just means he hates his brother. And I've gone and read too much into it and thought that...

It doesn't matter what I thought. It doesn't matter how he looked at me then because he won't look at me now.

I slam my fist against the door, letting the wood bite into my skin. "You need to listen to me. You need to give me a chance to explain. What you're doing right now is childish." *And hurtful.*

But I can't say those words out loud. I can't give him my vulnerability when he won't even look at me.

With no sound at all now, it would be easy to believe that it was never there and I'm yelling at an empty room. But I heard it before. I know it did.

"Do you think you can hide in there and I'll just forget and move on, looking for you somewhere else?" My voice rises in volume and pitch. I know I should bring it back down, but my hands are shaking and my chest aches and I need an outlet somewhere.

Something thumps against the other side of the door.

"Please let me in."

I splay my hand on the door while the other holds onto the knob. He has to let me in. He has to let me explain. He has to let me absolve myself of this guilt that wants to take me down.

"Come in."

The voice sounds deep and raspy, not at all what I'm familiar with from Aidoneus. But maybe I really upset him. He's been going through his own misery, now is not the time to judge him on how his body handles his emotions.

I turn the handle, but it catches and refuses to open. "I think it's locked."

"Open the door."

The pain in my chest gives way to tightness. Something feels wrong, I can sense it. But that doesn't stop me from trying to open the door again. The handle still won't turn all the way and the door stays firmly closed.

"I think you need to open it on your end." Without anger making me loud, my voice has become so soft that I'm not sure he can hear me. "You need to unlock the door."

"Can't," he grunts.

I turn the handle and pull harder but the solid door doesn't budge. "Do I need to get Jameson to help you out of there?"

A flurry of movement scuttles behind the door. "No. You do it."

Maybe this serves as my punishment for what I said before. I get to struggle with an impossible door while feeling creeped out. I guess it's original, but I don't like it. My heart beats harder against my chest and I wish Willa was here.

I tug on the doorknob again but it doesn't move. "Maybe you could try pushing from the other side."

He chuckles and it sends chills down my spine. My fingers feel cold and I can't grip the doorknob as well as I was before. I try to pull the door open anyway. If this fulfills what Aidoneus needs from me then I'm going to do it. My breath comes sharper as I keep trying with no success.

"Are you sure you haven't locked it or something?" I turn it as far as I can again, but it won't turn far enough. My face feels red and I'm not sure if it comes because of my efforts or the building desire to cry.

"Yes, locked."

I let go of the knob and sink to the floor. Resting my head in my hands, I try to breathe through the emotions so I don't end up crying. I don't need to fail at this and turn into a blubbering mess in front of him. It has to be one or the other and at this point, I refuse to entertain the idea of doing the latter. Even if I might not have much choice in it.

"Cora?" Aidoneus's voice comes from down the hallway

and sounds so much like himself that my head instantly jerks in that direction.

His hands are in his coat pocket, his shoulders straight, and his face smoothed of any negative emotions. If he struggles with what I said, he hides it well.

"Aidoneus? But aren't you in there?" I point at the door I'm leaning against and his eyes go wide.

He closes the distance between us in a few short steps and grabs me by the arms, lifting me onto my feet and away from the door. The scratching sound comes back, this time accompanied by heavy rattling that shakes the door in its frame.

Unsteady on my feet, I still try to move away. Instead, I trip over my dress and fall against Aidoneus's sturdy frame. He holds me, his gaze assessing how much of a threat the other side of the door should be.

"I—I'm sorry. I came looking for you, I only wanted to say I was sorry." Words spill out as I try to distract myself from the fact that my face presses against his all-too-firm chest.

"Hush." His grip on me tightens and he moves away from the door too quickly for me to follow.

I trip over myself and he uses his hands on my shoulders to hold me up. I expect to feel like I'm being dragged, but his strong hands hold me easily and it feels more like I'm floating down the hall instead.

"Aidoneus, I'm sorry. I shouldn't have said anything about your brother. I don't know the history between you two and I shouldn't have tried to interfere," I try again.

He stops walking, the darkness casting shadows across his face. His grip on my arms has pulled my sleeves up but I can't move to fix them without dislodging his grip.

"You have nothing to be sorry for." His voice resonates deep and quiet. "Things between my brother and I have always been turbulent. That doesn't mean your theory is any less relevant."

"But you got upset. You left when I talked about him." My mind swirls, trying to make sense of things.

I can only see half his smile in the dim light from the sconce closest to us.

"It doesn't matter how I feel about the truth if the truth stands." He glances down at his grip on me and for a second he looks like he might release me but then his hands close around me tighter. "You need to stay out of this area of the castle. I told you not to go exploring on your own."

"I didn't think I was alone. I thought I was chasing after you." Maybe that could be an oversimplification of things, but I really was just trying to fix things. And I really did think he came this way.

He shakes his head. "You could have gotten yourself killed. I've told you that there are creatures in this castle that would love nothing more than to find a way to hurt you."

"But you wouldn't let them." My voice stays almost a whisper in the darkness between us.

"No, I wouldn't."

He lets go of me and I miss his reassuring grip. I move to pull my sleeves down and he stops me with a firm hand.

"What are those?" He points to the scars on my forearm.

I try to tug my sleeves down and ignore his question, but he grabs my hands and doesn't let me.

"Who did this to you?" his voice is dangerously low and leaves no option for not answering.

"N—no one." I don't bother looking at the scars myself. I already know what I'll see there. "It was something that happened. I did it."

His brows come down. "On purpose?"

His questions feel worse than if he had seen me crying. I have nowhere to run from this and I can tell by his face that he'll only accept the truth from me.

"It wasn't on purpose. I just wanted to get away."

His fingers tighten around mine. "Your life before...it was difficult?"

"How would you feel?" I look up at him, eyes shining with unshed tears. "My father traded me to avoid his own consequences. My nanny took over raising me after that. I was worthless to him after that. He didn't care what happened to me as long as I fulfilled his bargain. And Nanny...well, she only hoped things would work for me as a bride. She told me that was my best-case scenario. How else was I supposed to feel?"

"But these... how did you get them?"

The memories come back as sharp as knives. "After I tried to run away Nanny suggested we have thorns and barbed trees planted. The only time I wasn't being watched was at night, so that's when I had to take the risk and run." Memories of my torn nightgown slick with blood come back to me, making me shiver. I'd pressed through, clawing at the branches and barbs with little concern. Thorns had dug into the tender flesh of my feet, but it didn't matter. My only thought: getting away from my father and the bargain he had made for me.

His eyes flash. "I had no idea. Cora, if I had known how the bargain would have made you feel..." His grip grows tighter as the guilt washes over him.

"I don't blame you." He lets me twist my arm so I can hold his hand. "It wasn't your idea for him to avoid whatever his punishment should have been. This isn't your burden to carry."

"It may not have been my idea, but I didn't stop him." Aidoneus's gaze stays permanently fixed to where my scars are even when he can't see them anymore. "I should have refused him."

I shake my head. "What's done is done. We have no reason to dwell on it now."

Maybe it's for the best that I never got away, not that I felt that at the time. I never even made it off my father's grounds.

The embarrassment had been worse than the injuries I'd sustained trying.

His jaw tightens and I know he wants to say something more, but even if he tries, I won't let him. He doesn't get to bear my father's sins.

He's the first person outside of Nanny who has seen my scars. Nanny was horrified and tried her best to repair the damage. The last thing she wanted was for a prospective husband to see how hard I had tried to get away. Aidoneus's response was so different. His desire to protect me was so strong for something that happened years ago and was completely outside of his control. It makes a warmth bloom in my chest that I can't get away from.

"Let me take you back to your room." His voice stays carefully quiet and his tone suggests the end of the conversation.

I don't bother arguing with him. I've done what I've set out to do. Aidoneus knows I wasn't trying to hurt him, and after all the scuffle with the door, I could use a rest with Willa.

She stands whining in the parlor, pacing back and forth as we come closer. As we enter the circle of light, Willa leans on my leg to lick my hand. I pat her head and her tail wags slowly back and forth. Everything is resolved for her.

I wish I could say the same for me.

Aidoneus follows me up the stairs, making sure I get into my room without further incident. Safely inside, I lean against the door and wonder more about the man who would get so worked up over my safety, even from incidents he had no control over.

I press a hand to my chest in an effort to get my heart to slow down. Something has changed between us. I don't think things will ever go back to the way they were again.

Fifteen

LYING in bed with Willa curled next to me, I hover between sleepiness and wakefulness. The fire pops in the grate, causing Willa's sleeping body to jump every time.

Nothing has changed, and yet it feels like *everything* has changed.

I've never had a man, or anyone else for that matter, treat me like Aidoneus has. Time after time he surprises me and forces me to recalibrate.

I'm not sure I would have had any of my adolescent troubles if I had known what kind of man my father traded me to. I expected someone who cared even less for me than my father did, but Aidoneus cares so much *more*. It exists in every moment he spends with me. And it feels so obvious that the behaviors he exhibits with me are contrary to his nature but he chooses to do them anyway. For me.

I'm safe here. I know that better than I know anything. But I'm only safe because of Aidoneus's protection and he won't be here after two weeks. Canaean will take him off somewhere to punish him. I can't allow that to happen. He takes care of and protects me. There has to be some way I can

144

do the same for him. I'm not sure how that would be, I'm just a girl and they're both possessed of the same strange magic that seems to infect this house, but there must be a way.

Pulling the covers up over my head, I press the blankets against my face and breathe in the light scent of soap that covers them. I count my breaths trying to find rest. Willa's warm body breathes with mine, lulling me into sleep, and helping my brain turn off for just a moment.

I can't deny though, that my chest warms to the idea of seeing Aidoneus again tomorrow. I hope he won't be able to tell the level of excitement that just thinking about him encourages in me now. It will be hard to hide, but I don't want to make him uncomfortable when he's been nothing but kind and caring to me. I'll be on my utmost behavior. He deserves that. And while I do that, I'll consider how to save him from himself.

We're *both* going to make it through this.

* * *

Despite a late night, I'm up early and get ready for breakfast in a flurry that leaves piles of clothing discarded on the floor. Ordinarily, I would take the time to replace everything and make sure the room was tidy, but I'm too excited to get down to the dining room to make time for organizing skirts and dresses.

My heart feels like it might beat right out of my chest as I descend the stairs. Even the castle feels brighter today than it has in the rest of the time I've been here. As though the building can match my mood.

The table is set with high flaming candles and trays of toast, eggs, sausage, and a tureen of oatmeal. Something about it feels more formal than the other days I've come down, despite the food being almost exactly the same.

Aidoneus sits at the head of the table, a place I've never seen him before, and our elbows almost touch as I sit in the chair to his right. I keep my gaze focused on my plate as Jameson dishes me so that my cheeks don't flame up and give me away.

"Did you have a better night after I left you?" Aidoneus asks.

Jameson halts for a second, his hand hovering over my plate before he deposits the sausage he'd been dishing me.

"I felt much better after our conversation."

He nods. "Good."

"I've been thinking though." I take a delicate bite of sausage to give me another second to think. "There has to be some way around the issues with you and Canaean. Surely we can put our heads together and figure out how to get out of your deal."

Aidoneus puts his fork down, his face strained. "I need you to pretend like you never heard any of that. It's really none of your business and I would rather you stay out of it."

It feels tempting to leave it alone and not make him angrier, but I can't let him accept his fate without trying. "I understand why you might feel that way, but as someone who was forced into a contract, I can understand why it would be painful and that you might want to explore your options."

"I did what was necessary." He kneads his forehead between his thumb and forefinger. "This is the best option for you. It protects you. It's best if you just leave it alone."

"Protects me for how long?"

His hand falls to the table with a thud. "What are you implying?"

"I think you're doing your best, but I also think you have no control over what happens with me when your time is up." I take another bite, savoring the spicy juices of the sausage.

"Canaean will not go back on my bargain with your

father. That one is done and over with. He cannot hurt you." He runs his hand through his silver hair and doesn't look at me.

I cross my legs to keep my foot from tapping out my agitation. "He will take you away. What if he doesn't send anyone back? Maybe I'll be safe from outright cruelty, but that won't keep me from perishing from neglect."

It's safe to assume that the only way to get him to see that now marks the time for action involves me. He doesn't care about his own safety, but he does care about mine. His sense of self-preservation is low, but he wants to take care of me. It's the same problem that got him to make his deal with Canaean in the first place.

"There will be someone here to care for you. Plus, Canaean cannot abandon this castle even if he wanted to. There exists work to be done here that cannot be ignored or avoided. He knows that." He pulls the napkin from his lap and places it on the table.

"And what exactly is that work?" My curiosity blooms anew.

"It's better that you don't know."

He stands from the table. I'm not sure what he runs from more, me trying to save him, or him having to say what he does. This time I don't rise to follow him. I didn't do anything wrong. Plus, I don't know how many more days after he leaves that I'll get a good meal, so now I have to take advantage of the food as much as I can.

When I've taken my time and my plate is empty, I sit at the table for a while longer. It's as good a place as any to think about what to do with Aidoneus. He won't help me, but that's fine. I'm sure I can handle this without him. If he was here he would just be moody and sulk around about it anyway, so maybe this is for the best. He'll get the benefits and I'll have a little more peace.

From what I know about Canaean, he won't do anything for free. Especially regarding his brother. The joy of putting him down would be payment enough for him to want to stay on his current trajectory. I don't have a favor to call in, or money to pay him off with. There has to be something though. Something he might want more than humiliating his brother. Which, I realize, asks a lot.

Still, I'm sure with a little thought I'll come up with something.

* * *

I decide to walk in the garden for a while and let the cool air outside wake my mind up to more possibilities. It truly captures the most beautiful part of the castle's essence. Every bud and leaf encased in a beautiful layer of ice that catches the meager light and brightens the whole space. If it weren't so cold out here, I could probably stay here forever. As things stand, I'm grateful Aidoneus gave me some warmer clothes or I wouldn't last five minutes out here.

Sounds like the tinkling of crystal echo through the garden as I run my hand along a few wayward branches. Willa runs alongside me, moving forward then back to make sure I'm still coming.

There has to be something Canaean will trade for his brother's freedom. Maybe there's a way I can figure out that will break his engagement to Teleia. That might be worth something to him. Although, I'm not sure I want to make more of an enemy out of Teleia and ruining the marriage she wants will surely do that.

I file the idea away in the back of my mind anyway. It's not a bad one and I might need it if I can't think of anything else.

Not much exists that I have control of around here. This was something that terrified me to think about before I came, but hasn't seemed quite so bad in practice. However, it leaves me without many options now. The only thing I can really manipulate is myself, and I fail to see how that will help anyone.

My shoes crunch in the white gravel of the garden as I walk further than I've ever gone before. Although it remains hard to tell because the planning and the plants remains identical throughout. Willa grabs a fallen branch and holds it in her mouth. Her tails wags back and forth as she comes back, proud of her find.

She drops her stick at my feet, sitting as she stares at me with her tongue hanging out of her mouth. I bend down to pick it up, a smile flitting across my face with her playfulness.

My hand goes numb as I hold the stick. She sits back, front paws in the air as she begs for me to throw it. I want to oblige her just to not have to hold it anymore, but I hesitate just before releasing it. The stick feels so smooth in my hand that it draws my eye to it. The second I actually look at it, I drop it with a shriek and it hits the ground breaking into a million pieces.

A bone. It was definitely a bone.

Willa didn't go that far from me to find it, so somewhere close by a body lays in the garden. Well, not much of a body anymore, but still. There are remains in this garden with us.

All the reasons for why I initially came out here flee my mind. I grab my skirts with shaking hands and turn back toward the castle as quick as I can. Willa follows after me, her tail still wagging like nothing has happened.

I'm not sure what happened myself, but I know enough to know I won't be coming back from what I've seen today.

Sixteen

SAFE IN MY ROOM, my hand still burns from where it touched the bone. I don't know if the burning is real or all in my mind, but the pain persists either way. I crawl into bed and clutch my hand to my chest.

As far as I know, there isn't a cemetery so close to the castle. I'm sure they have one close by, but not *that* close. Even if there were, bodies wouldn't just be lying around it for Willa to steal pieces of them.

Aidoneus told me that his castle was dangerous. I'd been warned that there had been others that came here before me but not for long. Has this been what he hinted at? All this time I thought people just didn't want to be here with him, but in actuality they just never leave. There could be a whole field of bones out there and I would never know. The weather here keeps me inside and when I go out it keeps me close enough to the castle that I am sure to stay out of trouble.

Willa jumps on the bed next to me, curling against my side and lending me her warmth. The horrible thought crosses my mind that this might be the work that Aidoneus disappears to care of. It doesn't sound like the work of a gentleman, but he isn't like any gentleman that I have ever known.

I just can't see him messing around with bones though. What would be the purpose of it? I can't think of any real job that would involve that.

He may not even know. I'm not sure what Aidoneus does outside, but he probably doesn't wander far either. He may not know what hides just outside his garden. But if that were the case then it would be my responsibility to tell him, and I don't think I could ever find the words for that. This definitely isn't a possibility I ever prepared for.

I rub my hand against my dress as though that can remove the taint of bone that still clings to my skin. Bile runs up the back of my throat and for a moment I'm afraid I'm going to be sick.

"Cora?" Aidoneus's voice comes out quiet and there's a faint knocking at the door. I just want to bury my head in my pillow and be done with this day.

I don't answer. I don't think I could even find the words if I wanted to. If I tried, I'm worried that the first thing to come out of my mouth might be screaming. I never prepared for this. Nanny had no idea how to prepare me for this place.

"Cora, is everything all right?"

Maybe if I stay silent he'll think I'm somewhere else. Or maybe that's why he came here. Maybe he worries that I'm somewhere else.

I sink farther into the bed. Willa's head pokes up, her ears alert as she monitors the door. Her tail wags, hitting against my side.

My focus shifts to my breathing when it remains quiet for long enough. If I can just get that under control, then I might be able to sleep. But I can't focus on that when I don't know for sure why he was at the door. What if he came by because he knows what I found? The pieces were so small, but that doesn't mean he wasn't in the garden and knows what I've discovered. But if that were the case, then wouldn't he have wanted to tell me that I'm not allowed in those gardens anymore? He could easily tell me to take Willa in the court-yard, where I was taking her before. But he didn't. So maybe that means that he doesn't know.

My stomach feels tight and my throat grows dry. Nothing feels right and I don't know how it ever could feel right again. I clutch Willa and pull her closer to me. Her hot breath coats my arm, warming me and pushing away the chill.

"I don't know what I would have done without you." My words are quiet against her neck. She licks my hand in response and it feels almost too much to bear. A tear squeezes its way out and drips down my cheek. "I couldn't have survived without you."

Squeezing her closer to me, I use her breathing to soothe me. She wiggles, pushing me to release my hold, but I can't. Not after what we've been through today.

Finally she relaxes and her letting go helps me to let go and we find sleep together.

* * *

When morning comes, I still can't leave my bed. My nightmares were plagued with images of skeletons and the undead rising to meet me as I walked along the garden path. They chased me between the rose bushes and even followed me back into the castle. The sound of them pounding against my bedroom door jolts me from sleep and no matter how much I want the oblivion of sleep, my mind won't give it to me.

Willa whines at the door, her tail wagging for a second before going still. She looks at me then looks back at the door, wagging her tail again.

I'm sure she wants to go to the bathroom, but I can't bring myself to take her. My reality could become worse than my dreams if I dare to leave this room.

Thumping comes from the door and for a second I wonder if I'm still dreaming. My body grows tense and the fire in the grate pops, sending me jolting.

"Cora, I know you're in there." Aidoneus's voice travels across the room in a hard line that feels nothing like my dreams. "Did something happen? Did you try one of the other doors? I told you to leave them alone."

My mouth feels too dry for words. My throat aches like I've been screaming. Willa paws at the door, ready for Aidoneus to join us no matter how I feel about it.

"I'm coming in." I'm sure he tries for politeness, but it still feels like an invasion when I'm not ready to handle anything yet.

The handle jiggles but doesn't open. At least in my panic last night I remembered to make sure the lock was in place. It's a small comfort that that lock would keep something as serious as Aidoneus out. Skeletons probably wouldn't stand a chance.

A thump makes the door shake and I'm sure he throws his body into it. Another thump and Willa whines at the door, her ears upright as she waits for him.

I sit up in the bed, but another thump doesn't come. Maybe he's given up on me and went back to doing his other work, whatever that might be. He might be right and I'm much better off not knowing.

Willa stands against the door, her small squat body not even reaching the doorknob that has started to glow blue. It gets brighter and brighter until I can hear the latch click. The blue fades away to nothing and the doorknob turns without issue.

Aidoneus stands like a dark shadow in the doorway, gaze

landing on me. His shoulders move up and down with his heavy breathing. Willa comes closer to him, but doesn't touch him. Her tail wags then falls as he continues standing there.

"It was smart of you to lock the door," he finally says, his voice deep and untroubled like the magic didn't affect him despite what I've already seen. "You never know what might be out here."

He takes a step into the room, patting Willa on the head when she comes to sniff him. "Would you like to explain why you were absent from dinner? And breakfast?"

I shake my head.

He moves to the end of the bed, his footsteps silent against the rug. "Something must have happened. I've never known you to miss a meal."

A small smile cracks at the side of my mouth.

He reaches out, touching the foot board of the bed. "If someone has done something to you, you must tell me." There's an edge to his voice that almost makes me afraid of what would happen if someone *had* done something to me.

I shake my head. "No one did anything."

If someone else had been there maybe it would have been better. Then I wouldn't have had to carry the burden of this secret on my own. But there wasn't. There was just me and Willa and the bone that shatters over and over again a thousand times in my memories.

The lines in his face tighten like he can see my pain as the image replays itself once again in my mind.

"I brought you something." He reaches into his coat and pulls out an apple. "I thought you might be hungry and I didn't want you to have to wait for Cook to make you something."

I doubt she'd be so accommodating anyway. I won't forget my first few days here when there was nothing and no one.

He holds out the apple to me without getting any closer, giving me some semblance of my space.

It feels like I've been here before, to these odd spaces in my mind. I practically lived in them when I was at home. So many days were spent in this lethargic inability to help myself when all I wanted was to break free of everything.

I didn't think I'd feel that way when I was with him.

Willa hops onto the bed to get closer to Aidoneus. She makes a grumbling sound and puts her head under his hand, wanting his attention. He doesn't give it to her though, his eyes remaining fixed on me.

The apple stays in the air between us until I'm sure his arm aches and I finally reach out of the blanket to grab it. For a moment the smooth skin reminds me too much of the garden and I want to throw it as fast as I can before it can shatter in my hand. Instead, I take a deep breath. This is just an apple. I'm safe in my room. Aidoneus would never give me something so horrifying. And if he knew what I'd seen... I don't know what he would do.

"Would you rather have something to drink?" he asks when I don't move to eat the apple. It sits in my limp hand like I would rather forget about it.

I shake my head. My stomach can't handle anything right now, no matter what form it comes in.

Aidoneus frowns, his brows coming down tight. "I don't know how to help you."

He's not alone. I don't know how to help myself either. This isn't a scenario I was ever prepared for. And now it feels like it's played in my head for too long, becoming bigger and worse than it was originally, and originally it was still bad.

Aidoneus curls his hand around mine, bringing the apple to my lips. "Please eat something."

Perhaps its the only form of comfort he knows. It

wouldn't matter what type of comfort he chose though, I don't know if I could take any of them.

Releasing the apple, I let it fall onto the bed. I do the same with my body, pulling the blankets up over my head. Aidoneus already knows something's wrong so I don't have to hide how I feel.

"Will you speak to me?" He kneels next to the bed, his hand still holding mine. "Please help me fix whatever has gone wrong."

If only I knew how. If only I knew what to do then maybe it wouldn't have plagued my nightmares in a never ending loop.

I stare blankly ahead, so unfocused that I can't even see him in my peripheral. His fingers tighten around mine as he tries to pull me back.

"Would it... would it be okay if I went into your memory?" His question is hesitant but I'm too numb to feel outraged by the idea of him going through things. I'm too numb to do anything.

He lets go of my hand and places his on either side of my head, framing my temples. His cool hands soothe my mind. I close my eyes to feel the sensation more clearly.

"I'm not going to dig around," he reassures me unnecessarily. "I'm only looking for reasons for this."

How convenient for him that he has this ability. Heaven knows I'm only slipping farther and farther away from being able to do anything or say anything. I've found my dark place all prepared for me like I never left and I don't know that it will let me go this time.

My head tickles as he starts, like a wave pulsing between his hands. I expect my brain to let me know what he's looking at, but it stays blissfully blank.

What will he do when he knows I've discovered one of the secrets of this place? It's a terrible one. More terrible than any I had imagined before. Even with his warnings of what lurked behind the doors here, I guess I never took it seriously that someone had ever actually *died*.

His fingers tighten for a second around my head. He probably found it then. Maybe my bones will be the next ones left discarded outside for the elements and nature to get rid of for him.

I feel so idiotic that I ever became comfortable here. I was never comfortable at home, so why should coming here have been any different. I let myself think I was safe in a place where I was openly warned that I wasn't. I've been a fool from the beginning.

His hands slip from my head and he bends down to look me in the eye. "I was hoping you would never have to deal with any of that."

So he did know. It wasn't a surprise to him that there were bones in his backyard. He just didn't want *me* to see them.

If I were a smarter girl, I would try to run away right now. I would use this experience as leverage to get away. How could he hold me to a contract when death looms as a potential? He couldn't.

"I don't know that there's any good explanation for that. Not for a girl like you," he says.

"A girl like me?" Those words help pull me out of the darkness. "And what would you mean by that? Do you think there are girls out there who wouldn't be phased by your murderous tendencies?"

His grin turns wry. "My murderous tendencies? How quickly you assume all the death lies directly in my hands. I assure you that is not the case."

"Then how else can you explain the bones at *your* castle? The bones *you* knew about?" It had to be him. Otherwise, he wouldn't have allowed them to sit here. Someone would have gone to prison. Only a man with as much power as him could have avoided that fate.

"This is a part of my job—"

"Are you a crypt keeper then? Because excuse me, I've never seen that kind of work done by lords, *my Lord*." I cross my arms over my chest, feeling my blood pumping through me faster than it has in days.

He sighs. "No, not a crypt keeper, but my job involves having dealings with the dead. I told you before that I would rather you not know my work. It's better for both of us."

"And yet you leave your work scattered around like you want it to be found."

"I assure you I did not." He sits on the edge of the bed, frustration evident in the tight lines of his body. "This has all been a mistake, one that you have had the unfortunate experience of being caught up in. I promise you, it will never happen again."

Not that there aren't any other bodies or bones around here, just that I won't have to look at them again. My stomach turns and his promise makes my mouth taste sour.

This man, this man I have found a way to trust... I don't want to question if he deserves it. He can't be the monster that's been in the castle all along. I refuse to feel stupid for letting him get close, but I can't linger on how I felt only yesterday. It will only make me sicker.

He reaches for my hand but I pull myself away from him.

"Cora, I'll keep you safe. I promise you."

I look down at my lap. "Can you keep me safe from yourself?"

The air feels colder against my skin. He stands from the bed, mouth thinning. He paces in front of me, his movements sharp and quick.

He runs his hand through his hair, silver locks falling over his forehead. "I'm doing my best. I told you I would keep you safe. Of course that included from me. Why else do you think I stayed away from you for so long? It was better for you to not have me around and I knew that. But you continued to poke and prod and then it became the better option to be around you. I've struggled every day about how best to help you." He kneels by the bed. "Don't you see? Don't you see how I have tried?"

I can't get distracted by the way my heart grows warm and my chest grows tight with his words. None of those explain why Willa found a body in the garden. He can't be so self-righteous with me but allow others to die.

"Do you even know who the dead person was?"

The words fall between us in limp syllables.

He looks away from me, his face growing smooth as he tries to distance himself from the answer. I pull my legs up to my chin, wrapping my arms around them to hold myself in place. Everything feels like it burns and I just need him to say it and allow the pain to wash over me so I can move on in some way.

"Yes. I always know. It's my job." The sparks in his eyes glow brighter as he stares into the fire. His hands curl into fists and everything about him looks taut like he wants to run away.

"But you say you didn't kill him?" I'm not sure it would be better to just think he has a known murderer living somewhere around here that he lets loose from time to time rather than having it be him.

"I did not. That does not fall within my job description." He glances at me but doesn't make eye contact. "I only do what I am tasked to do, as distasteful as it may be."

"Are you trying to tell me that Canaean has bodies sent here and it's your job to take care of them?" I can't keep the incredulity from my voice. None of what he says makes sense.

My neck heats with embarrassment for ever wanting to

believe him. I can't believe I was ever such a fool. Canaean and Aidoneus probably deserve each other in the same way Canaean and Teleia do. I've just been too much of a fool to see Aidoneus's faults clearly.

"No, no, nothing like that." Aidoneus opens his mouth to say more, but the words don't come.

"If not that, then what exactly *is* it like?" I straighten my neck to look at him better. My voice grows in volume the longer I speak as the fury building within me finds an outlet. "Because I deserve to know. You forced me to come to this nightmare castle and now you think I'm better off if I go through it blindfolded. The time has passed for that. Your secrets are out. Tell me what I need to know or release me from this place."

"It's not that easy. None of it is." He comes next to the bed but still can't look at me. "There are things I am incapable of saying. If I could, I would have told you from the start so you could understand what a dangerous position you are in. Even now I can't speak the words that will free you while dooming me. But I want to." He reaches for me again but I don't let him. "Please know that I want you. And please believe me when I say that I'm not the killer. I never have been. That would be part of why Canaean found so much joy in giving me this assignment."

"You can't be very good at your assignment if even Willa can find the evidence on a casual walk." I wish Willa would come back to me on the bed, but she rolls around on the rug, too busy trying to get Aidoneus to notice her. Traitor.

He shakes his head. "Hiding isn't a part of my assignment and I don't always have control over where things end up. My dealings don't involve the bodies themselves. Not usually."

I think I'm going to be sick. I clamp a hand over my mouth as bile rises up the back of my throat. My eyes burn and

I just want him to go away. It's obvious nothing he can say will make any of this better. He only seems to make it worse.

"Just leave—"

"But!"

"Go, now." I glance at him and he finally looks at me, eyes shining. "You need to leave. If you can't fully explain yourself then we have nothing to talk about. You're the monster in the castle you warned me about and it's time I made sure I was protected."

His shoulders slump, his fists opening and closing. He hesitates like he might say something else but in the end only shakes his head. Silver hair falls over his eyes hiding the emotions that are on the verge of being free. Part of me wants to comfort him, but I can't, not without inviting him back in in a way that will only hurt me more.

His footsteps are heavy and slow as he moves towards the door, as though giving me time to change my mind. But I can't. And he knows that.

Distance between us will be best. I'll still try to free him from Canaean's bargain, but there can be nothing more between us. We'll all have a better chance of survival that way.

Seventeen

HELPING Aidoneus without having anything to do with him proves problematic right away. Especially when I can't help but be distracted by the 'job' he claims to have. It just doesn't make any sense. I can't think of anything that would require him to deal with the dead, not in the way that he describes it, or doesn't for that matter.

I wander the halls, being sure to stay far away from any doors. I hear movement behind a few of them, but I won't be tricked so easily this time. It helps that I don't have any desire to actually see Aidoneus face-to-face right now anyway. It's been relatively easy too when he decides not to show up for the same meals that he hunted me down for avoiding. I'm not the only one who isn't ready for a rematch.

In every room I go to, I'm still drawn to the books. I'm not sure why I have such confidence that they'll help me at some point. Each one I open displays the same language I can't read, far from helpful, and yet I keep going back. It doesn't help that Aidoneus has books stashed everywhere like some sort of treasure hunt. Every room has at least one somewhere. It makes the temptation to open other doors that sound quieter inside even greater. What knowledge could they be hiding? The only book I could possibly read could be waiting behind any of these doors, full of answers, but there's nothing I can do about it.

Willa follows me through the dark hallways, her ears alert and her tail high, though not wagging. Wandering may not be her favorite activity, but it isn't one she'll let me do alone. Especially not when sometimes we end at the kitchen and the cook throws her a nice scrap. She may not like me, but she loves Willa.

The smell of mildew coats this part of the castle. The air sits cold like the rest of it, but the layer of dust on the trim implies a not often-used section. I'll have no trouble avoiding Aidoneus here.

The light changes, becoming brighter just ahead. A door on the left hangs open and my breath catches in my throat. An open door could go either way. Either I'm safe and there was nothing in there, or I may be in imminent danger with the creature that was inside now on the hunt.

My steps slow as my body refuses to get any closer. Willa waits with me, her body still but not any more tense than it was before. I try to take my cue from her. If there was something beyond, she wouldn't let me wander into it blind.

Steeling my will, I take a few steps forward. However anti-climactic it seems as nothing immediately changes. There's no intake of breath or scraping along the floor or anything to even remotely imply there something waits in there for me.

Without new stimuli, the tightness in my chest eases. It's hard to maintain heavy fear when there's nothing immediate to keep feeding it. Plus, if Willa's okay, then I must be okay.

I make this my new mantra as I press forward, one foot in front of the other. My hand trails along the wall, ready in case I need to hold myself up.

The light grows brighter, almost like in the kitchen. That

room shines the brightest of any in the castle that I've found, with nothing even remotely close to compare, but this new room might just do that. My shadow lengthens behind me as I get closer. I expect the light to be warm after spending so long in the dark, but it feels just as cold as the rest of the castle which only leaves my skin more chilled.

I reach the open door frame, my fingers resting on the cold wood. I take a deep breath before turning to face the room beyond.

Inside lies a room very similar to mine. A four-poster bed sits against the wall with a fireplace opposite it. Dark emerald wallpaper lines the room, making it feel like the inside of a jewelry box. Heavy black curtains have been pulled away from the window which shines brighter than anything I've seen since coming here. I squint to make out the rest of the room's much smaller objects. A half bookshelf sits next to the fireplace with only a few books sitting on its dusty shelves. A nightstand leans beside the bed where a glass has been placed. If I peek just right around the bed, it looks like a copper tub might be sitting between it and the wall.

The bedroom seems so normal for a moment I'm stumped. I expected more to be hiding behind these walls. After everything that Aidoneus said, it doesn't seem possible now that they would just be normal rooms. Like he keeps a hotel running for dangerous creatures. Or maybe this would be considered a glamorous prison. I don't know.

I step into the room, my shoes sinking into a plush rug that looks almost exactly the same as mine. Nothing happens. No creature rushes at me from the corner. No beast leaps from under the bed. Everything seems perfectly normal.

With that fear assuaged, I make my way to the window, eager to feel the sun on my skin. I've grown so pale after staying here. I didn't have much color before, so in the brighter light I'm sure I'll practically become translucent.

Warmth lingers in the light, more than I expected. It tingles along my skin and brings a smile to my face. It's so full of life, something the rest of the castle lacks.

I take another step towards the window, unsure why this window can be so bright when the others are not. Mine always offers a dusky dark light that offers more shadows than it does sun. I doubt the issue is that my window just faces the wrong direction, because at some point the sun would swing my way. No, I feel something special about this window. Probably about this room if I take a second to survey it. Later, I'll look at it later, when I've had my fill of letting sunshine dance along my skin and warm the parts of me that have been icing over in this dark place.

Blinking a few times to clear my vision, I lean over until my forehead rests against the warm glass. It feels like heaven. Like the first spring day after a long winter.

I expect to see the courtyard or the garden outside, but I never would have guessed what lies beyond the window. Instead of the wintry chill that I've come to expect every-where, this window looks out on warm sand and bright sun. People mill about outside, greeting each other and carrying heavy packages that look like they came from a market. The sun reflects off the water in the distance, giving everything a sparkle. Tall palm trees frame a stone walkway. Like a vision into a whole other world.

"It's part of my punishment I suppose."

I gasp as Aidoneus leans against the window beside me. My heart beat ricochets but he doesn't even look at me, his gaze focused on the world outside the window.

"I can see part of the home I should have had instead of being out here. Clever really. How else would Canaean keep me miserable except with such a stark comparison." His voice stays dry but his eyes hold longing as the sparks swirl within them.

"Sorry," I mumble. "I didn't mean to bother you. I'll just go."

I have to get out of here before I make another mistake.

"You didn't mean to bother me? You came to my bedroom." He gives me a wry smile. "I'm not sure I've ever had a visitor here before."

My face flushes and my hands grow clammy. "I didn't mean to. I didn't know it was your room. I just saw the light and—"

"And you had to see for yourself. I don't blame you. But what were you doing down here in the first place?" He turns from the window to face me, resting his hand against the ledge.

I straighten my shoulders. "Exploring."

"Exploring," he repeats. "Looking for anything in particular?"

I don't know if my face will ever return to its normal color. This marks the moment to stand my ground and put distance between us. I don't want him to look at me like he did before… I'm not strong enough for that. "I'm looking for answers."

"Ah." He looks down at his hand. "Not to be dissuaded I see."

My mouth feels dry. "If you thought my discovery before would kill my interest in figuring this place out, you were wrong."

"Obviously."

"It has only made me feel like I need to know more than ever." *Time is running out.* I can't look at him or he'll see the words I can't see hiding on my face.

He kneads his forehead between his fingers. "It seems nothing I can say will stop you. Nothing you can find will stop you."

"So why don't you just tell me what's going on and save me the trouble?"

His smile stretches until it looks painful. "I can't. I have explained all I am capable of. Plus, you're a strong and capable girl. Imagine all the fun and sense of accomplishment you would lose if I could just give you all the answers."

"Are you... teasing me?" I brace a hand against my hip with a frown.

He sighs. "If you have to ask then I haven't done a very good job at it."

I feel my mouth lift and a giggle presses between my lips. He raises a brow at me and the giggle forces its way free. My shoulders shake and for just a moment everything feels lighter.

Then I remember I'm standing alone with him in his bedroom.

My giggles dry up and I take a step back from him. His smile disappears back into the hard lines of his face.

"I should leave."

The words hang between us. I'm not sure what I want Aidoneus to say.

He nods. "I suppose you should. But wouldn't that defeat the purpose of why you came?"

He takes a step toward me and my chest feels so tight I can't breathe. "I..."

"It would be such a waste if you didn't get to snoop around now after going through all the trouble of getting here and having to put up with me discovering you." His mouth twitches at the side.

My mouth feels dry. "I can't exactly start going through your things while you're watching me."

"But you might be able to ask the right questions if I'm here." He shrugs. "All up to you."

"Are you giving me permission to go through your room?"

He nods.

My face feels hot. I really can't do that while he stands there. This is his *personal* space. His *private* space. I have no idea what I might discover here. And with him watching me... it all feels too weird.

But a larger part of me wants to look. I've come all this way and what if I can't find this room next time? This would have all been a waste. I would have wasted all my time looking out a magic window instead of searching for answers.

I back away from him until I bump against the bookshelf. He watches me with a small side smile. It's hard to look away from him to begin my search, but I have to do it. I can't waste any more time.

Taking a deep breath, I turn my back on him and look at the sparsely lined shelves. If there was going to be any clues, Aidoneus's room would be where they were lurking. I feel sure of it. I'll find my answers and get out of here and work on my plan. Easy. What proves difficult is ignoring the heat of his body as he comes closer to watch me.

I run my finger along the spines of the books, all written in the same unreadable language. "You seem to have an affinity for books."

"Yes," he breathes and I swear I can feel it on the back of my neck. "They have been my friends and company for many years now."

"Why didn't you just rehire servants to stay here? Then you might not feel so lonely." I pull out a book that looks promising, an embossed pomegranate splayed across its cover.

"If only it were that simple. Unfortunately, my ability to have servants comes from the deals I make."

I clench the book tighter in my hand without opening it. "Your deals? Jameson, the cook, they're here because you made deals with them?"

"And they all felt like doing work here would be better than the fate that awaited them."

My skin grows cold. "Is that what I'm supposed to be?"

Have I been treated like a guest when I'm supposed to be

nothing more than a servant? Is that why I've had such issues here? I'm not supposed to live like this. Everyone who lives in the castle knows it but me. I'm living in a delusion and everyone else laughs at me.

It feels like a rock drops into the pit of my stomach.

"No." Aidoneus reaches for my hand and this time I don't pull away. His fingers are cold as they wrap around mine. "You are not supposed to be a servant. You were never supposed to be a servant. That was not the contract your father made for you."

I don't think I can believe him. How could I? He's so full of secrets and half-truths that this just feels like another moment when I'm being duped. He shouldn't worry so much about trying to protect me. The moment for that is over. Has been over for years.

My body feels empty, like I'm swirling down and down and down on a dark sea of thoughts that won't let me go.

"Cora, are you listening to me?"

Even if I listened the way he wanted me to, it wouldn't matter. It all feels like lies.

"Why do you want to protect me so much?" The words burn like poison as they come out.

He squeezes my fingers. "You're special. How can you not see that? You hunt me down when you think I'm in trouble. You live and *laugh* in this castle like it's a normal place even though we both know it isn't. You've made me want to live again. You've forced me to stand up to my brother. How can you not see how special you are?"

"All I've done creates more problems for you." I scowl, my voice sullen.

"No." He shakes his head. "Those problems were always there. There was nothing you could do with Canaean and I that would have changed anything. For the better or the worse."

I don't believe him. Not for one second. Without me, he would have been able to live in this castle forever. He wouldn't be forced to leave his home in two weeks. Two lousy weeks that don't feel long enough to accomplish anything let alone the massive undertaking I've placed upon myself. It seems so stupid that I thought I could change everything.

Aidoneus bends down to look me in the eye. "None of the fault lies with you, Cora."

"It's all my fault," I whisper, looking down so I don't have to see the worry etched in his face. "I should have stayed in my room like you told me to."

He shakes his head. "That was never going to work. I think we both know that. I was living in a daydream of my own that I could keep you safe from him. It was never going to happen. Not in the way I wanted it to."

We've both been living in a daydream. A place where our actions were pure and our motives untouchable. Where we would win our fight just because it was what was right. That's not how real life works. If it were I wouldn't be in this position in the first place.

"Cora, none of the fault is yours. There was nothing you could do that was going to change what happened. Maybe your being here sped some things up but it didn't change anything. Canaean has been waiting for this moment for years. Nothing was going to stop him from seizing it." He tips my chin up, forcing me to look at him.

The sparks in his eyes spiral faster, matching my beating heart. My breath catches in my chest as his gaze flicks over my lips for only a moment before he draws back up to my eyes.

This certainly feels like playing with fire.

I pull my hands away from him so I can catch my breath. I can't recover and I can't think clearly, not with him that close. Not with the smell of him burning in my lungs.

He lets me go even as his jaw grows tighter.

"I... I need to go." There are no clues here that will make any of this worth it. Staying here any longer will only drag me down.

I don't look back at him as I run down the hallway, putting as much distance behind me as I can until I don't feel his presence anymore.

Eighteen

MY MIND IS a swirling mess and I don't know what to do. My thoughts won't settle and my body feels electric. I pace through my room, the jittery feeling under my skin making it impossible to sit down. Willa watches me with her head cocked to the side, her tongue lolling out of her mouth.

I refuse to acknowledge what I'm feeling. There's no way. It doesn't make any sense. This doesn't represent me. I don't do this. I don't feel like this. This isn't right.

Flopping on the bed, I kick my feet in the air to try and get some of the burning moving sensation out of me. It doesn't work and I just feel like I could levitate right off the bed.

He has no right to look at me that way. He can't look at me and hold my hand and tell me that I matter and I mean something. Not only would that be unbelievably inappropriate, but so forward. Or it would be if this was a normal place where normal rules apply. Instead, I don't know what counts as normal and what would be okay here. Anything he says as master of the house probably.

What would Nanny do if she could see me now? I can't imagine how disappointed she'd be. I've been *alone* in a man's room. My reputation would never recover. Not that it matters since I'm never going home and the man in question is also leaving.

And nothing happened.

But did I want something to happen?

I shouldn't. I know I shouldn't. At the same time, I don't even know what I would want. What did I want him to do? Why does my body feel like it could run for days and never tire?

It's ridiculous and I'm ridiculous and maybe it's for the best if we just never see each other again. Good thing I know Aidoneus will honor that desire. Not. He won't let me avoid him.

Night passes in slow increments that I can't escape. Sleep refuses to come as my mind continues to swirl around and around with thoughts I wish I could rid myself of.

The look in his eyes as he tried to help me captures me the most. There was so much there like he wanted to say things but couldn't. Would I feel better if he had?

I roll over, burying my face in the blankets. The air comes hot and thick to my lungs. It would be so easy for this to be the end. Fall asleep and let the air slowly fade from my body. Then I would never have to think about any of this again. It would be brilliant if I felt like I had any real chance of follow-through.

No, for one of the first times, those thoughts have come and I haven't cared. Whispers of an easier way out have no affect because life feels... interesting? Worth living? There's something there that I can't avoid even if I want to. And all of it comes down to Aidoneus.

I want to scream.

I never asked for this. I never asked for any of it, but I *really* never asked to *care* for him. It's ridiculous. Without him, my childhood would have been infinitely better. I wouldn't have had this threat hanging over me that made the thoughts come in the first place. And yet... somewhere along the way I've stopped holding Aidoneus accountable for his part in the bargain. I don't know what it was or what my father did, but I know Aidoneus well enough now to know that he wouldn't have asked for me. He wouldn't have made it easy for my father to get out of his troubles by borrowing against his daughter. That's not Aidoneus. I'm not sure how the others managed to get themselves caught up in being part of the castle, but that story doesn't match what I know of Aidoneus with me.

He would have protected me.

The thought hits me hard in the chest. I'm not sure I've ever had someone willing to protect me before. The way he reacted when he saw my scars... it was never his problem and he shouldn't have cared, but he absolutely did. There was death in those eyes. A threat I didn't understand before. That promise that he would bring down the world to get back at whoever hurt me... I tried to ignore it, but it was still there nonetheless.

There's something between us and I can't ignore it. Not with the look he gave me tonight. His time here is running out because he wanted to protect me.

He can say it would have happened if I was here or not, but I think we both know better. He wouldn't have gotten in his brother's way if not for his desire to protect me.

I wanted to help him before, but now... it's not an option not to. I have to save him. From himself and from me.

Blowing out another long breath, I stay face down for a moment longer, letting all the thoughts of staying here fade away until my mind and my body agree, we have to save Aidoneus.

* * *

I wait until I know Aidoneus will be at breakfast before I try making my way to his room again. It's childish of me to hide my intentions when he was more than willing to share with me, but I can't dig around the way I want to with him standing beside me. It's far too distracting for far too many reasons. No, it's better this way.

Willa huffs as she walks next to me, finally getting over some of her fear of the castle. It doesn't feel as scary when she moves by my side. I know if something peeks from behind the locked doors, Willa has enough teeth for both of us.

I expected it to be hard to find his room again, but my feet memorized the journey even when my mind was distracted. It doesn't take long before I can feel that I'm standing in front of his room, even if the door stays closed now. Light peeks out from under the door through the narrow crack.

The window Canaean left behind represents one of the most awful things I could imagine a brother would do. Punishment on punishment exists for Aidoneus even when Canaean has already won. Why show him the world he can never have? It feels so wrong it hurts, and that's saying something considering the family I came from.

I close my eyes to say a quick prayer that Aidoneus has gone to breakfast, so as not to be waiting for me inside. An image of him standing before the bed, getting dressed, flashes through my mind and my cheeks get hot. I open my eyes and pull open the door before I can think any more about what Aidoneus does when he's in his room alone.

Luckily, the room remains just as abandoned as it was yesterday, even if the door was closed this time. I cross the floor quickly, my gaze darting toward the open window where a breeze filled with the smell of salt and hot sand floats into the room.

Distracted, I move toward the window once again. My

fingers curl against the frame as my body longs to lean forward and taste the air.

I didn't realize the window could open. *Could Aidoneus climb through if he wanted and land back in his home?* The image veers toward ridiculous and makes him seem so much more like a boy than the man I know.

I doubt Aidoneus has been climbing out windows though. Not unless that's where his 'work' hides.

It's hard to pull away from the window and the group of ladies standing below me, their voices carrying in the breeze like bells, but if I don't move now I might not get another chance.

I don't go back to the bookshelf. I've had far too many dead ends with books to want to try that again.

The shelf with a few knickknacks holds nothing of value, at least not for figuring out what to do. I pick up a hand-carved figure of a three-headed dog with a chuckle. Aidoneus has more imagination than I thought he would.

Moving to the middle of the room, I brace my hands on my hips with a scowl. Willa sits next to me, tail-wagging despite my mounting annoyance.

How can there be nothing here? Surely he must keep a record of things somewhere. Unless he keeps that in the books I can't read.

I look around the room again, gaze snagging on the small table next to the bed where yet another book lies. I don't remember it being there when I was here with Aidoneus before. It sits at an angle like it was put down haphazardly after reading it in bed. It makes this one feel more important than any of the others. This one is being read.

I'm careful not to knock over the half-full glass of water sitting beside it as I grab the leather cover of the book. It feels smooth in my hand, the leather well-worn from use.

Biting my bottom lip, I open the cover. The writing

mirrors the writing from before, completely unreadable, but this time words aren't the only thing on the page. Pictures spread across the pages as I turn them, my breathing coming faster.

While not a picture book like I would see for kids, there are still too many words on every page for that and the thickness of the book makes it one a child would have a hard time holding. The pictures are detailed and beautiful, if a little dark. Several of them involve skeletons, and not even skeletons laying in death. No, these ones are up and moving, walking the barren land on several pages.

My stomach feels unsettled as I dig through more pages, looking for more than just fairytale images. There has to be something in here that can help me understand Aidoneus and Canaean and what I can do next to put things right.

The breath leaves my lungs as I land on an image that looks all too familiar. Aidoneus's castle, complete with the hazy twilight that always covers this place and even the horse-less carriage that brought me here. The picture looks so real, that it feels like I could fall right through the image and land outside.

Why is his castle in this book?

I know I'm running out of time. Aidoneus has finished breakfast by now, if he actually even sat down and ate anything with me gone. Which could mean that he might come looking for me. He's not an idiot. I'm sure he might suspect where I could be.

I want to pocket the book and take it with me, but it was on his nightstand. There's no way he wouldn't notice it missing. But there's just so much more I need to know.

My fingers grip the book even tighter. I can't put it back, I won't. Not when there could be answers here. Not when Aidoneus's *castle* lurks on within its pages. There is something here.

I make the split decision to take the book, knowing that it will be immensely difficult to remove it from the room in any kind of secret manner. It's too big to hide under my arm and too heavy to fold into my skirt. But if I don't figure something out and stay here with it, Aidoneus will eventually catch me. At least by leaving the room he'll have to confront me if he wants it back. He told me I could snoop. Maybe he wants me to take it.

I try to make a pouch with my pettiskirt, tucking the book in it and then tucking it into the band of my skirt. It hangs awkwardly, knocking against my legs, but it does hang and that's all I need it to do.

I close my eyes and count to three before I move again as panic threatens to set in over what I'm about to do. I half-expect him to be waiting just outside his door, but when I enter the hallway it remains empty.

My heart pounds so hard and so loud that I'm sure Aidoneus will find me no matter where in the castle he resides. Willa keeps close to my feet, her tail down like she knows what I've done.

The paintings in the hallway look down on me, their faces seeming to stretch into frowns that weren't there before. The walls feel like they're moving in closer and the ceiling doesn't feel as high as it has. It feels like I'm being suffocated by the castle itself as punishment for taking Aidoneus's book.

I gasp as my petticoat slips, the book slamming against my thighs hard enough to bruise. Willa cocks her head at me, but I give her a quick pet to quiet her even as I bite the inside of my cheek to keep from groaning.

Behind me, the already sparse lights begin flickering out. Darkness floods the hallway and I grab my skirts in my hand to run. I can't breathe, I can't think as I run faster and faster, desperate to get away from the impending sense of doom that follows the darkness behind me.

Ahead I can just make out the light of the parlor. Willa bounds ahead of me with ease, reaching the bright room with a wag of her tail. I'm close, so close, when my petticoat comes free and the book slips from my grasp, knocking against the floor with a loud thud. The light beside me goes out, leaving only the parlor to illuminate my hands as they search along the floor for the book.

In the darkness, the door beside me rattles. My hands shake as I widen my search for a book that wouldn't be hard to find at all if the lights had only stayed lit.

"Cora," a whispery chorus rustles from under the door.

Every muscle in my body tightens, making it impossible to move.

"Come Cora."

I want to move, want to scuttle towards the light, but my body refuses to cooperate and I still don't have the book that I came for in the first place. Willa barks behind me in the parlor but doesn't come closer.

"Join us Cora," the voices persist, their words brushing against my cheek like a gentle hand. "Stay with us."

I try to swallow, but my throat grows thick with fear. Cold sweat trickles down my back like spiders. The floor beside me creaks and in the darkness, I can't tell if the door has actually opened or if fear has made me crazy.

"Cora!"

A hand comes down on my shoulder and I flinch, letting out a sharp scream that makes Willa back away with a cry.

"Cora what are you doing here?" Aidoneus's voice strikes harsh against my ear. His fingers tighten until they're painful.

"Get away from me!" Finally, I can move, I shove away from him, if it proves to be him, and crawl toward the parlor, toward the light, toward Willa, toward safety.

"Cora." He reaches out for me, trying to slow my movements.

I can't stop. Now that I can move, I can make it to safety. My body keeps inching towards the light. Toward where Willa waits with her tail wagging.

"Cora." He moves to stand in front of me, blocking the light. "Cora, I promise you're safe."

But I'm not. Not really. And what good are his promises? Soon he'll be gone and I'll be alone with no protection at all.

Hot, fat tears well in my eyes, threatening to spill over. I wipe at them and shove Aidoneus out of my way.

This time he lets me pass, his attention snagged on something else.

"Did you take this from my room?" His voice is hard as he bends over to pick the book from the ground.

I don't turn around, I just keep moving toward the light. It's tempting to want to move toward his voice to find the book again, but part of me feels like if I do that, I may never see the light again.

My knees scrape along the floor as I crawl, making far more noise than feels comfortable, but I have no other choice right now. The tightness in my chest eases as I get closer and closer, my fingers almost grazing the transom between the parlor and the hall.

"Did you take this?" he asks again, his voice right behind me now.

I can't stop. This conversation will feel so much better if we can have it in the light. I can't stay in the dark hallway with him wondering if death waits for me in the shadows.

He moves with me, his steps slow as I finally collapse in the doorway to the parlor. Light brushes against my face, drying the stray tears that escaped.

"What you did was extremely dangerous." His voice grows so low I can barely hear him. "I told you that you could go through my things when I was there. What made you go back alone?"

I lay on the floor, my back pressed into the plush rug. "I didn't want to go through your things with you watching me. That would be weird."

"It may have been uncomfortable, but it was also safe. To go back alone, to *take* something... do you not care for your life at all?" He moves closer to me, but I can't see him clearly, not with the comfort of the light in my eyes.

I roll over so I can at least see his black shoes, the light from the chandelier reflecting against the polish. "I didn't think it would be that bad."

"You didn't think there might be others in the house after the same knowledge that you are?"

I sit up, hands resting in my lap. "Why must it be such a big secret? If you would tell me just a little bit, then I might understand. You can't even tell me why your castle is so dangerous. Ordinary people don't live like this."

"Do you think I don't know that?" He collapses to his knees beside me. "You've seen the window. I know what much of the world resembles, and yet it does not change my fate. I am a prisoner here as much as you."

My jaw goes slack.

He pulls at his hair, the swirling in his eyes moving even faster. "You know this place was not my first choice. There are many reasons for that. Many reasons I'm trying to keep you safe from. But you're such an inquisitive girl. You haven't made it easy to keep you alive, despite all that I'm doing."

"I'm not trying to be difficult. I'm just trying to help—"

He holds up a hand to stop me. "I know. Of course, I know. It has only made you all the more precious to me."

Silence descends so heavily around me that for a moment I fear my heart has stopped beating.

He reaches out, his large hand cupping my cheek. I stare into his eyes, breathing in the smell of him until he has consumed me altogether.

"I never wanted you to come here." His breath mingles with mine, our faces far too close together. "I never wanted this for you."

"Why didn't you want me?" The words come out small.

"It was never that. It was always that I didn't want to risk…"

"Risk what?"

He shakes his head. "I'm not allowed to say."

My chest grows hot. "Then why did you agree to the contract in the first place?"

"I'm a selfish man." He takes my hand in his. The chill of his fingers permeates my body, cooling the anger building in me. His hand is so smooth. A gentleman's hand. "Once I had the opportunity to have you, I couldn't let it get away."

He leans closer to me, until all I can see are his eyes. They're dark, almost black, but they have flashes of white in them like stars. Or like souls.

"I-I…" I can't get any words out. Everything sticks in my throat. I can't do anything but stare into his eyes.

His hand tightens in mine, his eyes grow impossibly large. I can't stop. I can't look away.

"No," he gasps and thrusts me away from him.

I stumble back, almost losing my footing at the rough movement.

"What did I—"

"Get out of here." His voice is hoarse and he won't look at me. He rests his head in his hands, eyes screwed tight. "Get out of here now."

"But I just want to—"

"Now," he raises his voice to a yell and I only hesitate for a moment before turning and running.

Tears I don't understand stream down my cheeks but I don't stop. I can't. I must get out of here.

Nineteen

ONLY LATER WHEN I'm lying in bed do I think of the book again, it feels safer than letting my mind rest on what happened after I found it. There must have been something important about it or everything wouldn't have reacted the way it did. The only thing different I noticed about it was the pictures and those were the only thing that even made me want to take it because I might finally understand something.

I shake my head, rolling over and pulling the blankets tight around me. The image of him, of his desperate face as it moved closer to mine grows larger in my mind. It makes my heart ache with an unspoken need that I can never have.

It's all too ridiculous. I shouldn't linger on those thoughts for even a moment. They shouldn't be important to me at all. *He* shouldn't be important to me. Nothing about this makes sense and yet it has all felt so natural. So easy. I'm drawn to him in a way I don't understand. All I know is that I shouldn't want to be near him. I shouldn't want or think about any of this.

But for a moment I...

It doesn't matter. I won't let it matter. It will only distract me from my goal, from saving him. I know he won't help himself, so I'll stay focused to do it. I don't have time to sit around thinking about what ifs and ruminating on the moment where I thought he might... where I thought he might kiss me.

I should be stronger than this. I shouldn't be caught up in this frivolity for a moment. This was never my plan. Nanny wanted this, but I never did. So why would this happen now?

Pulling a pillow over my face, I press it against my mouth until breathing becomes difficult. It feels soothing in an awful sort of way. I feel calmer, more able to think, and only then do I release the pillow so air flows normally.

I can't let him affect me like this. Thinking it doesn't change how I feel though. And I know, deep down I know that I'm not just interested in saving him to ensure my own survival. I'm saving him because I *care* about him. The thought lodges in my brain and won't let go. It makes me feel sick and giddy at the same time. But it's all pointless, a distraction.

There's no point to any of those thoughts, not when the threat of him leaving hangs over us and I'm still grappling with my own mortality here. We need to focus on staying alive, not on how I feel when he's near me. Not what I wish he might do or say when we're together. Not on what he's *already* said.

I've never had someone talk to me like that before. He said he was selfish for keeping the bargain with my father. Why does that make my chest tight and my face warm? He could have saved me. Doesn't that make me mad?

No, it doesn't. He *wanted* me here. Something lingers so powerful in that that it wipes out all the rest.

And despite everything happening, I... I think I want to be here too.

Just letting myself think that makes me have to bite my lip to keep a smile from spreading across my face. I know it shouldn't be this way. It doesn't make sense. And yet... I can't help it. I know I shouldn't *want* to stay in the very place where I'm trapped, where monsters roam and dark corners hold terrible secrets, but I *do*.

I want to stay here and I want to be with him, in whatever capacity he'll have me. He's made it clear that while he wants me here, he doesn't want the same closeness from me that I want from him. But that's okay.

Delving deeper into the blankets, I let their weight press against me, soothing some of the wild beating of my heart.

This has all gotten so much more complicated than I ever imagined it could, but I don't think I would ever go back to the way it was before. I wouldn't trade the safety of my father's home for never meeting Aidoneus. I can't imagine my life without him now. I hate to think what Nanny would say about all of this, but I guess that may be part of what makes being here nice too: I never have to tell her.

The thought makes me giggle as I tuck the blankets in around me.

I will survive this place. I know I will. And Aidoneus will too. I'll make sure of it.

* * *

I show up for breakfast in the morning, my heart nearly beating out of my chest at the idea of us being alone in the room together once more. My steps are quick and my face can't stop smiling as I turn the corner and enter the dining room.

My steps falter as I take in the empty room. Only one domed platter rests on the table and Aidoneus isn't in his usual spot waiting for me.

I feel my chest deflating even as I try to tell myself that him not being here yet doesn't mean anything. Maybe he's running behind. Maybe he was nervous to see me this morning. But as I take my seat and wait for him, I can't help the flood of disappointment that washes over me.

Possibly he feels even more upset about the book than I thought he would be. I probably should have apologized more for going into his room when I knew he wouldn't be there. That was rude of me, no matter how lax the rules of propriety are in this place. He has every right to be upset with me if he wants to.

I pull the dome off the tray, desperate to do something that could possibly get me out of my own head. The dome rattles against the table as I put it down, the sound so jarring that I nearly jump out of my seat. My pulse skyrockets even as I take in the nearly empty tray that holds only a few pieces of toast.

Puzzled, my brow wrinkles with questions. I take a piece of toast from the tray and don't even bother to put it down on my plate before taking a bite. It's already been buttered and my body needs this this morning.

I try not to think about Aidoneus the longer I sit eating my toast. It could all be fruitless anyway. It's more than possible that he already ate because he had business to attend to.

As much as I try to tell myself all the many possible reasons why I'm not the reason he's gone, the more the thought makes itself known in my mind. He must be mad at me. He told me to leave yesterday, did he mean leave his house altogether? Even though I thought he might have really wanted me, maybe that was never the case and I simply misunderstood him. If that is the case, then my hanging around still would be embarrassing for both of us.

I rest my arm against the table, something I was never allowed to do at home. But here no one to tells me not to and

I need the extra support right now. I need more than the feeling of being adrift that seems to follow me in this place.

"Will that be all?"

Startled, my arm slips on the table, driving my elbow into the corner and causing a flare-up of pain that makes me wince. Jameson stands next to me, his hand extended for my plate.

"Did... did the Lord already eat?"

Jameson's eyes narrow slightly in pity as he watches me. "I was only told to come and assist you this morning."

An answer that isn't for what I asked, but for what I feared. He *is* avoiding me. Of course he is.

My face grows hot and my eyes burn. If I don't get out of here soon, I'll make a fool of myself in front of Jameson.

"Yes, I'm finished here."

My chair scrapes against the floor as I stand and make a run for my room.

* * *

Despite Aidoneus staying away from me, I still have work to do. I may not have that book to study anymore, but I know there has to still be something I can do or remember from it that can help me free him from his bargain. Even if I didn't feel so confused about him, I'd still feel the need to save him from the deal he made to save me.

It was so stupid of him to do that. I still don't understand why he would. It didn't benefit him at all. It only saved me.

I press my hands against my cheeks to keep them from getting warm again. I can't get distracted by that right now. I have to stay focused and think.

Pulling a notebook out of my trunk, I lay it on the bed and with a charcoal pencil begin drawing some of the images from the book that I remember. I may never get another opportunity to hold the original again, so these copies will have to do. Something has to be hiding here.

I work on page after page of skeletons illustrations, both with them coming out of the ground and with them spinning in a black void. The bodies in those ones pictures didn't look so decayed, so skeleton probably isn't the right word for them but for some reason my brain prefers that description to thinking of them as the *dead*.

It takes a little effort to not focus completely on what I'm drawing either or I may lose my will to sketch altogether. Today could be the first time I've ever been grateful for Nanny making me take so many lessons. She firmly believed that accomplished ladies made the best matches and as such made me learn how to master many skills that didn't have any practical use. It didn't matter how many times I told her that my ability to do anything was useless when my father had already traded me away.

The next image that my mind pulls up for me flows across the page, my quick sketches retaining just enough of the original image to help me remember what everything looked like in person. There are more skeletons in this one, but instead of them being alone, like they usually were, this time the image holds a regular man. He stands beside a hole where they rest, his hands in his black jacket pocket.

I try not to focus too much on what I'm doing until the image sits finished in front of me. Another one comes to mind, but I pause before I can turn the page to start work on the rest of them. Something catches my attention about this one...

My eyes squint up and I lean closer to the page as I try to peer deeper at the picture I've recreated. Something feels familiar about the man in the picture. It's so different from the other ones I've already drawn. Why is he there? I've never had a 'normal' looking person in any of the others, no hint that humanity existed anywhere else. His hair is light compared to his clothing, but with only the charcoal to draw with, I didn't have to make any color decisions.

As I stare at him, the image seems to move. He turns his head to face me, his eyes a dark charcoal with light specs moving through them. He runs his hand through his hair and his shoulders sag before he turns back to the hole he was watching before and the image stills.

I let out a deep breath, my chest feeling unbearably tight as I scramble back from the notebook.

I've seen magic before, obviously, I came here using magic, but there's never been any magic in something *I've* done before.

Across the room, the pages look solid and unmoving, but I don't trust them now. If I go back over there, anything could happen.

The man looked so familiar in the shape of his face, the line of his jacket, and those eyes... I've stared at them a hundred times before. But it doesn't make sense why would *he* be in the book? There must be something I've missed and it all seems to go back to Aidoneus.

It doesn't matter if he wants me here or not, we have to talk. I could have wondered if it was him or even just marveled at the similarities between him and the drawing, but to have it move, to see those *eyes*... it's him. I know it's him. And I feel like the magic wanted me to know that too.

My fingers tighten into fists as I move out the door, the muscles in my neck growing tight. He may not want to see me, but that doesn't matter anymore. He can't avoid me now.

Twenty

THE CASTLE FEELS DARKER than it has since I first got here. The mists in the hallway swirl at over waist height as though begging me not to go. I wish I didn't have to. I wish I could spend more time nursing the wounds of my rejection, but we're almost out of time. If he hadn't wanted me to get involved, he never should have protected me.

Around me, the sconces set against the wall go out. This isn't the first time the castle has tried to scare me like this. It's not even the first time this week. Without the whispering voices and threat of the walls moving in on me, the darkness doesn't feel nearly as intimidating as it once would.

My steps only grow with confidence the farther I get from my door. If the castle wants to give me a hard time, it must be because I'm getting closer to answers. The only time it's left me alone was when I haven't wanted to figure something out. Unfortunately for the magic around me, I only feel better than I did when I left my room, not worse. I don't even need the light as much. It's never very bright around here and I've been in the castle long enough that I've started to figure things out for myself.

I count my steps all the way to the stairs. I know Aidoneus isn't in the dining room and he may be in his own bedroom, but I've *never* gone down the other hallway up here. I've always been too eager to go downstairs to make it to the safety of my own room.

The other side stretches out before me, the mist curling back just enough that it feels like an invitation. I swallow down the lump in my throat asking me not to do this and walk past the stairs.

The layout mirrors the same as the side my room occupies, just another long expanse of walls and doors. I don't hesitate by any of them this time. I'm not stupid enough to make the same mistake twice. I don't need to give the whispers any opportunity to get to me.

Keeping my pace brisk, I move through the hallway until I reach the dead end. This side has a window at the end of the hall that looks out into the gardens behind the castle. I'm tempted to look and see its beauty again, but a part of me might be afraid of it now. I don't like not knowing what I might see. There could be a field of bones behind the garden that only this view can show me.

I turn from the window even as my mind whispers to me that I'm a coward. How can I claim to be looking for answers if I'm not even willing to *look*? But no amount of shaming can make me do it.

It does have an effect on me though, even if it isn't to run back to the window. No, instead I run back to my room where Willa waits to support and comfort me.

Only when her face is buried in my chest do I begin to feel a little silly. Hitting a dead end shouldn't have bothered me so much. Finding a window shouldn't have bothered me so much. It wasn't the first time I've encountered any of those things here.

But that's not what's really bothering me, not really. It's

me that feels like the problem. I made a goal and I haven't achieved anything significant with it. Not only that but I ran away when I didn't find answers right off the bat. I'm a disappointment to myself.

Fat tears roll down my cheeks in the privacy of my room. I don't have to hide them here, don't have to pretend to be stronger than I am. It's just me and Willa, the same as always.

She whines and I pull her body onto my lap.

There has to be a way to help Aidoneus. If only Canaean was still here. I could take things up with him directly and stop looking for clues that don't feel like they're coming.

Except that isn't true.

There was magic in my drawing. Magic I didn't put there. Something wants me to speak to Aidoneus. He's a part of this, that I already knew, but he's a part of the bones too.

He said it was his job but that he wasn't responsible for what happened to them that got them here. He hasn't said anything else about any of it. I need to try harder to think of jobs that would encompass that, and that might explain why he's featured in that book. It has to be him. I won't accept any other options. Otherwise, what would the magic even be trying to tell me? Someone else might be responsible? Who? We're the only ones here unless Jameson happens to be the man on the killing spree, and honestly, he just doesn't seem the type.

When the tears stop coming, I know the time has come to pull myself back together and get some work done. Just because I've disappointed myself once doesn't mean I need to keep doing it. These moments don't have to be the end, even if they feel like it. I can persevere.

This time I decide to take Willa with me. I do my best work when she's around and she likes Aidoneus. She might help me look for him just because she'll be interested in finding him herself.

The hallway remains dark but the mist grows thinner. I like to think the castle knows I'm going to look no matter what, but it feels hard not to listen to the whisper that says the castle doesn't care because it doesn't believe I can do it. But then what do I care? It's still just a building even if it *is* infused with magic.

Willa walks with a jaunty gait, her tail upright and unbothered as she moves towards the stairs at an even clip. Part of me worries she'll just lead me towards the door and want to go out, but when we get to the main floor, she ignores the looming front door altogether.

Just glancing at it causes a shiver to run down my spine as memories of the beast that also lives here flits through my mind. It's probably that monster that's responsible for the skeletons. I should have thought more before I went to blame Aidoneus for that. I know there's more going on in the castle than is obvious, so I shouldn't have made an obvious, and wrong, accusation. Even if it was only in my mind.

The dining room table is laid out with a simple spread of silver domes. It must already be lunchtime even though I don't feel like enough time has passed. Time moves differently through the castle, this I already know.

Willa moves into the dining room, putting her stumpy legs up on the side of the chair while her tail wags back and forth. I guess I should have thought about how food can be equally distracting to her and been more concerned about that.

I take my spot at the table, Willa settling on the floor beside me as her black eyes watch me for signs of snacks. Pulling the domes off the trays, I can't help but think of Aidoneus and miss even just his company. I don't need to have answers if it means I can't see him at all. This castle feels too big and too lonely when everyone else who lives in it actively avoids me. It's the only reason I can come up with for why he'd miss so many meals. Especially after he made a big deal about me missing some.

This is our place of civilization, where we choose to remember what propriety entails and follow its rules even though no one knows what we do here. It's made for a fun little game and I miss it. For that, I even miss Canaean even though being around him felt similar to waiting for a snake to strike.

I pile my plate with fruit and sandwich slices, trying to move forward and ignore the pang of loneliness. Just one more thing in a long list of things that I don't need to focus on. It's not important, not right now.

"I feel that an apology might be in order."

My body goes tense with shock as Aidoneus pulls out his chair and sits across from me. His hair looks haggard, his suit coat wrinkled like it's been slept in. He dishes himself while I wait for him to explain.

He glances at me and then shifts back to his plate. "I should not have acted the way I did about the book. I never told you not to remove anything from my room. I suppose I didn't think I needed to, but that was a big assumption on my part, particularly when I know how inquisitive you are."

I don't know where to look or how to feel. I don't remember ever getting an apology before. Nanny and father would never. They were right even when they were wrong. This new experience ripples over my skin and makes the hollow places in my heart feel warm.

"The book in question that you were taking happens to be one that many would like to get their hands on. If you had chosen anything else, there wouldn't have been a reaction like you experienced."

Of course, I picked the one thing sure to take the castle down. I have to fight to keep a scowl from creeping over my face. If only I had had more time in his room with it. If only I wasn't reduced now to looking at pictures from my memory and wondering if they are accurate.

He clears his throat. "I should not have been so upset about it. I should have taken the time to explain what was happening. I'm just not used to having to explain myself."

No, he wouldn't have to explain himself, not when the others that have come here have all ended up as servants. The question of why I wasn't treated the same way lingers on my tongue but I tamp it back down. This isn't the moment for that.

"As such, I'm sorry, and I hope you can forgive me."

I stare down at my plate, one of my finger sandwiches tipping over in the silence as he waits for me to respond. My mind can't find the right words. Nothing feels like it explains what I was doing well enough. The desire to absolve him of guilt flares strong. I want to take that away just like I want to take away the bargain he made with Canaean. But I also want answers. I want to know why his face was in that book that I may never get a chance to look at again.

"I appreciate your apology." I do, I really do. It still sits against my skin like a foreign thing. I can't stop noticing it. "However, I would like to talk more about the book in question."

His gaze flicks over to me, indecision and the faint lines of hurt marring his face. I know I should have spent more time on his apology, but I don't know when I'll get another chance to ask him about the book and I'm a fool if I don't take advantage of it.

"Are you hoping to see it again? Because unfortunately, that will not be possible. It needs to be somewhere safe at the moment until things have adequately calmed down." He takes a bite from his sandwich, probably as an escape from having to talk to me.

"I don't think I need to look at it. I've been making drawings based on my memories of what I saw before and—"

He spits out his food with wide eyes. "You've been doing what?!"

"Well." I play with the edges of the napkin in my lap. "I didn't know if I would ever get to see the book again so I had to make sure that I could remember what I had already seen."

"You are a wonder," he says in a dry voice that doesn't make me feel very wondrous at all.

My shoulders grow tight and I grip the edge of the table to keep myself under control even as rage boils beneath my skin. "I am doing my best to help you and everyone here. The least you could do is keep your negative opinions to yourself and answer my questions when given the opportunity."

"That all?" he asks in a dour tone.

"Yes." It's hard not to stand from the table as my emotions grow even heavier. "And it would be wonderful if you were grateful at all. I understand that may be asking a lot, but basic decency would demand that you be appreciative of someone going out of their way to try and help you."

He turns his flashing eyes toward me. "And why exactly are you helping me? What is the reason for all this interest? There must be a reason for wanting to solve this mystery. Would you care to share?"

I feel my face go hot. "Can I not simply want to help you?"

"No," he says simply.

My breath comes quicker as words bluster around inside my brain, never making it to my mouth.

I want to turn this on him, to demand that he see himself as worth being saved, but I know that won't save me. It couldn't now that he's asked the question aloud. It's too much for the pressing of my own emotions. Why am I doing this? It could be because of guilt that he's done this for me.

That's the answer I've been using since it happened, but there's a twinge of untruth to that. It doesn't sit exactly right with my conscience. There's more to it, whether I'm ready to admit it or not. And for that reason, I don't feel ready to reveal myself in front of him while doing the same to myself for the first time.

My chair scrapes across the floor as I finally allow myself to stand. Aidoneus's face stays impassive as he watches me. My body torn between being locked up and wanting to run away, makes me sway on my feet.

"Why is it so imperative that you help me?" he says quieter this time, almost gently.

I can't look at him or the truth of what I feel might explode and then I'll never have the opportunity to take it back.

"It's the right thing to do."

"I can guarantee you that it is not." I can hear the smile in his voice.

My face feels hot and my tongue grows heavy. The force of my secrets presses against the back of my throat, choking me as I refuse to let them out.

"I got you into this mess. It wouldn't be right to leave you to deal with the consequences." I'm sure I look like a mess as I choke out just enough words to appease his questioning.

"What happened between my brother and I was no one's fault but our own." I glance up in time to see him frown. "It arises from our own history. I won't have you hold yourself responsible for our sins. As I told you before, we have had issues long before you came into our lives. There is nothing you need to do to help me."

I bite my bottom lip, taking a few deep breaths before I can continue. "But you would not have made that bargain if not for me."

"And you would not have been here to cause distraction if

I hadn't let your father make one on your behalf. We have all made questionable choices and it seems only fitting that I be the one to rectify them all." He looks at me, his mouth a tight line of determination. "I wouldn't have it any other way."

I clench my hands together under the table. I can turn his question back on him. "And why would you do this for me? I guarantee you I'm not worth it."

His head jerks up as I use his own logic against him. "I made a deal I shouldn't have with your father, which is the same reason why you are not treated the same as the others who have come before you. You deserve better than what you got. I should have been stronger when I talked to your father, but I'll be stronger now and protect you from my brother. It will be my penance."

"What did my father do to you?"

The question hangs between us. He looks away from me, but I don't back down, not this time.

Nanny and father never answered why I had to go. They never said why a deal had been struck that had ripped me from the home where my joy had already been stunted on its behalf. It is time for someone to share some honesty with me. Aidoneus owes me that much if he's going to choose not to help me help him.

He runs a hand over his face, dragging his hair over his forehead. "It isn't my place to tell and would come far too close to the things I cannot say."

I reach across the table for his hand, blushing at my own boldness. "Say what you can and I'll do my best to fill in the gaps."

What I would fill them in with I have no idea, but it's a promise that makes his excuses all the more weak.

His face grows anguished. "I would tell you everything if I could. If I thought it wouldn't rip the tongue from my body and cause you to run just because of the awful truth of it all.

In truth, I'm grateful I can't say anything because I don't want you to look at me like the monster that I am."

"Surely it can't be as bad as all that." I try to keep my tone light as though that will help him see how ridiculous his point proves and continue. I've seen a monster on this property and it wasn't him.

"It is *exactly* as bad as all that." The sparks dull in his eyes as he looks at me. "You would never suffer to be close to me again and that would be worse than any pain Canaean can put me through."

His words make my stomach tingle, but I can't be distracted by that, not now. Not when I'm so close to finding out the truth of everything. "I deserve to know."

"Of course you deserve to know, but I have loved not having to be the one to have to tell you."

"Whatever the issue is, it will sound better coming from you. I guarantee it."

In this I am absolutely sure. Finding out his faults from someone else will feel like a betrayal. One that is wholly unnecessary when he's right here to tell me the truth of himself.

"I'm not that scary, I promise you."

He closes his eyes. "But I absolutely am. I am worse than the creatures that haunt your nightmares."

I shake my head. "I won't let you be so self-deprecating. It helps none of us and only continues to feed the awful things you think of yourself that have no bearing. I refuse to believe you are a deliberately bad man. I have lived with you for several weeks now and have seen nothing that could confirm the evil you seem to think you are."

"I didn't want to be a bad man." He presses his hands into his hair, looking down at the table. "It was why I fought so hard to have Canaean's position. But I lost and now I have no choice but what I have been given. It has made me bad. Unspeakably bad."

I pinch my lips together. "Talking like that won't help your case with me, I assure you."

"It stands better this way than that you know the truth." Real pain hides in his eyes as he looks at me. "Hate me without knowing me, for I can bear that. I cannot bear you hating me with the full knowledge of who I am."

"Then everything can be one-sided for you." I rise from the table with the force of my anger. "I am laid bare before you. All my secrets were traded away years ago and you can't even do me the decency to give me the few answers I'm looking for. You have the advantage over me and are content to keep it that way. I cannot continue this way. If you will not talk to me, then I refuse to continue this farce."

He reaches across the table, even though my hand presses tightly against my side. "Hate me if you must, but it is better this way."

"No." I shake my head and move for the doorway, the food on my plate long forgotten. "It is only better for you."

Twenty-One

I WANT to sit around fuming and raging at the man I can't seem to get off my mind despite how he refuses to be any help at all. He may have given up and accepted a version of himself that deserves it, but I refuse to do the same.

Willa rolls around on her back on the rug, watching me pace with beady black eyes. I plop next to her, rubbing her belly while she whines for attention.

"At least you don't mind my help." I pat her head as she grumbles at me. "What would you do if you were me?"

She growls low in her throat.

"Yeah, I wish I could just give up too. It would be so much easier if I just didn't care about him." I stop and press a finger to my lips.

I've never so much as hinted out loud before that I care about him or anything else. It's been a private thought and I've been happy to leave it as such. It felt safer and left me more capable of denying my feelings when things started to get out of hand as they feel they have now.

"Willa, I didn't mean to say that." I lay on the ground next to her and she scoots closer to lick my face.

It's not that I don't feel it. I know I do. I just also know I shouldn't. It's not wrong per se, it's just not appropriate right now either. It's a distraction that will keep me from focusing on what I need to do to save him. It's the reason why I want to linger so much on our interaction when I thought he might kiss me despite never showing any inclination to do so before.

I need to let it go. I need to forget it ever happened. He obviously has. The only one getting tripped up by their emotions around here is me.

Sliding across the rug, I grab my notebook where I left it on the edge of the bed. I flip through the pages looking at image after image that I've carefully recorded from my memories. The book falls open naturally on the image of Aidoneus that he refused to talk about.

It doesn't move this time, which gives me a greater ability to inspect the image itself.

He stands by a hole in the ground where ethereal bodies swirl around in a downward motion. Around him, nothing but emptiness and a few skeletons.

My brow furrows as I try to understand what any of this means. The magic that came to me last time that showed under no uncertain terms that the man in the image is Aidoneus happened for a reason. I just need to figure out what that reason is.

I lean closer to the page, my neck straining as I narrow my eyes and search for answers.

He stands by the hole like a guard maybe? Or a protector? There's nothing around so it's hard to say, but I know his presence is determined by the hole itself. So what is so special about the hole and why are there bodies in it?

The other images all had some sort of death in them like the skeletons that Willa found outside. A chill runs down my spine. What if these aren't just images? What if all of this is real?

The temptation to slam the notebook closed pulses through my fingers but I ignore it. If the images in this book where real, then could this have been a sort of journal? That would make sense considering its placement next to the bed and not on the bookshelf and based on what Aidoneus has said about his work.

My head starts to throb as I process everything and try to make sense of it. If this is his job, then what exactly *is* it? Why would he need to stand in place to guard the dead?

I think about Aidoneus and his otherworldly castle and his relationship with Canaean that feels older than it should. My skin grows cold, but not as cold as I've felt Aidoneus's, which is *also* odd.

The answer is right there, staring me in the face, but I don't want it to be that. I want it to be anything else but that. I want Aidoneus to be a normal Lord like I thought he was when I found out I was coming here.

And if what I think proves to be true, then my father must have known all along. He knew what Aidoneus was and never even gave me a hint of the truth to protect or prepare me.

A tear burns down my cheek as the truth of my relationship with my father becomes clear in a way that I never wanted it to be. He never cared for me. I always knew that in the back of my mind. If he had he never would have bargained my life away. But I always hoped that there was another reason for his actions. Something I just didn't know about that made what happened necessary. But even if it was, he still chose not to tell me *anything* when he could have prepared me so much better. He could have told me *exactly* who Aidoneus was and not left me to figure things out on my own.

Maybe he didn't expect me to ever have the time to figure it out. Perhaps he thought I would end up in that swirling mess of spirits where he was supposed to go.

The thought brings out a startled laugh from my throat.

All those years when I had a death wish and that was exactly where I was going to end up.

I slowly close the book, the answers already in my mind now. Aidoneus said he couldn't talk about it, but now that I know, couldn't I? Not that I'm sure I want to now. Asking him about his place as the ruler of the dead doesn't sound like an exhilarating conversation, not when I know how much he hates it. And for good reason.

No wonder this castle is so empty when only the dead come through. The servants he has must be people who made deals to prolong their lives. I must have been a deal like that. My father must have found a way to cheat death by using me.

It's sick. It's so sick. I couldn't imagine doing the same for anyone that I love or care about. But that's the thing, he never loved me. He couldn't have.

The tears come heavier now, splashing down on the cover of my notebook.

It's too much. Too much to think about, too much to absorb, too much to deal with by myself. But no one could help me with this anyway. I can't wish for Nanny, not when she must have known. She tried to prepare me for the best, but she must have known what bargain my father had struck. Did she really think she could save me from my fate by teaching me how to simper and coo and make a man feel good about himself? It's disgusting, all of it.

I've got to get out of this room. I can't keep sitting here in my discovery. I'll never feel better this way.

Marching to the bedroom door, I wrench it open with such force that it knocks against the wall with a bang. Willa takes a step back, her head tilted as she watches me. I don't bother forcing her to come with me. If she wants to come she will. She knows she can. Unlike me, Willa has always been free.

As I enter the hallway, Willa hesitates for only a moment

before joining me. Her squat black body lends a comfort I'm not sure I deserve as she trots beside me towards the stairs.

I'm not completely sure where I'm going, only that I need to get out of here. Not that there are many places I can go. There are hallways I shouldn't go down, and monsters I'd rather not face today. In my current weakness, I'm not sure I would be able to say no to them like I need to. My self-preservation cracks, forcing me to take risks I shouldn't.

It's not hard to find the back exit of the castle. Despite thinking I would never go there again after what Willa found last time, it's the first place my feet take me now that my brain remains otherwise occupied with its own sorrows.

The garden sits beautifully in the quiet stillness. It really is a special place out here even if I haven't come prepared for the cooler temperatures. My hands turn red then white before I tuck them into my armpits. I follow row after row of roses, the garden becoming much bigger than I remember as I get farther and farther from the castle. But it's a good thing. I need a big place to lose myself in to avoid my big emotions. Not that I'm doing a particularly good job. The only difference now, the tears are no longer hot burning tracks on my face, instead, they're frozen tight lines that make my face feel permanently stretched in its own sorrows.

Willa barks at something, and I half-turn to see what distracted her, causing myself to trip on my own dress. My knees drop into the white stones of the garden path, their uneven ridges digging into my skin. Willa doesn't come to check on me like she normally would. Instead, she stands by my feet, tail attentive with the most minor suggestion of a wag.

"Willa?" I want her here beside me. I want to bury my face in her neck and cry some more until the pain of what my father did doesn't cling to my bones anymore.

She looks at me and wags her tail once before turning back to the rest of the path, her pointed ears at complete attention.

Scowling, I drag myself over to her, not even bothering to get up, not bothering to worry what crawling along the ground will do to my dress. Such small things don't seem to matter as much, not compared to the fate I've found myself sold into.

Willa barks once in warning before Aidoneus comes around the corner. His black suit looks as crisp as ever, his hair back in perfect order. Looking at him now it would be easy to pretend that I never existed to him at all. I'm nothing more than a wraith briefly drifting through people's lives before disappearing altogether.

His eyes narrow as he sees me on the ground, the pristine white stones thrown asunder around me. "Cora? What are you doing out here?"

I shake my head. There's no point in telling him anything. He doesn't care. Not really. And there's nothing he could do to fix things anyway. Plus, if I say anything he'll want to make it all his fault and that's something I couldn't even pretend to deal with right now.

"Cora?" He pats Willa's head as he meets up with us, her tail wagging with more earnestness now. She must have sensed him coming and that caused her to pause.

"I tripped."

It's a stupid thing to say. I'm sure he could surmise that just based on my position on the ground. But it's a safe thing to say. It's something that doesn't make me feel like crying or wailing or raging against the world.

He nods and crouches down next to me, forearms resting on his knees. "I can see that. Could I perhaps help you up?"

He doesn't extend his hand to me as though he knows how fragile I am right now. As if he can tell that something as simple as a touch could tear me down and destroy me completely.

I shake my head. It's the most I can do without giving myself away entirely.

"I should apologize for our last interaction," he says with a sigh. "I shouldn't have given into my own self-loathing like that. It's not your place to fix my wounds or tell me that I'm a good man. I shouldn't have put that burden on your shoulders. I should have been able to focus better on your questions and your needs."

My tongue feels thick in my mouth and nothing I can say that will make this better for either of us.

He gets closer to me, making sure I can see into his swirling, unearthly eyes. "You deserve to have all the answers. You deserve to know what happens around here. I wish that I could be the one to tell you. I wish that I could have that immense privilege. Unfortunately, I'm not sure Canaean will release my tongue until it is too late for both of us. You deserved so much more than this life, Cora. I wish it didn't have to end this way."

"And how will it end?" Curiosity finds a way to loosen my mouth and find words.

He glances at the ground. "I fear you will be left alone in this castle for a long time. I doubt Canaean has found anyone else he hates enough to force to live here and take on my responsibilities."

I didn't think I could sink any lower than I was before he said that. So now if I fail, not only will Aidoneus be taken, but I'll be alone. Alone in a house that has no loyalties to me. I can't imagine I'll last long in that manner myself.

Looking down, I know this is the moment. This is it if I ever want a chance to say anything to him. If I wait any longer I may not be able to get the answers I need now to save us both. And I need confirmation at least on what I already know.

"I know something." My voice comes out so quiet even I

have a hard time hearing it. Aidoneus leans closer and I wait a moment before continuing. "I know something about *you*."

"About me?" he repeats, a crease forming between his eyebrows.

"Yes. Something I don't think you can talk about, but I *can*."

He settles back, the stones beneath him grinding together. "I suppose you could. It's really not necessary though, Cora. This isn't your fight." He glances at my purple lips. "You really should go back inside."

"Not this time." I take a deep breath. "I know it's you in the book."

He goes so still that if I weren't watching him closely, I wouldn't even know he was breathing. He closes his eyes, mouths something and opens them again, his jaw growing tight.

"I know that your job lies with the dead. You told me that, but I also know that your work is more serious than you implied before. You're in charge of them somehow, and you have been for a long time." There should be so much more to say, but my mouth feels dry and I lose the strength to continue.

He runs his fingers through his hair. "You never should have seen that book. I should have been more careful with it—"

"No, I'm glad I did." I reach out and grab his hand. My fingers are so cold that I don't even notice the chill in his. "You were never going to be able to tell me and I had to know. It's the only way we'll be able to find a solution and—"

He stands, dropping my hand. "There is no solution. There never was, not where Canaean is concerned. He'll never change his mind and I will never take back my bargain with him. If I even tried I can't imagine what he would do to you."

"You don't need to protect me." I have far less grace than

him as I stand, rocks flying out from under my feet. "Especially not from him. We can do this together. Let me help you."

He shakes his head. "It's much better for you that you stay out of it. And when I'm gone, I need you to promise me that you will stay hidden from him. Don't let him provoke you into making a bargain. You will never be able to escape him."

"Did that happen to Teleia?" I haven't thought about her in a long time, but the image of the sad, worn down girl comes to my mind anyway.

He frowns. "Yes."

"But I thought he had no interest in actually marrying her."

"That doesn't mean he won't punish her for trying to force him into the arrangement," he scoffs. "My brother is nothing if not brutal."

I look at the ground, at the mess of the garden path I've made. "But you do work with the dead, don't you? You watch over them?"

It's a leap, but the way his eyes grow wide for a second before he can hide it tells me I'm on the right path. I'm going to get answers out of him, whether he likes it or not.

"I..." the words still won't come as his mouth hangs limp.

I'm going to have to guess or I'll never learn anything.

"You protect them?" I try.

He shakes his head, not looking at me. I think about the image of him standing by the hole to the underground where the bodies swirled. There has to be more there. If I can find the right questions, then he'll have to answer me.

He already basically confirmed that he watched them, but for what purpose? He's obviously more than a man. He and Canaean are probably much older than they appear. So what would more than a man be doing here with the dead.

"You make sure they get to where they need to go?" It feels

like a weak guess, but he gives me a barely perceptible nod. A chill runs down my spine and an answer I don't want runs rampant through my mind until I'm forced to say it. "You're the keeper of the dead."

He looks away from me but doesn't say no.

I thought that might be the case earlier. It's what made me so upset to think of my father trading me away for dead. But something about actually *knowing* that makes my stomach twist until I think I'm going to be sick.

Taking a deep breath of the chill air to clear my lungs, I swallow down the bile that had been making its way to the surface. Aidoneus watches me with sad eyes. He doesn't say anything, but he doesn't have to. His greatest secret lies out in the open now. I can see him clearly as he is for the first time.

I wait for the knowledge I carry to change the way I feel as I stare into his swirling depths. The illness is still there, but it isn't about Aidoneus himself. No, it's more about realizing I've been spending so much time with the God of death. It's knowing that Jameson and the cook... everyone I've met here is essentially already dead.

But Aidoneus... he's still the same man I've felt an increasing pull toward. Even knowing what he does doesn't stop me from glancing down at his pale lips and wondering what could have existed between us in another life.

"If this is your position and your power, then how can Canaean have any control over you at all?"

Aidoneus laughs with little humor. "He was given position over us all. While he may not be able to interfere in my work here, that doesn't mean he can't interfere with me... with you... with anything else he can find around here during his visits."

Canaean was given position over them all... He's a god of gods.

The thought concretes itself in my mind but still doesn't

feel right, doesn't feel real. I'm nothing, nobody. I shouldn't be in the presence of these men. My mere presence shouldn't have forced Aidoneus into a very binding contract.

A cold tear slips down my cheek. "You never should have let me stay here. You should have let me take my father's place and had it be over. I have done nothing but hurt you by being here."

"No." He takes my hand, clenching it tightly between both of his. "No, this is not your fault. You have not brought pain to me. You have merely exposed the pain that has always been there. You have brought *life* to this castle, and to me."

I can't look at him, even if my eyes weren't blinded by tears.

"Cora." He places his hand under my chin and guides my face gently up towards him. "I could not have chosen a better way to die than to do it for you."

"I—"

He closes the distance between us, his solid chest crashing against mine. His lips come down on mine and they feel like an icy fire. I can't breathe, can't think. I'm a part of him, melting and icing over until we're one. His fingers trail down my spine, pulling me closer to him as though that will save us.

My hands creep over his shoulder, touching his hair where it curls against his neck. It feels soft under my fingers like down and I only hesitate for a moment longer before burying my hands in his locks.

He groans, his lips on mine becoming harsher, the tenderness fading away with his need. His hands drift to my hips, digging into the fabric of my dress. I'm burning. I'm on fire for him and nothing is close enough.

"Cora," he sighs, pulling himself away until his forehead rests against mine. "You're freezing. Let me take you inside."

I push myself to my tiptoes, trying to kiss him again. He

shakes his head with a chuckle and shifts his position, threading his fingers through mine.

Without him pressed against me, I am much colder than I realized. My body tingles with the chill and my lips practically vibrate with the memory of what just happened.

I squeeze his hand tighter as the castle comes into view and he returns the pressure with a smile.

Twenty-Two

MY BODY REFUSES to rest despite the hours I spend in bed trying to. How could I possibly sleep after what happened? I can't go back to my regular life now, not when the culmination of so many thoughts has finally happened.

I have laid in this same bed and tried to tamp down the thoughts about him that I couldn't explain. Now I don't have to wonder what it would be like if he stared at me with the full focus of his magic eyes. It happened. It happened because *he* wanted it to.

My legs grow restless and my toes tingle. My mouth pulls tight as I try to stop smiling but can't.

Not only do I have this moment to relive, I also have answers now.

I expect the thought to sober me enough to focus, but all it does is increase my excitement. I know who he is now. I know who Canaean is. That means I have a chance of being able to *do* something. I can change the bargain that has been made now that I know who the players are.

Aidoneus keeps telling me to leave it alone, but I can't. I won't. Especially not after what just happened. I can't let him go now. I can't say goodbye and live in darkness again. I won't accept that fate. I allowed it to permeate my whole life up to this point, but no more.

Aidoneus will just have to deal with it.

Sleep forgotten, I climb off the bed and open my trunk still filled with books. I never thought to look for answers here because this was the material that I brought with me. But now that I know more, there's no reason why my *own* books in my *own* language can't help me.

The notebook I was drawing in slips to the floor, landing open on the page with Aidoneus. I choose not to pick it up and put it away. With the image of him watching me, I can only be more motivated. He is who I'm doing this for after all.

And for myself.

It's a sneaky little thought that comes through my mind. There exists an element of selfishness in my desire to save him. I know that. I want to save him for myself.

Just the thought makes a blush spread across my cheeks.

I turn back to the trunk to distract myself from myself. So many of the books that I brought are frivolous. Just stories that I enjoy and not works that could offer any information on anything. If I could go back in time and go through the library at home, I would have packed completely differently. But if I could go back in time I would have done a lot of things differently. I wouldn't have shown up for the meal that caused Aidoneus to make the deal in the first place and then I wouldn't have to go through all of this at all.

Making neat piles, I take my books out and categorize them. The side of the trunk digs into my underarms as I grab more and more from the bottom.

I thought the piles would make things more manageable, would help me know where to start, but instead it makes me want to sit back on the floor and feel more frustrated with myself than I probably deserve.

I didn't know what I would need when I came here. I packed for what I thought would be a lifetime, but that hasn't turned out to be the case. Nanny prepared me for all the wrong things.

A heavy tome with a romantic title on the front sits in the pile closest to me. With a shout, I pick it up and heft it across the room. It hits the edge of the fireplace with a solid smack. The binding loosens instantly, letting pages fall over the dark rug.

A sob catches in my throat and I swallow it down. I can't give up yet. I can't let tears thwart the progress I'm sure I can make. There has to be something here.

My knees rub against the rug, burning them as I crawl over and put my pages back together. It wasn't this book's fault. This poor book's only sin was being an escape for me during a time when I thought that was all I could hope for. Now I know so much more waits for me if I can only figure out how to reach it. I just have to save Aidoneus and then the world will be mine.

Well, maybe not the world. More like the *underworld*.

Just the thought makes a shiver run down my back. I still haven't been able to process that little fact. I can accept Aidoneus for who he is, Lord and all, but of the *underworld*? It still feels strange.

But it explains so much. His life has been here in shadows and loneliness with only the dead for company. It only makes sense that he would grow reclusive and sad and angry. Who could he have survived any other way? Every time he disappears to be alone, he must deal with the souls and bones that find their way to his castle. It's a nightmare that I would rather not imagine. He deserves so much more than Canaean was willing to allow.

Turning back to my stacks, I'm able to see them from a new angle. Without the covers to read, I only have pictures and binding styles to guide me. I can tell by the sizes which are novels and which are reference books, so I head to that section first.

The first book falls open easily and reveals ink sketches of faraway places I hoped to visit one day. Little did I know that I would never go anywhere on the earth again. I left it behind without even knowing in my carriage without windows.

I expect the thought to sting more than it does. Instead, it feels more like a fleeting thought than the death of a dream. I have something new that I want more than anything. It used to be that I dreamed of freedom in new places, and now I would remain captive forever if I could remain captive with *him*.

I put the book down and open another one. This one too is full of pictures of places, but the images look less real than they should. Flipping the cover over, I take a moment to read the title: Fairy tales for the Very Young.

A frown prickles my brow. I don't remember this book and I definitely don't remember packing it if it was a book I actually enjoyed when I was young. I flip through the pages with steady fingers despite the chill that rolls down my spine. There are plenty of pictures to go along with story titles like Jack and the Giant, Trevor Learns a Lesson, and Mary's Seashells. I stop turning before I get to the end of the book as an image that seems all too familiar spreads across one of the pages.

Aidoneus appears by the hole again. This time the picture doesn't move, but it's undeniably the same image. But I feel like I would recognize him anywhere now. I know him by the angle of his shoulders, the fall of his hair. There's an intimacy there that didn't exist before and would make a blush come to my cheeks if I were the same girl who first arrived at the castle. Now there's nothing to be embarrassed about. I am his as I feel like I was always meant to be.

The story that goes with the picture starts on the page opposite it, the title standing out in thick, black ink. **The Watcher at the Well**.

The well? If that's nothing more than a well, then why did Aidoneus agree with me when I asked him if he was a keeper of the dead? I rise up on my knees as though that will alleviate the pressure and help me find answers sooner. It could be possible that someone once saw the same picture I did and made up a different story for it. It could have nothing to do with Aidoneus at all except that it used his likeness.

Even trying to find answers that exclude him lying to me makes my stomach twist and nothing quite right. There can't be any answers, not when I still haven't read the story.

It takes a lot of focus to bring the words together when part of me doesn't want to know the story at all. But this is what I'm here for. These are the answers I've been seeking and I can't afford to be squeamish about it now. Not when I'm so close and we don't have hardly any time left.

The story has all the usual child-like qualities one would expect with rhymes and a simplicity that make it hard to discover the true underlying meaning.

There lives a watcher at the well,
He would count every soul that fell.
All would be caught in his spinning gaze,
There was no escaping the fiery blaze.
Down the swirl into the world below,
Where they would leave behind all they know.
The watcher sits with a heavy heart,
Not wanting to make them have to part,
From the lives they love, and all they were given.
But this is as he was bidden.
There is no escape for those below,
And no escape for the watcher who knows,
That this is the end for all who dare to tangle

With Gods and their determined angle.
All deals lead to the well,
So beware when Gods offer to help you accel.

My throat feels thick, my stomach heavy as I flip back to the picture of Aidoneus by the opening to the underworld.

He knew. He always knew what making a deal with his brother would mean. He never thought he would end up anywhere but in the same opening he had to keep watch over.

And his eyes...

Souls

The word whispers across my mind. I've stared at them, been caught in them as I admired Aidoneus, but what I was seeing was a reflection of the well he watches over.

My stomach threatens to lose it altogether and I stand and pace to keep it from spilling its contents.

This shouldn't be such a big deal. I knew there was more to him, I knew about his dealings with the dead. This *children's book* doesn't change that. If anything, I should be celebrating because the answer I've been looking for was waiting for me there. If I want to save Aidoneus from his bargain, then I'm going to have to make a bargain of my own.

My mouth feels dry, but my pulse feels steady. This is right. It only makes sense that it falls to me to make a bargain. Everyone else keeps making ones on my behalf, now it's my turn to take charge.

I try not to picture the well with the swirling souls that will soon hold mine too. This is where I was meant to be and then Aidoneus can watch over me too. There's a comfort there even if it is a small one. He'll make sure I'm okay. He'll make sure I'm safe. And then he'll be able to live as he always has. It may not be a perfect solution, but it's the best one I have and that makes it right.

When Canaean comes to collect, I'll be ready for him.

Twenty-Three

"YOU'RE AWFULLY QUIET," Aidoneus remarks as he puts his breakfast spoon back on the table.

I swirl my porridge around in the bowl, my mind lingering on what I discovered the night before. I thought that when I saw Aidoneus again all I would be able to think about was the way his lips taste, but instead I'm distracted by how I'm going to get Canaean to agree to my bargain.

"Just thinking." I put my spoon in the bowl and give him a smile.

"Of good things?" A hopefulness grows in his voice that threatens to break my heart as he looks at me with searching eyes.

I look away from them before he can catch me in the swirl of souls that reside there. "I would like to think so."

"If you think I have taken liberties with you, I—"

"No, nothing like that." I should have known he would have thought I regretted letting him kiss me. Kissing him back myself. He wouldn't know that my thoughts have been stuck on the information I've discovered in my room.

I bite my lip, wanting to tell him what I know but

knowing that doing so would probably backfire on me later. The last thing I need is for Aidoneus to stop me from making my own bargain with Canaean. I'm doing this whether he like it or not. It never should have been him. It always should have been me. My life has been functioning on a stunted timeline anyway. I want my life to mean something. I want it to give something to Aidoneus.

Aidoneus watches me with a careful gaze when I don't say anything else. "If it is not that, then—"

"Don't worry." I give him the brightest smile I can muster, filled with the joy that he has brought me since I've come here. "That remains one of the few things I could never regret."

The faintest touch of pink grazes his cheeks. My smile grows different, sinking further inside my soul, filling me with a warmth that makes me want to explode. I look down at my plate to keep myself from doing something, not that I know what I would even do, but a vibrating in my soul makes me want to *move*.

"I was worried I had gone too far. I know that you were raised a certain way and I never wanted you to think I was taking advantage of you." His words carry more confidence now.

I laugh, I can't help it. "The way I was raised was a complete mess. I don't think you have to worry about that."

"Surely you were taught certain things—"

"Oh I was taught a lot of things, but my nanny wanted nothing more for me to be settled with the man my father bargained with. I think she would be plenty pleased by the developments thus far." I give him a smirk as his mouth falls open and he stares at me for a few minutes.

"Y-your nanny wanted you to form a relationship with me?" His voice comes out in a squeak.

I spear some egg with my fork. "She seemed to think it was the best way to find me an advantageous match. She did her best to try and find a way to control the situation despite neither of us having any control over it at all."

Aidoneus looks a little green. "That is an odd way to handle one of my bargains."

I chew my eggs thoughtfully. "I suppose, but I think Nanny just wanted to do her best to ensure that I moved forward and found some sort of happiness."

I never actually asked her about any of it. I'm not sure how much she knew about my father's bargain. If she was trying to set me up with the Lord of the Underworld knowingly... she's a much more interesting woman than I ever realized.

"You never should have been raised to take over your father's bargain." Aidoneus's face falls as he tips back towards his own self-loathing.

"Somehow I don't see you raising me until the appropriate age though." I try to tease him to bring him back out of it.

He drops his fork on the table with a clang. "There used to be others here. I'm sure they would have handled all of that. But that isn't the point. I never should have let your father weasel his way out of it with his talk of his beautiful daughter."

"Beautiful?" I snort. "I was so young."

He shrugs. "It wouldn't have mattered, I hadn't seen you anyway."

"Then why agree to it?" I know I shouldn't go down this road, but I can't help myself. "I'm sure others have tried to bargain their way back to life before."

"Many have tried, many have succeeded." He clasps his hands together. "But none have been like you."

I can feel the blush blooming under my cheeks again and I swallow so that his compliments don't drown me and cause me to lose focus. "What makes me so different?"

"Your soul..." he trails off, his eyes closing. "Your soul is so pure... full of so much strength. It was a shock to my system.

Nothing was ever going to be the same for you after that. You were never going to be one of the regular souls here."

It feels weird to have him talk openly about something that has been part of his job, but it doesn't make me want to run away, so that's a good sign that I can deal with his assigned work. I look around the room to make sure Jameson isn't here though. I can't imagine how he would feel knowing how his soul measures up to mine and the fate he could have avoided.

"Is that why you stayed away from me when I first got here?" I try to keep eating as though that will keep this conversation more casual, but my stomach doesn't want any of it. It's content to live on the butterflies swirling around in it.

He runs a hand through his hair. "I had no idea what to do with you when you got here. I thought it would be safer for you if I stayed away."

"Definitely safer to leave me alone in your deadly and mysterious castle." I give him a smirk that softens my words.

"It probably wasn't the most intelligent of moments I have had, but it seemed right at the time. You were so..." he stumbles over his words. "I had never met anyone like you."

I hold my fork so it sits upright on my plate, focusing on the tines as they scratch across the china. "And I'm sure you've met many people over the course of your time here."

"More people than you could possibly imagine. Just a day can hold hundreds of souls."

"And you watch over them all?"

He looks up at me, eyes swirling. "I want to make sure everyone ends up in the right place."

Despite everything, my heart can't help but break for him. He bears the weight of souls on his shoulders. No wonder why he has a hard time laughing or smiling. Every moment he spends with me is one he isn't using to watch over the well to the underworld. Where would people go if he weren't there to help them?

Perhaps that remains the real reason why this house proves so dangerous.

I'm not sure what to say to him. I can't say he's doing a great job. I don't really know if he is, I can only assume that he takes his responsibility very seriously. And I'm not sure that's the comfort he would be looking for anyway.

"I'm glad there's someone like you watching over them." I stick to honesty without trying to make him feel better. I can tell by the slight twitch of a smile that it's the right thing to say too.

"I'm sure my brother will find someone just as capable to take care of them." He tries to wave away my comment with reality. But it's a reality I'm choosing to reject.

"I doubt he has people lined up ready to watch the underworld for him."

He pushes his plate away. "Maybe not, but that doesn't mean that there aren't plenty who are capable."

"Sometimes capability goes down with lack of desire."

"If that were the case then I probably have done a terrible job for years." He gives me a wry grin that doesn't meet his eyes.

I shake my head. "If that were the case then this place would be overrun and I have yet to *see* any ghosts." *I've just heard them.*

But I have seen a monster.

I try not to think about that day and the presence of the monster that made sure I stayed in the castle when I was ready to run away. I'm not sure now whether to be grateful to it or not. It would have been nice to have the choice to leave and choose to stay, but given the choice I may not have gotten to know Aidoneus better. Last night might never have happened.

My lips tingle just thinking about it and I look down at my plate to keep my cheeks from becoming hot. The last thing I need is for him to ask why I'm blushing.

I need to get out of here before I embarrass myself.

My chair scraps against the floor in a loud screech and Aidoneus stands as I do, his face tilted in a question. He doesn't outright ask me why I'm leaving though so I don't have to actually answer him. It's a saving grace that I'm all too grateful for.

I trip on my skirts as I leave the table, my eagerness to not embarrass myself transmuting itself into clumsiness. Apparently, I'm going to be embarrassed either way. This will be fine. I'm more than happy to face plant on the floor if I don't have to talk about my feelings.

"Cora?"

Aidoneus hasn't moved from the table. He stands with hands on the wood to brace himself as he watches me. I hesitate, waiting for him to continue, but he says nothing more.

Released, I breeze from the room before I can say anything I might regret.

* * *

"I have no guarantee that Canaean will take me up on my offer." I lay on the floor, face to face with Willa. Her hot breath brushes my face as her dark eyes watch me. "He has no real motivation to listen to me. I'm not the best bargaining chip."

She whines her agreement, forcing me to smile.

It's a problem I've been thinking about since I got back to my room. Why would Canaean give up Aidoneus for me? If he's going for power, he has no reason to do it. I'm nothing compared to Aidoneus. I'm not a god. I don't have magic. It's a poor trade and I know it.

I roll over onto my back and trace my gaze over the trayed ceiling.

It will be a hard sell. I might have to find something else to entice him. Assuming he comes back to fulfill his deal with Aidoneus at all. It could just happen and then where would I be? Without Canaean here, there's absolutely nothing I can do.

The thought travels down my spine in an itch that makes me itch and sit up to stretch it out. Willa watches me but doesn't get up herself.

"Lazy girl." I scratch her belly with a smile. "I don't know what I would do without you."

She scootches her back on the rug, releasing a low grumble from her chest. She's beautiful and her black matches the tone of the castle so well. In a weird way, she belongs here. Just like I wish to.

It's a stupid dream that I should let go of because it won't happen. There is no way for Aidoneus and I to both be here together and I shouldn't even spend time thinking about it. I just never thought there would ever be a time that Nanny and I would want the same thing, and yet here I am wishing I could be with the Lord of the castle, just like she hoped for. What would she say now if she were here? I don't deny that she probably could have crafted a wily way to force Canaean to see her side. She was always doing that with my father.

But she's not here and I have no way to contact her. I'm not sure what I could say even if I *could* talk to her. There's no reasonable way to explain any of this to her. I can barely manage thinking about it myself. To put pen to paper and try to reason this out? I couldn't do it.

I grab the notebook I was drawing in and open it again to the picture of Aidoneus. The magic has never come back to get him to turn and face me again, but I keep hoping anyway. My heart aches and I tear the page from the notebook with shaking fingers.

I don't know what will happen after I make the deal. I don't know how long things will take or if I will ever see him again. If I can never see him in person again, then I want to at least keep this side profile image of him that I've created. If there's a bottom to that well and I find stillness in my afterlife, I want the option to look at it. I want to keep the reminder of why I made the choice that I did close to my heart.

Folding up the page, I stick it in my bodice. The paper slides roughly against my skin, but I'm grateful for the contact. Just that bit of discomfort helps ground me and remind me I'm still alive. At least for now. And keeping it on me will help me remember and be prepared for whenever Canaean shows up to call in his bargain. Because he must do that. Maybe he wouldn't with every deal, but this one is important to him. This one means something because of how much he hates his brother. And I have to meet that hate with how much I... how much I care about him.

Willa whines placing a heavy paw on my leg. I scratch her head and try to ground myself and not feel so much like I'm going to float away on a cloud of distraction and despair.

I want to do this, so the heaviness doesn't come from that. I know it isn't rooted in regret. No, I think it has more to do with the life I haven't lived that I want to now. There are things I never cared about before that I do now. So much I want to experience because I have someone I want to experience it *with*. A cruel twist of fate for me after so many years of not caring and of pushing myself towards death anyway.

But I can't stay here wallowing. If I do I run the risk of missing Canaean coming. I can't even imagine how I would feel if I had finally made this decision only to miss Canaean coming to collect and not even be able to offer it. No, I'm going to have to be stuck like glue to Aidoneus until the time comes.

That's not such a bad way to be for my last days anyway. I might have picked it if given the choice.

Willa grumbles as I rise to my feet, but I can't stay here. I must find Aidoneus. My body is tired and I can't remember the last time I really slept, but I don't have time for it now.

I lurch for the door, hoping that he'll want to see me again. Hoping that he'll allow me to be with him. And the dark part of my heart hopes that if we're together he might want to kiss me again, giving me fresh memories to take to the underworld with me. If I can be selfish in one thing, that's the one I choose.

Twenty-Four

I FIND him in the study that goes down the long hallway to his room. It feels much darker than the parlor on the other side of the hallway and not one that I've chosen to spend much time in before.

He sits at a shining black grand piano, his long fingers deftly picking out a tune while his eyes are closed and his back hunches over the keys. The music acts like a siren call, drawing me closer to him from the safety of the foyer. I pad across the thick woven rug, its black pattern displaying the same fruit painted on his China plates. My footsteps are so quiet that I don't think he hears me approach, not when the music doesn't even begin to falter.

"Cora." He says my name like a gentle caress and I stop in place. The music still continues to pour from his fingers, the song deep and beautiful in a way that makes me want to cry.

"I didn't mean to disturb you," I whisper. It's a lie and it isn't. I meant to find him but I didn't realize he'd already be busy.

He turns his head toward me, cracking his eyes open just enough to see me. "You're not disturbing me."

He motions toward the space on the bench beside him with his head. My palms feel sweaty as I move closer to him. I don't know what I'm nervous about. He just wants me to sit next to him as he plays the piano. Nothing wrong or weird about that.

The wood is cold under my hand as I brace myself to slide onto the end. He nods at me, eyes closing again as he delves deeper into the music. The melody makes my heart ache despite never having heard it before. A part of me wants to break this moment to break away from the feeling of sorrow it builds within me. I want to mention I didn't know he could play or that I didn't realize there was a piano in this room the last time I was here, but the music proves too beautiful to stop, no matter how it makes me feel.

I close my eyes too so I can hear the music with no distractions. Tears stream down my cheeks as he plays a particularly delicate passage. My body sways with the music, lost in a place where only his melody can take me.

It takes me a few minutes to come back to earth and realize the music has stopped. He sits beside me, fingers still stretched over the keys without moving. His chest heaves with heavy breaths, his eyes still closed.

"That was so beautiful," I say when I can finally find my voice again.

He bends over until his forehead touches the black wood of the piano. His fingers trill against the keys, the rhythm swirling through the room.

"I used to come here often." His eyes are still closed as he plunks out another tune. "It was my escape in this house."

"I thought that's what the garden was." At least that's what it felt like when he showed it to me the first time. It became part of my escape... until...

He gives me a smile like he can read my mind. "The garden lies too close to my job to be a real escape. It isn't rare enough to find something there that I would rather avoid."

My mind supplies the image of Willa with a real bone right away. Yes, there are things there that I would rather not deal with as well. "It's still beautiful."

"Yes," he murmurs. "There are many things and places around here that contain beauty, but that doesn't make them any less dangerous or deadly."

I bite my lower lip. I'm not sure I agree. While I would rather *not* find a bone when I'm out walking, I wouldn't necessarily call it *dangerous*. Disgusting yes, unsavory definitely, but not deadly.

"I'm glad you've found places of peace here." I really am. He'll need it when I make my deal with Canaean. This could be the thing that helps him survive.

He shakes his head. "I would not describe it as peace. Merely an outlet to the depths of my soul."

My heart feels tight in my chest. "And what are you needing to let go of today?"

He looks at me, eyes swirling and mouth tight. "I am taking the time to say goodbye."

I wish I could tell him right then that it isn't necessary to do that, that it will be me in the end who says goodbye. But I can't have him thwarting my plan and I can see in his eyes that he will do just that if he knows what I'm going to attempt.

"Did you write the music yourself?" I try to steer back into safer territory.

Aidoneus shrugs. "It comes to me. It always has. It is probably some twisted gift given to me by those who have come before."

"Can the dead do that? Leave you gifts?" I can feel my eyebrows shoot into my hairline.

"They may not intend to, but if someone is particularly

strong that I have to ferry, sometimes they leave something behind in the struggle."

"Like the music?"

He nods, turning back to the keys. "Like the music."

It's strange. Despite yearning for death before, I never thought much about what would come after. *Would I have been one of the ones to struggle? Trying to claw my way back to life full of regrets for throwing it away?* If I had, I wonder what gift I could have left behind. Probably nothing he would have even noticed. My talents aren't great enough for something like that.

The music stops again and his cool fingers touch my chin, guiding my gaze back towards him.

"What did you think of? I felt the chill come off you." His brows narrow as he looks at me.

I shrug. "Just bits of the past mingling with the future."

"Ah." He releases me to play the keys again. "That drew me to the piano in the first place. I hope that you are able to find a release for your thoughts as well."

I'm glad he doesn't look at me because I fear he would see what I'm really planning in my eyes. There will be no release, not for me. My future will ensure the possibility of his and I am glad for the trade, but I don't need him to see that. Not yet.

"If I could play as well as you, I'm sure I would be happy to release my thoughts." I want to turn his attention, but it's also true.

Nanny tried to turn me into a lady which involved many lessons, but that never turned into any kind of proficiency. Not that that stopped Nanny from trying.

Aidoneus stops playing and reaches for my hand. I give it to him, butterflies churning in my stomach as he runs his fingers along mine.

"You have great hands for a pianist. I'm sure we could teach you in no time." He says the words but stops himself from saying anything more. We both feel the clock ticking above us.

"Here." He positions my hands on the keys. "No better time to start than now."

He slides further down the bench, pulling me along with him until I'm in the primary position in front of the piano. He moves an arm around my back to nudge the fingers of my other hand as I get them into position. His body is so close to mine that I can feel the breaths he takes before the air he breathes out even has a chance to touch my shoulder.

"This one made me think of you." His voice stays quiet, but it doesn't have to be loud for me to hear him. I'm so attuned to him in this moment, my body stiff and hyper-aware.

He presses my fingers to tell me which keys to play, moving with me up and down the keys. The song that comes out bounces along like Willa's tail on a walk. There is joy to it despite my inability to play it. Still, he guides me with infinite patience, taking me through every note until it finishes. I take a deep breath as the last light note fades into the silence.

"That makes you think of me?" I reach a hand up to my face, noticing tears I never meant to cry.

"Everything good in my life makes me think of you." He brushes my hand away and wipes the tears from my cheeks himself.

I lean into his hand and the breath catches in his throat. He pulls his arm from around my back, and I feel the chill of his absence immediately. I don't draw back from him though, I can't. My body longs for his presence in a way I've never felt before. All I want is to be near him. I lean closer and he doesn't back away. His hand cups my face, the chill seeping into me working as more of a comfort than a warm fire ever was.

"Cora," he whispers, his body leaning closer to mine.

My body is fire and ice and full to exploding. I don't wait for permission, I don't wait for him to come close enough to me first. Instead, I lean close enough that our thighs are touching, my fingers reaching for the silky softness of his hair. I want to taste his lips and hold him tight enough to me that the memory can never fade. He clutches me back as though he wants the same thing.

My elbow jabs a few keys, jolting Aidoneus away from me and back to the present. I reach for him and he takes my hand, holding it against his face.

"Every good thing I have was first a part of you," he whispers again.

My fingers grow more chilled as he holds me to him, but I don't pull away. I could never pull away from him. This moment feels more right than anything I've ever experienced before. There is nothing in the world but him and I. Nothing but this moment.

"Aidoneus, I—"

He presses a finger to my lips. I try to speak again and he taps my lips with his finger. A part of me wants to be hurt, it would be easy to be hurt when he refuses to hear what I want to say. His words to me are so beautiful that I want to add words of my own. Words he can carry with him later when I'm not here to remind him how much he deserves life and happiness.

"Aid—"

He finally covers my mouth with his own, his lips harder than the first time he kissed me, more desperate as he clutches me as close to his body as the piano bench will allow. He cups the back of my head with his hand, tilting my face to allow him better access to me.

My hands drift down to his jacket, the desire building within me to pull it from his body, when a chuckle fills the room. Aidoneus pulls away from me so quickly that without his firm grip on me, I might have fallen into his lap.

"I see you've been having quite a bit of fun since I've been away." Canaean strolls into the study, his eyes gleaming.

Aidoneus releases me, sliding as far away from me on the bench as he can. "What are you doing here?"

Canaean pouts. "Is that any way to address your brother? Not even an ounce of pretending you missed me while I was away?"

His mouth shifts into a catlike grin that makes me feel sick. Without Aidoneus's presence to buoy me, I feel adrift and alone under Canaean's gaze. I'm cold for all the wrong reasons and all I want is to reach out and take Aidoneus by the hand and force him to protect me. But it wouldn't do any good. Not when I'm looking to make a deal on my own. I force my spine to straighten and do my best to make sure my face stays impassive.

"What are you doing here, Canaean? There are still a few days before you can call in your bargain." Aidoneus sounds tired as he stares at his brother.

"I know." Canaean steps closer, brushing lint from the gold jacket he wears, the light reflecting from it bringing out the warmth of his skin. "That is why I have come. Did you really think I wouldn't want to spend time with my poor dear brother before he had to leave?"

Yes, exactly as I thought. I bite my lip to keep the words from escaping me. It won't do any good and will only hurt my plan if I build animosity between us. But could he not have given us the last few days alone together?

"Do you want honesty?" Aidoneus asks dryly.

Canaean chuckles. "You know, I might actually miss you. You've always been such a fun tease."

I glance behind him in the hallway, looking for signs of Teleia. There's nothing but him though, not even bags to suggest he's planning on staying. After how he acted when he was here before, I have a hard time believing that Teleia let Canaean on a long enough leash to let him come here alone. *Does she know he's here or did he finally break things off with her?*

Aidoneus stands from the piano, his shoulders tight. "Did you come here for something specifically or to ruin my last days at home?"

"A little of both." Canaean smiles, his gaze drifting between Aidoneus and me. "And it seems my time here will not be wasted. You've been busy while I've been away, haven't you?"

Aidoneus steps in front of me, narrowing my field of vision to the strength of his back. "You have made promises about Cora and I expect you to keep them while you are here."

Canaean sighs dramatically, shoving his hands into his pants pockets. "Always so touchy. I do think our little bargain might be just what you needed to bring you out of all this doom and gloom."

If not for Aidoneus's hand shooting back and gesturing for me to stay put, I would have shot off the bench and given Canaean a piece of my mind. If Aidoneus has been gloomy, it is only because Canaean put him here alone, and not only that but left him with a magic window that showed him exactly what he misses day after day. How could letting him sink farther into the underworld save him from melancholy that Canaean had a huge part in creating?

I can feel my neck getting hot as the anger builds within me at a rate I've never felt before. It's a good thing Aidoneus is in front of me because there's no way Canaean could have missed it or the murderous intent growing in my eyes.

"It is not time for our bargain yet, and I will have you

remember that this is still my castle," Aidoneus says, voice low and gravely.

"For now." Canaean smiles, revealing all his teeth. "Only for now."

236

Twenty-Five

AIDONEUS QUICKLY USHERS me from the room before I can say anything too damaging. My blood feels like it's boiling and I trip over my own feet in my desire to look back and tell Canaean exactly what I think about him. Aidoneus keeps a tight grip on my arm, wrenching me to my feet and practically pulling me up the stairs.

"It will do you no good to antagonize him." His words are hot in my ear as he keeps his voice low. "And I need to know that you will be safe here without me."

I'm glad he can't see my face once again. All my secrets would be laid bare if he could only see my face where they lie in wait.

It's a good thing that Canaean came here even though I wish he had waited until the last minute instead of coming to enjoy the last few days before the bargain is due. But it's better this way. Now I don't have to spend days fretting about what I'm going to say and how I'll convince him. I'll be able to figure something out right away. I'll be able to talk to him and have time if he says no to say something else. This will be better even though it feels like my heart is shriveling in my chest.

I know there's no way we'll ever be able to get that moment in the study back. I don't know if he'll ever look at me the way he did sitting on that bench. My lips still pulse where he kissed me and I hold onto the sensation, savoring it because I know with Canaean here he'll never feel comfortable enough to take that kind of risk again.

His body next to me is so tight as he maneuvers me through the hallway and I'm not sure he knows how tightly he holds onto my arm. If not for the long sleeves of my dress, his fingers would be pressing into my flesh and I still wouldn't say anything to him. Not when I can tell how stressed he is.

The sooner I can talk Canaean into seeing things my way, the better.

When we get to my bedroom, I expect Aidoneus to drop me off and leave, but instead, he lingers in the doorway, his arms braced against the frame as he releases me inside. His body is so tight that I fear one wrong move will break him entirely.

In the shadows between us, I can't even see the souls swirling in his eyes as he looks at me. "I need to know you're going to be safe."

If my heart weren't already trying to pull itself in and protect itself, I know his words would have broken it. I want to tell him I'll be safe, just to give him permission to relax, but it would be a lie. With him staring at me like that, I can't take the risk of lying. He'll see me and he'll know.

"You don't need to worry about protecting me anymore." I keep my voice low and he has to lean closer to me to hear my words, making my breath catch in my throat.

His smile turns sad. "I think I will always worry about that, even when the time is long past when I am capable of helping you."

I have to look away. I can't stare into his eyes with the knowledge that what I'm trying to do will destroy him in ways I never realized when I first came up with the plan. All I wanted was to save him. I never wanted him to pay for my mistakes, and that was before... before I knew what it was like to be held in his arms and feel his breath mingle with mine. With the way I feel now, I have no limit to what I would be willing to do for him.

"Aidoneus..." The words are there, just waiting on my tongue. The words that will tell him how I feel about him and cement this growing bond between us. *But how can I tell him when what I decide to do with Canaean will be a betrayal he will never forgive me for?*

He stands there, watching me in the darkness, waiting for me to continue even though my tongue feels too thick for speech. I just can't do it. I can't make any of this hurt more than it already will. I can't leave him with the burden of my heart to carry when I am gone.

I shake my head and he gives me a nod. "It would be best if you stayed here while Canaean is around. It will protect you from the games he likes to play."

I know what he's really trying to say though: it will protect you from his ire and punishments and deals I can't protect you from anymore. Aidoneus is already his, he has nothing of value left to barter, save for a few extra days. I don't think those would bring Canaean any satisfaction, and so Aidoneus has nothing. I would be on my own. And I'm going to be, he just doesn't know it yet.

"You want me up here for your last few days?" The emotion in my voice turns real as I imagine losing the rest of the time we have left.

He looks away. "It's for the best. It will keep you safe from Canaean, and from me."

"I don't want to be safe from you."

His fingers dig into the wood of the door frame. "You should have stayed away from me this whole time. I'm not what you should want, Cora. You deserve so much more than this. So much more than I ever would have been able to give you. My leaving will be the best thing for you, I promise."

My shoulders shake as I try not to let out the hot tears I can feel building. "It's not. I *know* you, Aidoneus. How can you not see yourself clearly at all? You are an amazing man who deserves more yourself than what you have been given here. Don't let your brother convince you that you're nothing."

How can he not see the kindness I see in him every day? He is gentle and sweet and so much more than the lord of the underworld. I can see it, so why can't he?

The smile he gives me feels sweet with its sadness. "Soon it won't matter. I will simply be nothing."

"No!" I can't stop the outburst from coming out of me, not this time. "I won't let you."

He leans against the door frame. "It isn't your choice. It never was."

That's where he's wrong. It will be my choice. I have already decided. And this time he can't stop *me*.

"Will Canaean be here the whole time? Will he stay until it's over?" I need to know how much time there is to make my deal.

Aidoneus's smile turns grim. "It would make sense for him. Despite being a god of life, he does enjoy misery."

"Maybe *he* should be the one that stays and becomes god of the underworld."

The souls flash in Aidoneus's eyes. "He would never do that, no matter where his enjoyments lie. It is far too isolating here and far too unsavory for his tastes."

"It seems to be that way for everyone. Surely there must be a better way."

"And yet... this is the way that was prepared and what we must do now. I could never willingly abandon my post here and abandon the souls to chaos."

I can't help the smile that grows across my face. "Because you're a good man."

"If one could call the god of the underworld who deals in bargains that." He looks away from me, his face dark. "You should probably get some rest. It will be good for you to stay away for a while."

I nod, knowing my voice will betray me. I couldn't possibly say I would follow his advice without him being able to hear the lie in it. I can't stay away, not from the work I need to do. Not from the deal I need to make.

The burning in my chest grows as I confirm to myself again that this is my destiny. This has been my purpose in life. I was born to save him. Just thinking it makes me feel stronger, fuller, and ready for the task ahead of me.

He gives me a long look, his gaze studying my face like he expects to never see it again. My thoughts drift back to the moment on the piano and for a second all I want is to hold him in my arms and feel his kiss one more time. But he doesn't move and neither do I. It's for the best. I don't need any other distractions right now, not when I'm so close to achieving my goal.

He grabs the doorknob in a white hand and nods to me before pulling it closed behind him. I stand there for a minute, long enough to assume he's no longer in the hallway on the other side of the door. Then I grab the doorknob and slip out into the night.

* * *

Darkness fills the castle, making it blacker than I've ever seen it before, as though even the walls know of the threat to their master. I place a hand on the wallpaper, feeling the urge to comfort it even though I know that would be crazy. It's just a building, even if a little odd. Still, the touch of my hand makes the darkness ease just a little bit.

Willa stands in the doorway about to follow me, but I motion for her to stay. I don't want Canaean to get the wrong idea about what he's allowed to barter for.

Peering down the hallway, Aidoneus is nowhere to be found. He must have been moving fast to get away from me. No, not *me*. More likely because he thought he was saving me from himself. It doesn't matter his reasoning though, because it's a good thing. I don't want to have to explain why I'm out of my room or why I'm looking for Canaean. No, he can never know that I've been out here. It's best for him if he doesn't find out until I've finalized everything. Then he can feel betrayed, but not before.

I'm not sure where the other guests stay when they're here and my chest feels tight as I move down the stairs in my search. I don't want to end up at the wrong door again. Not that I would be so stupid as to try and open any of them myself, but still. A tingle runs down my spine at just how close I was to the end just a few days ago. This is not a house I can turn my back on. I know that now and I won't make the same mistakes again.

The light in the parlor dims, making the black upholstery look nearly invisible. I can feel my pulse in my chest as I linger in the doorway to make sure no one hides in there. But even as my eyes continue to adjust and roam around the space, I can't see anything. Not a hint of breathing or any suggestion that anyone is in there.

The tightness in me lessens only minimally. If he's not here, then where did Canaean go?

I try to think back to when he was here before and all the places that I saw him then. There weren't actually that many. Then again, I was doing a better job of actively avoiding him.

It's odd to think about how much has changed since I first came here. In so many ways I'm still the same, but I wonder if the version of me would even recognize myself anymore. Actively seeking danger was never something that I longed for, in fact, I often tried to choose what I felt was a lesser danger to avoid what I was afraid of. It's funny now to think how unafraid I was of death like I always knew Aidoneus would be there waiting for me.

I ignore the warm tingle that wants to drift through me and turn my focus back to finding Canaean. The castle is big, but there are very few places I can actually go, so this shouldn't be hard. As long as I don't run into Aidoneus first.

I pick up my pace, running through the dark hallways. All I can hear is the thumping of my feet that have taken over the sound of my heart.

I stay away from Aidoneus's room. I'm not sure if he's there, but it would make sense that that would be where he would want to hide from Canaean himself. If he wants any peace during Canaean's stay, he'll be there. My intuition presses on me though, telling me that Canaean will keep himself close to Aidoneus, no matter where he is. He will do his best to keep Aidoneus as miserable as possible until time runs out and the bargain comes due.

My footsteps slow and I slink towards the shadows as I get closer to his room. I put my hand over my mouth to cover the sounds of my breathing that threatens to get louder and reveal me.

Aidoneus's door sits closed, but light, real light, comes from under his door. The window in his room must be showing a wonderful day. I wonder if he stands there like I did, hands clenching the windowsill as he stares at what he can never have. It breaks my heart to think of him that way. If it were possible to save him from the fate of being trapped here, I would do that too, but unfortunately, I know what I'm asking for will be pushing my luck anyway. I need to stick to what I think is possible. Maybe when I do Aidoneus will find a way to be able to free himself.

Farther down the hallway, another door sits open. Aidoneus isn't in the habit of leaving doors open, so it must be Canaean. I swallow, my throat feeling so thick that the motion hurts the roof of my mouth. My body that was so eager to move before now feels stuck like my legs are wading through jelly.

This is it. I've been waiting for this moment since I discovered a way to subvert Aidoneus's deal, and now that the time has come, it feels so much harder than I thought it would. Not that I thought trading my life away would be an easy task, but I didn't think I would hesitate.

I move so slowly past Aidoneus's door to Canaean's that I'm sure I'll get caught. The floor squeaks under my foot and I freeze in place, waiting for Aidoneus to throw open his door and catch me in the act of doing the one thing he asked me not to do: talk to Canaean.

He must be absorbed in his own thoughts though because no motion stirs from the other side of his door. Not even a shadow shifts through the light to suggest he's inside. Maybe I was wrong about what he would do. Maybe I did him a disservice by assuming he would hide. Aidoneus is strong, I know that.

My mind whirls in a war of emotions, each fighting for dominance in my head, each proclaiming that they're the right one. But the fear, the sorrow, and the guilt win out. I'm breaking Aidoneus's rules and I'm thinking of him like a coward to do it. It's wrong, so wrong, and I know it. I should believe in him more, trust in him more. Maybe if I had in the first place, none of this would be happening.

If I were never here in the first place, Aidoneus's life would never have had a chance to be in danger. It's the same circular thought I get stuck in every time. It's the thought that finally gets me to move forward again.

It doesn't matter how strong Aidoneus is, that was never what was in question. The real question now is how strong *I* am. *Can I actually do what I set out to do now that I'm face to face with the reality of it?*

The floor under me squeaks as I take another step, but I don't slow down this time, I don't hesitate as I take another and move squarely into the open doorway.

Twenty-Six

MY BREATH TRIES to catch in my throat and my lungs do their best to seize up as I stare into the room, but I don't let them. I must be strong now. There's no turning back and I don't *want* to turn back. There's no point in giving so much voice to my fears if they're not going to change my destiny anyway.

"Cora? What are you doing down here?"

Instantly my heart sinks as I see Aidoneus perched in a chair in the corner of the room. My mouth suddenly feels dry and I can't even smile.

He stands, his long legs crossing the distance between us far quicker than I'm ready for.

"I thought I told you to stay away." He glances into the hallway behind me as though he can see Canaean lurking there. "I needed you to stay upstairs, safe."

"I...uh..." I still can't find words to explain myself and he just keeps watching me, his face patient as he waits for me to speak.

He comes closer and takes my hand. The cool chill of his palm snaps me back into myself, unlocking my body.

"I didn't want to be apart from you, especially considering..." It's a lie and a mean one at that. I can see in the warmth that comes to his face how much my words mean to him. Not that I don't want to be with him, but I *can't* right now. I can't until I get everything organized with Canaean and I have no idea how long that will take.

Aidoneus squeezes my hand, his other hand moving to cup my face. "I know how you feel, but it just isn't safe right now."

And it never will be if we leave things the way he's asking me to.

"You're right." The lie burns my tongue and I pull away from his grip even though I just want to stay safely cocooned with him. "I'm sorry, I should have stayed in my room. I—I'll just go there now."

His eyes narrow as I move for the doorway. My shoulders feel tense as I wait for him to call me back and reveal my lie. But he doesn't say anything as I move back into the hallway. He just watches me go, his hand tightening into a fist. He knows more than he's saying, but it's clearly a fight he doesn't want to have.

It's exactly what I wanted, so I don't know why it hurts so much as I leave. I don't want to get caught up in staying with him and not be able to do what I need to with Canaean, but I guess I want him to want me to be with him more. Lingering on these thoughts is purposeless though, especially because if he were to take more of an interest in me right now, it would be to personally escort me back to my room where I'm safer. It wouldn't be to do what I want him to do most: hold me in his arms and tell me how he feels. No, even with the deadline looming I can't see him doing that. But it doesn't change the fact that I want him to.

Leaving without him makes the castle feel darker and colder as I resume my search for Canaean. My heart feels like a rock in my chest, refusing to beat now that I'm away from Aidoneus.

"What else am I supposed to do?" I whisper to myself, clutching my chest where it hurts so badly.

There's no answer, but of course there isn't. How could there be? I would have to be the one to come up with it and if I had a better way to fix things, that's what I'd be doing now, not searching for a man that I know wants to hurt me and is more than capable of making that happen.

I grind my teeth together and force myself to keep moving. It doesn't matter how much I want to go back to Aidoneus and force him to help me fix this, the only way out is the one I'm already taking. That's why I'm doing this. That's why I spent time thinking and creating a plan. I can't just abandon it now, no matter how much better it might feel in the moment. I can't leave Aidoneus to make all of this better, because I already know what path he'll choose. He'll do anything to save me and I can't let him.

I have to leave this hallway altogether or run the risk that he'll come out and see me looking for Canaean. I don't know if I can keep lying to him if he persists in asking me what I'm doing here.

The high gloss of the piano gleams in the low study lights as I make my way out of this section of the castle. As terrible as it is, I *do* wish I could go back to that moment before Canaean got here. Sitting with Aidoneus as he played will have to be a memory that I use to keep me together throughout whatever comes next. I can't linger around him hoping for another moment like that, at least not until I've done what I need to do.

My body feels worn and beaten as I move through the study. I'm not sure where I should go next. There's so much of the castle that I haven't seen yet, but I don't want to just explore. I need to find Canaean. I need to find him now before I lose my nerve.

Even from the foyer I can hear pots and pans banging around in the kitchen. Would the cook know where Canaean stays when he's here? I know she doesn't like to be disturbed and I'm pretty sure she doesn't like me in general. I mean, how could she when she was sent here to pay off debts and I've existed in this world as a guest? I don't think I could look favorably on that situation either. I'd be angry and annoyed too if my Lord took an interest in someone else when his interest could have saved me from servitude. Although, he did say that I was different because it wasn't my debt. I may understand that, but I'm not sure how the others see it.

If only I could find Jameson. He's less aggressive for sure, even if he can be unreliable. I suppose he might go right away and tell on me to Aidoneus too, which I would rather avoid. There's just no winning if I'm looking for help outside myself, no matter how much nicer it would be.

I can check the dining room though. It may not be a proper mealtime, but that *is* where I've seen him the most. Plus I'm already on this floor, so it would be easier than climbing the stairs and investigating the rest of the castle. It feels more dangerous to stay on this level though, like Aidoneus could choose to follow me at any time and discover what I'm up to. And he can't know, he just can't until it's already over.

I swallow the thick lump building in my throat but it doesn't budge. I guess if this is what I want to do, then I'll bear the physical consequences even before I make my deal.

Checking the other parlor across the foyer, it remains as empty as it has always been. I let the heavy curtains blocking it off fall back into place as I bite my lip. The dining room isn't far away but it *feels* farther. Just stepping into that room where it all happened feels like too much of a reminder of what already happened and the consequences of me not knowing how to keep my mouth shut.

My shoes click along the wood floor as I leave the safety of the hallway behind and move into the dining room. I don't really expect anyone to be there. Why would they? It's not time for a meal and I already left Aidoneus behind in the other section of the castle. And yet, like my thoughts called him to me, Canaean sits at the head of the table like a king.

He grins and my breath catches in my throat. "I would have thought my brother smarter than to let you linger during this visit. He does realize he has nothing left to bargain with me, right?"

I step closer, grabbing the back of the chair to hold me upright while I do my best to look self-assured with my chin raised. "He doesn't control me."

"Definitely not." He runs a finger over the fine wood grain of the table. "Otherwise you would not be here."

"I fail to see how my location can be any concern of yours." An edge coats my voice that I know I need to soften. Canaean won't listen to me if I do nothing to encourage him. "Be that as it may, I was actually hoping to run into you."

He leans forward, eyes lighting up. "Truly?"

My heart beats hard against my chest and for a moment I'm worried my words won't come and I won't be able to do what I came for. "Y---yes." I straighten my spine. "I was hoping to make a deal with you."

With the words finally out after so many days thinking about them, I feel like I can finally take a full breath. Canaean smiles and I feel like a fly caught in a spider's web. But that's okay. It has to be. I wasn't lured here. I came because I wanted to.

"What kind of deal were you hoping for? Were you hoping to find a way to fly away, little bird?" As he speaks I could count each one of his teeth if I wanted. "Were you worried about being left behind in this droll castle? If you wanted to make a deal with me, I would let you. I would take you home with me if you so desired."

The direction of his thoughts would make me laugh if I wasn't so afraid. He's crazy if he thinks he can get both sides of what he wanted when Aidoneus first struck his deal in this very room. Aidoneus tried to protect me, why would Canaean think I would give that up for nothing besides not having to live alone. Sure this castle can be creepy, but I like to think that we've... made peace together.

"It's not for me—"

"You haven't come hoping that I would save you?" The smile fades until nothing remains but a shadow where Canaean's glee used to be. "What could you possibly want then? I'm sure you know that there's no way for you to return to the human lands. It is far too late for that. As such, nothing you can trade would affect those you left behind. Your life is already forfeit to the gods."

I try to ignore the sinking feeling in my stomach. There has to be something I can offer. My life can't be completely useless yet.

"I have come to trade for Aidoneus." There's no point in being coy now, not if he doesn't think there's anything left for me anyway.

Canaean picks up a knife from the table, digging its point into the wood. "You have come to trade for my *brother*?" He bursts into a snarl. "And what do you think you could do for him?"

I dig my fingers into the chair, my knuckles growing white. "I want you to release him from his bargain. I want to take his place."

"Your life holds a different value than his," he says with a frown.

"Perhaps, but not having to replace him would be a nice

reprieve. I'm sure there isn't a line waiting to take over his role of watcher of the underworld."

He taps a long finger against his chin. "You are right there. It has been hard to find any even willing to consider the role. And as I'm sure you know, the dead must have a keeper, lest they run rampant and find their way back to the living realm."

"Precisely. Let me take this from you, from both of you." *Let me right the wrong that was created by me coming here in the first place.*

"This would also hurt my dear brother, would it not?" The gleam in Canaean's eye takes on a manic tint.

I try again to swallow. "Yes. It would."

Aidoneus hasn't said as much to me, but I feel like enough has passed between us that I can assume it. If the memory of his lips against mine means anything, it's that *I* mean something to him.

Canaean claps his hands together. "Perfect. I thought it might get boring around here without Aidoneus to... visit. This could solve everything. Imagine the torment he will find himself in when he discovers you have traded yourself for him. It will be delightful." He lingers over the word, making it take longer to leave his mouth.

I chew the side of my cheek to keep from taking back my request. This will be hard enough for Aidoneus without Canaean there to further add to his pain. I hope this will be worth it in the long run, even if Aidoneus feels like cursing my choices when he finds out what I've done.

"You'll let me take his place then?" I reach my hand out for him to shake and seal this agreement between us.

Canaean studies my hand. "It will be a waste to lose you, my dear."

The way he glances at me feels slimy and makes me want to take my hand back, but I keep it straight and strong. "I must have your answer."

"You need an answer." He looks at my hand, his mouth turning up in a smile that sends chills down my spine.

I can't breathe, can't think while I wait for him to make a decision. This is it. If he doesn't agree, then I have nothing left to bargain. It was a long shot anyway, I know that, but I want it so desperately, I can't imagine what I'll do if he says no. I try to keep my hand steady, to not show how shaky my nerves are to this man who will only use them against me, but I can see my fingers twitching. I only hope he's not paying enough attention to notice.

"Fine." He grips my palm, his hand like touching hot coals. "This should be fun."

I open my mouth to thank him, but he holds up a hand to stop me.

"I relinquish Aidoneus of his bargain and replace him with Cora. She will pay the price of his insolence and commit herself to his punishment. All further bargains regarding her person will belong to me." He squeezes my fingers so tightly that I gasp from the pain. "Now bring my brother to me."

Twenty-Seven

MY HEART LODGES in my throat as I make my way back to Aidoneus's room. My body feels stiff and my gait becomes uneven, like my body has already begun to shut down now that it knows it belongs to Canaean.

This is exactly what I wanted, and I'm grateful that he was willing to take me up on my deal, but it's important to keep reminding myself that this was my idea as my feet fall like lead against the floor with every step. Aidoneus may never forgive me for this, but at least he will *live*. I would be willing to give anything for that, and I am.

The door to the room he was in before sits closed now, all of them are and there's only the whispers of the rooms I'm passing to keep me company. Only a few hours ago their presence would have been enough to scare me, but I have no reason to fear them anymore. The deal has been struck and I don't belong to them any more than I belong to Aidoneus anymore. They can't hurt me, not more than I've already been hurt.

I stop in front of his room, the light peeking out from under the door so bright that it hurts my eyes after the darkness of the castle. My fist feels like a rock as I knock against the door, hoping he's there and hoping that he's not.

I should have assumed that Canaean would have wanted to do this in front of Aidoneus. The only reason why he even took the deal was to hurt his brother. But I really didn't think that far ahead and if I had, I wouldn't have assumed that I would be the one sent to tell him.

The door creaks long and loud as Aidoneus slowly opens it. He peers around the edge of the door and when he sees me he opens it without hesitation, a brightness coming to his eyes. It makes all of this feel so much worse. I wish he hadn't found a way to trust me, but then again if there hadn't been a connection between us then I wouldn't have been interested in saving him from his bargain with his brother, so thinking about that will only send us around and around in a dizzying loop.

"Cora, you said you were going back to your room. What are you doing here?" No edge lingers in his voice this time, only curiosity. I can see in his eyes that he hopes I've come here for him.

My stomach lurches and I think I'm going to be sick. "Canaean sent me to fetch you."

Instantly all traces of a smile flee his face. "What have you done Cora? I asked you to go back to your room. What did he do to you?"

He closes the distance between us and grabs my arm as though to make sure that I'm real and okay. I shake in his grip, feeling the reality of what I've done come crashing down on me. He'll never forgive me for this. I know he won't.

"I made a bargain with him." I keep my voice steady even as I can feel my heart breaking with the disbelief that flashes through his eyes.

"You can't do that."

"That's not really something you can tell me anymore. It's

done." I shove him away, my hands hitting his chest like a brick wall. "If you had wanted a say in anything I did, you should have done something while you still controlled my contract."

He frowns, reaching for me again. "It's never too late to stop you from doing something stupid."

"This isn't stupid. It's the only way." I hate the tears burning in the back of my eyes. All I want is to be strong right now and prove I mean what I say. One lone tear and he'll never believe me. He'll never believe I made this choice. Even though I have.

It's the only way. The only way for him to survive. I don't know how he can't see that.

I step away before he can reach me, even though it kills me.

I want things to be like they were, but that's impossible. Too much has happened. Too much has been said that I can't take back now.

The knowledge burns deep in my chest. A pain grows there that I don't think will ever go away. And I don't want it to. If it did I would forget why I was doing this. The pain lingers as the only thing I have left to push me into doing the right thing.

"This won't change his mind," Aidoneus whispers. "All he's ever wanted is to punish me."

I close my eyes so I can't see him. He's not that far off with what motivates his brother. I wish it were different but if Canaean didn't enjoy his pain, I never would have been able to make my bargain in the first place.

"Assuming I'm doing any of this for you." The words feel like acid in my mouth. I can taste the lie in them. But the tightening of his jaw says he can't tell like I can.

He finally grabs my hand. "Don't do this. Don't go with him."

"There's nothing I can do. He bought my contract."

I have to get out of here. If I don't this will all come tumbling down and my sacrifice will mean nothing. I just hope... I hope he can forgive me someday. I hope he can understand why I'm doing this. I want him to know how special he is. He deserves this, even if he can't see it.

I just won't let his brother destroy him. I can't let it happen. I've given up everything to keep him safe from his brother, and I don't regret it. I could never regret allowing him to live, to survive.

"Will you come with me? Canaean wants to see you." I straighten my shoulders and gesture to the hallway.

Aidoneus's eyes are pitch black as he follows me. There's no hint of the souls that usually reflect in them. My body feels cold like I've already given my life. The lie of not doing this for him still feels sour in my mouth. I don't want to go to my death with that between us, but it's the only way I can keep him from pushing his point and breaking me down. It's the only way I can make sure he doesn't try to go over my contract. Canaean would have a field day with all the bargains he would be offered. I can just imagine how his eyes would brighten as each of us grew more and more desperate.

My back tightens with each step as I wait for Aidoneus to grab me and force me to stop and tell him the truth. The truth burns on my lips, making me want to tell him how much of what I said was a lie. But it's a lie I can't take back. I can't do it and still be able to go through with my bargain with my head held high, and that's the way I want to do this. I want Aidoneus to be proud of me. That won't be possible if I'm a blubbering sappy mess of emotions.

Aidoneus doesn't stop me, doesn't touch me as we make our way to the foyer where Canaean stands with his hands braced on his hips and a wide grin on his face.

"Welcome brother." His words are far too warm for the

reality of the relationship between them and I can feel Aidoneus flinch behind me. "So good of you to make it. I'm most excited for this evening's entertainment."

I glower at him, feeling my cheeks burn with embarrassment. I may have made the deal, but I didn't agree to be some sort of spectacle. Although, I *did* know he wanted this bargain just to make Aidoneus feel bad, so in some way, I suppose I did know that it was going to be a show.

Aidoneus moves past me to face his brother. "What are you talking about? Our bargain still leaves me a few days."

"That's true." Canaean taps a finger against his chin. "But you see, I've had a better offer."

Aidoneus goes paler than usual as he turns to look at me, his hands tightening into fists. "No, Cora."

"Cora, will you take the place of Aidoneus and free him from his bargain?" Canaean asks despite knowing full well that I've already done it.

"I will do it." I stand in front of Canaean, holding myself as straight as possible. "I will pay the price."

Aidoneus goes white. "You don't understand what that will mean."

"Whatever I need to do, I am prepared to do it."

Aidoneus strains forward but Canaean waves his arm and a wave of magic slaps across his chest and stops him in his tracks. "Cora you can't do—"

"I can do whatever I wish."

Canaean steps forward and grabs a lock of my hair, twirling it between his fingers. "And this is what you wish? To give yourself away for him?" He jerks his head back to where Aidoneus struggles against the magic to stop me from doing this.

"Yes." I can feel a tear make its way down my cheek. "This is what I want."

"No Cora!" The muscles stand out in his arms and his

chest puffs with the effort of getting closer. "Don't do this! You can't do this!"

I shake my head. It's already done. It's always been destined to come down to this from the first time I saw him. I knew there was more to him than he showed everyone. It took some time, but I got through. It was always going to be me who paid this price.

"What do you need from me?"

He takes out a knife and slices it through my hair. Curling brown locks fall into his waiting hand. His smile seems to stretch across his face as he closes his fist. I resist the urge to let out a breath of relief. Hair. That's not so bad. I'm more than willing to sacrifice my hair for Aidoneus.

Canaean steps back, shaking his fist full of my hair at Aidoneus. "Oh brother, what did you do to get her to decide you were worth the sacrifice? You who were thrown away by the rest of us without a second thought. You've been stuck here in your cold and lonely reprieve for years, following the rules and doing what you're supposed to do until this girl comes along. Just a few months with her and you're ready to risk it all. But then maybe you always knew you weren't risking yourself. Maybe you always knew she'd be the one to pay the price for you."

My eyes narrow as I glance between Canaean and Aidoneus. Canaean keeps his wide grin but Aidoneus won't even look at me.

I may have encouraged him to live his own life, but I never thought it would come down to this. I never thought his brother would rather punish him than hear him out. But Aidoneus must have known. He knew and followed my suggestions anyway.

Closing my eyes, I bite my lip to keep from crying. Pain ripples through my chest but I don't take back my decision.

Regardless of what Aidoneus has done, he deserves this. I will protect him, just as I promised.

"Awe, poor girl." Canaean touches my hair where it sits above my shoulders. "It seems you didn't tell her everything."

"I never intended for her to take my punishment," Aidoneus bites out. "And you shouldn't have accepted her."

"How could I not? It was too delicious to resist. You should have known that," Canaean says.

His shoes clip across the tile and I open my eyes again to track where he's going.

"You know, it's a little funny." Canaean turns to face Aidoneus as he tucks my hair into his pocket. "This feels more like a reward to you than a punishment. Just think, she'll be here forever." He gives him a side smile and strides from the room.

As soon as he leaves, the magic holding Aidoneus disappears and he runs for me, grabbing me by the shoulders. He shakes me, my short hair flying around my face.

"How could you do that? You have no idea what you've done!" His mouth stretches into a frown, anguish written in every line. "You should have let him hurt me. I would have been okay. But you..."

I try to laugh but it comes out too squeaky to be convincing. "All he did was take my hair. That's not so bad. I don't know why you're so concerned."

He shakes his head. "It won't just be your hair. You have no idea what he could do with it."

"What could he do with my hair?"

His fingers dig further into my arm. "He's going to punish me by keeping you here. Near me but not with me. I'll never be able to... you'll never..."

"What are you talking about?" I try to pull out of his grip but he only holds me tighter.

"I won't let him." He stares into my eyes, the lights in his flashing faster than ever. "I don't care what you said you would do, I won't let him."

He lets go of me, striding across the floor to confront Canaean. I take a step to follow him, but my body feels strange. I look down at my feet, but I can't see them.

"Aidoneus?" My voice comes out faint, quieter even than his footsteps.

I hold up my hand, watching it fade away until I'm left looking at the outline of my skeletal fingers. "Ai—A…"

There are no words. There's nothing left of me. I can't see anything but my own skeleton. What has he done to me?

I sink to my knees, and instead of hearing my skirts swish against the tiles, there's only the clack of my skeleton.

"Cora?" Aidoneus turns back, eyes wide in horror. "Cora, no!"

He runs to my side, sliding across the floor. He grabs my hand, the bones nestling into his flesh.

"I won't let you do this to her," he roars at the ceiling. "You can't take her."

It becomes harder to focus. My vision goes fuzzy and it doesn't feel like I'm in the castle anymore. Instead of the familiar black wallpaper, the walls around me look more like stone, like I'm sinking through the floor and into a cave.

Aidoneus tries to follow me, but his body refuses to sink like mine. He keeps his grip on my hand and I focus on that. I focus on his flesh instead of the lack of mine.

I slip further through the floor and the cave around me expands. Down here lacks the touch of elegance that the castle has. Instead, the rocky walls descend forever into a swirling mass that looks uncomfortably like Aidoneus's eyes. Sparks twist and fall in a spiral that goes further down inside the cave.

My feet hover just above the line of sparks that flow like a fluid through the cave. I try to hold my feet up as primal instincts warn of danger lurking below.

Aidoneus braces himself against the floor above, still holding onto me with all his might. His face turns red and his cheeks puff with the exertion, but he doesn't let go.

My body fades further until I can't even see my skeleton anymore. "What's happening to me?"

If I had tears I'm sure they'd be falling, but I can tell that functioning part of me ceases to exist. Colors are replaced with shades of grey, but somehow even without color Aidoneus looks perfect. His silver hair glimmers in the sparks from the flow below me, his eyes reflecting the light back to me.

"I'm sorry," he pants as he tries to lift me higher. My body refuses to follow his command. I can feel the pull into the fluid beneath me. That's my ultimate destination. "This never should have happened. You weren't supposed to take the fall for me."

"I wanted to." I try to smile with whatever I have left. "I wanted to save you."

He chocks on a sob. "Save me? No Cora, I'm going to save *you*. I could never be anything different than what I am. It's my nature, but you, Cora, you are better than this, better than me. I will *not* allow this."

The cave walls shake with his words, sending rocks splashing into the fluid. The sparks shift around it, flowing closer to me. Aidoneus watches them, the panic growing in his eyes. His grip on me loosens and I slip lower until my toe touches the fluid.

Sparks fly to me, attaching themselves to me, pulling me farther down. Aidoneus grabs me tighter, his momentary distraction over.

But it's too late.

Up close to them, I can tell that the sparks aren't sparks and the fluid isn't fluid. They're all souls. Bright souls and dim souls, their faces twisted in anguish as they flow past me into the spiral that tunnels further down into the cave.

They grip me tight with their own skeletal hands, forcing me into their misery before my time.

"Let her go," Aidoneus roars, the cave shuddering with the power of his voice.

Some of the bright souls release me, continuing their journey, but others are more than happy to take their place.

It isn't going to work. I can see it in his eyes. He'll continue trying until nothing remains of him too. I can't allow that. This was my sacrifice to make and I stand by my decision. I will save him, no matter what that will mean for me.

I release my hand and hang like a dead weight. Aidoneus tries to hold me tighter to make up for the difference, but I slip further into the stream anyway.

"Let me go," I whisper, eyes burning with tears that can't even fall. "Let me do this for you."

"No, I won't lose you."

I fall further and he only has me by one hand now as he struggles to stay planted in the castle.

"It will be okay. Let me go."

I don't know how I know that, but I do. I don't feel afraid of what comes next. I've done what I wanted to. Canaean may have tricked me into something far worse than I could have imagined for our deal, but I stand by it. It was worth it and I don't feel fear.

More souls attach themselves to me, increasing my weight and pulling me down. Aidoneus stumbles, barely catching himself before he falls in with me. My hand slips through his until he only has me by the fingertips.

"I love you," I whisper.

Aidoneus wrenches me from the grip of the hole where the souls move in the same spiral reflected in his eyes. My feet trail in the mess, my skirts feeling water-logged with souls.

Despite his hold on me, I can feel myself slipping further into the hole.

"Let go, Aidoneus," my voice strains.

I don't return his hold, letting my hand hang limp. His eyes narrow with exertion as he tries to heave me up.

"You don't get to do this. I told you this was my burden." His words come out in heavy pants.

"It was always going to be this way. From the moment my father signed that contract, this was my destiny."

I always knew my path would lead here. To death. I thought I could escape this, but it was never going to be.

Behind Aidoneus, Canaean watches with perplexed interest. His hands clench and unclench and for a moment he almost looks like he'll reach out for Aidnoeus before he stops himself.

"You are a survivor, Cora. This is not the way it ends for you." Aidoneus's muscles bulge as he pulls at me.

I *am* a survivor. Death never got a good hand on me before. Not before Aidoneus. It was always a part of my life, living on the fringes before I came to be with him at the castle. But none of that matters. This is right. I was meant to take this burden from him. He deserves so much more than Canaean was willing to give him.

"Release him." My words are directed at Canaean; despite how quiet they are, I know he hears me.

His mouth twists, his shoulders pulling back. He won't do it. I don't know why I even asked. It would take a heart to make that choice, which I already know he doesn't have. If he did, he never would have made the bargain with his brother in the first place. He wouldn't have left him here to rot the way he has.

I slip farther into the underworld, and for the first time, I wonder what Aidoneus will do without me. I was so worried about saving him, that I never stopped to question what I was saving him *for*. I can see that same problem reflected in his eyes. He doesn't want to do this without me any more than I wanted to be in the castle without him.

"I cannot do this without you." Aidoneus's face turns red as my dress drags me further down. "I never should have let you come here. It should have been your father here years ago. I should never have been so selfish. Forgive me."

Phantom tears run down my cheeks. "There was never anything to forgive you for. This was how it supposed to be. I would rather die here with you than live a hundred more years alone."

His cold grip grows clammy against my skin. I give his arm a last grip of comfort before I fall in altogether.

Canaean steps closer, the toe of his shoe nudging the edge of the hole. He takes Aidoneus by the arm, his face twisting.

"You really care about her? This human girl?" His lips curl up in a sneer.

"More than anyone in this world, past and present," Aidoneus breathes.

Canaean looks from him to me and back to Aidoneus. Whatever he sees there softens his face. "Truly?"

"Eternally."

My hand falls through Aidoneus' until only our fingers are gripping each other.

His words hang in the air as I slip further into the stream, my head submerging in the flow as our hands come apart. Souls swarm over me, threatening to carry me away into darkness. The memory of my fingers tingles where he last held them.

My vision grows even hazier and things go dark. And then I'm no more.

Twenty-Eight

"YOU CAN'T LET GO like that," Aidoneus yells as he heaves me from the swirl and forces me back to consciousness. "I won't let you do this. Take my hand and help me get you out of there."

But there's no way for me to do that. I can't. The bargain has been made and I must pay it. I won't leave Aidoneus open for Canaean to come back for him.

"I love you," Aidoneus whispers, his words falling on me like a plea.

Canaean looks at Aidoneus like he's never seen him before. The concept of love feels so foreign to him that he can't even process it.

I slip farther in Aidoneus's grip. "You need to let me go or you're going to fall with me."

"I would rather live with you in the underworld than exist in life without you," he says, his face twisting in a grimace as he braces his feet against the floor.

The wood splinters beneath his feet, and he stumbles forward, almost losing both of us completely. Canaean's face breaks and panic causes him to flush. He grabs Aidoneus by the arm.

"You need to let her go," he says, voice grim and bewildered.

Aidoneus stares into my eyes, his mouth tight. "Never."

"S—stop this," Canaean sputters. "She's just human girl."

"Not to me she isn't." Aidoneus's fingers wrap even tighter around me.

Canaean glances at him and looks at me, his eyes wide. Aidoneus isn't going to let me go. He won't get the sad broken man he hoped for. He'll lose both of us instead.

I sink further into the swirl and Aidoneus cries out in pain as it becomes even harder to hold me up.

"I release you," Canaean says quietly. "I release you!"

The hole around me shudders as pieces of the castle fly back into place. Aidoneus regains his footing as the floor shifts back into place. He steps closer to me and wrenches with all the strength he has left. My body shudders, the transparency of it shifting back to real flesh as the souls swarming around me part as though they can tell that I don't belong with them anymore.

I'm living. I'm real. And I'm not going to be lost to the underworld today. I grip his hand, not wanting to slip through his fingers now when I've been let go at last. Canaean watches us, watches his brother struggle to pull me out of the opening to the underworld his deal made in the middle of the castle. I grab the edge of the floor, the sharp ends of the wood digging into the very real flesh of my palm as I help Aidoneus pull me up.

My chest heaves as my body falls onto the solid ground and the hole finishes filling in with a sharp clack.

Aidoneus falls to his knees beside me, his shoulders going slack. He scoops me into his arms, resting my head against his chest. His body feels warmer than I've ever felt it before, with no hint of the sharp chill that defined him before.

"Why did you do that?" Aidoneus demands, grabbing me by the shoulders. "Why would you ever make that kind of deal?"

I give him a weak smile. "I had to. I was never going to let you pay the price for me. I never should have been here to even force your hand like that."

He shakes his head. "I wanted to, I wanted to save you. That's why I have done everything in my power to protect you while you've been here, and you were going to throw that all away."

"It was worth it. I would have given more to save you. You deserve it, Aidoneus. You deserve everything I have to offer."

His hands slide into my hair, tugging me against him as he presses his lips against mine. I rest my hands against his chest, feeling the steadiness of his heartbeat under my palm.

I would do it all over again for this moment. I give my life to feel him safe beneath my hands and know that he would be given life in my place.

His fingers tangle in my hair, pulling me so tight to him that I can't breathe. And it still doesn't feel close enough.

Canaean clear his throat. "Lest you forget you're not alone."

Aidoneus struggles to his feet, pulling me with him. He extends a hand to his brother, the moment feeling so similar and so starkly different than when I did the same thing earlier. "Thank you. Thank you for releasing my heart from your bargain."

Canaean shakes his head. "I just don't understand. How could you feel this way for a mortal? I don't even..."

"Cora isn't just a mortal. She's the most incredible woman I've ever met. She has a fire in her that refuses to be extinguished. The way she looks at me..." Aidoneus looks at me and smiles. "I could live my whole life in her eyes."

Canaean frowns. "I suppose I am happy for you, brother."

"I won't forget this." Aidoneus shakes his extended hand.

Canaean looks at it, his back curving in just the barest amount before he clasps Aidoneus's hand. Their grip is strong, the motion drifting close to violence.

"I will have to return," Canaean warns. "I still have to ensure that you are living up to your duties."

"Of course." Aidoneus gives him a crisp nod.

Canaean wanders through the front door, still shaking his head. He glances back at us, looks at his brother's arms curved around me as though he still can't process what lies between us. He flings the door wide despite the weight of it and slams it closed behind him.

Neither of us moves for a moment even after the door clicks closed. Our heavy breathing fills the now-fixed foyer. After everything, it feels good to just feel him again, to feel *me* again. I'm real and I survived, just like he said I would.

"What happens now?" I turn to face Aidoneus and he cups my face in his palm.

"Will you stay with me?" The words are quiet, just for the two of us as he ducks his head closer to mine. "Will you stay in this land between the living and the dead?"

I look down at my hands, a million thoughts flitting through my mind. "Do you mean that I could go home?"

His eyes grow dark and he looks away from me. "You are released from your bargains. You may go wherever you wish."

"In that case, I would like to go home." I keep my voice firm, forcing him to look at me.

He nods and releases me, my body feeling cold in the dark room without him. "I will arrange a carriage for you. If you will give me a moment."

He takes a step away from me, his hand flexing like it

remembers how the curve of my face felt. He keeps his face carefully positioned away from me as he moves towards the door so that I can't see how my words have affected him. He knows I was willing to give everything for him, and yet his self-doubt remains so strong that it takes nothing at all for him to believe that I don't want to be with him. I bite my lip and take a step closer to him even as he tries to move away from me.

"That will be a short trip then," I say, trying not to smile and give myself away entirely.

He glances at me with a frown, his hands tightening into fists as though that will hold his pain all his pain in. "The journey between here and the mortal lands stretches long, as well you know."

"It's a good thing I don't consider the mortal lands home then, isn't it?"

His eyes narrow and he takes a hesitant step closer to me. "You mean..."

"I need to stay where my heart remains, and it hasn't been in the mortal lands for quite some time." I try not to smile, but a small one still makes its way to my face.

"What are you saying?"

I take his hand in mine, my smile breaking wide. "I want to stay here, with you, for as long as you'll have me."

He closes the distance between us, an answering smile on his face. "Truly?"

I nod, feeling the warmth of tears against my cheeks as I feel my heart open wide for the first time.

He smiles, his eyes bright with more than just the souls inside them. "Then prepare yourself for eternity, for I will never tire of having you with me. You are my heart, my love, and the first reason I've had in my lifetime for living. Without you, my veins would continue to pump only darkness."

I tilt my face up to him and he rewards me with a kiss,

slow and soft, that promises as much time as we need to explore what lies between us.

Willa barks from the top of the stairs, her tail wagging as she watches Aidoneus embrace me. She runs down the stairs, her stout body bouncing on each step. I laugh and Aidoneus raises a brow at her as she reaches the foyer and runs to us, jumping up so her front paws rest on my legs. I pat her head and rest my head against his chest. His hand curves around my back, holding me tight and keeping me close.

The shadows of my heart fade away at his touch, and together we are home. Finally, I am where I belong and I never want to leave the warmth of his heart again.

Acknowledgments

Thank you dear readers for going through this journey with me. This book felt like such a joy to write and I dreamed of you reading it even before it was finished.

A huge thank you goes to Megan. You believed in this book when it was just a concept floating around in my head and no one has loved it more than you.

Thanks to The Fellowship of the Ink. You guys have been there for me when I didn't know how I was going to make it through a manuscript or even through the next week. Thank you for listening to my manic craziness and comforting me through the tears. Steve, Bonnie, Rachel, Lexi, Joel, Ashley, you guys rock!

Alan, every book exists because of you. You've read everything I've ever written without complaint and continued to be a support to me even when I should have been supporting you. You have been a true friend and I'm so lucky to have you.

Laura, thank you for believing in this book. It literally couldn't have made it without you. Thank you for always believing in me.

Thank you to my family for listening to me talk about this book and let me work out plot problems in the middle of dinner and at all hours of the day.

Most of all though, I'd like to thank my Heavenly Father for giving me the gift of turning characters and stories into books. Thank you for listening to all the prayers and tears and helping me pull it all together.

And again, thank you readers, without you, none of this could've been possible.

Standalone Novels:
Out of Time
Curse of the Forgotten

Burden of the Banished Duology:
The Exile's Promise
Fight of the Fallen

The Lost Trident Duology:
Seeking Neopolis
Losing Neopolis- *Coming 2025*